MW01137143

Echo Island

E M Walton

Copyright © 2011 E M Walton
All rights reserved.

ISBN: 1460956923
ISBN-13: 9781460956922

In memory of Mary K. McMahon, the conduit of Lake Opinicon and the McMahon clan.

For my children Spencer, Eavan and Delaney. Follow your dreams as far as they will take you. And for the unconditional faith of my loving husband Mark. Because of you I dared to soar.

Acknowledgements

Lake Opinicon served as my muse while writing this story. Much of the story was written while listening to the loons, waves and rain on the Rideau. It is a beautiful place that I recommend for anyone's bucket list.

I need to thank my family: Mark, Spencer, Eavan and Delaney and also my Dad, Dan, Carmen, my aunts, uncles and countless cousins who listened to me go on and on about the Callaghans as they quite took over my thoughts for some time. Also for reading, editing and encouraging me endlessly. I thank Tom and Dorothea Harblin in particular, for spurring me to move forward with publishing.

I thank my mother for opening the world of the Rideau to my family and providing such a rich childhood there. I think she would be proud that some of that youth was captured here.

Thank you to Alan Hutchinson for allowing me to weave his words about loons into the fabric of this story. The loons still watch for the Callaghans to return each year.

The Callaghans became quite a part of my life – refusing to let me leave them alone for too long at any time. They still haunt me occasionally as there continues to be much life left for them. I hope they capture you as well.

Quotations taken from:

Just Loons: A Wildlife Watchers' Guide.
Alan E. Hutchinson. Willowcreek Press, Minnocqua, Wisconsin, 2003.

Prologue

"The most dramatic loon displays are performed when they sense danger to their nest or to their young"

Echo Island
December 1, 1986

A wintry gust swept over the cold, blackened lake. Patches of ice drifted aimlessly on the surface. The fallow tree limbs arched and struggled against the bitter chill, rocking forward and back in pained synchrony. The youngest branches, which in spring had boastfully displayed their neonatal blooms, snapped and fell to earth, doomed by their own youthfulness and fragility.

The same icy wind snapped at the back of Kit Callaghan's neck. She stood, a lone figure on the empty boat dock, and burrowed deeper into her coat. To a stranger, she would have appeared merely affected by the harsh elements, but those who really knew her could discern that the light behind her gemstone eyes had gone dark.

She was tall and thin, often referred to as statuesque. Her complexion, which had always been fair, now lacked the peaches and cream sheen and recent weight loss hollowed out her cheekbones. Her dark auburn hair, always impeccably groomed was tousled, stray strands stood on end against the steel gray sky. The effect made her almost unrecognizable.

She gazed up the hill at the majestic stone and log cottage feeling the emptiness in her soul, a cavern where the cold winter air entered and circled, echoing its own forsaken rumbling.

She had insisted on remaining down at the dock, preferred the numbing cold and angry winds to the warm rooms that had once been her second home.

Even now though, the building could take her breath away with its arched entryway and cobblestone paths. The upstairs windows, once aglow on a warm summer's eve were boarded over and closed for a long winter slumber. The front window was the only view in, one lazy eye of the sleeping giant. It had been their sanctuary, their escape. This was where Kit felt closest to her family. It was here that she could blissfully take for granted the blessings bestowed upon her. Strange how one's mind could see things so differently in just a single, frozen moment of time. The cozy retreat had become the one place Kit could no longer bear.

She had a vague and tattered memory of the beginning of this past summer. When everything had been as it always was. The family opened the doors to their cottage in late spring and traveled there every weekend. Even Patrick, the oldest, had shown some benign excitement about spending his last summer before college with the family. Kit had been certain he would resist, wanting instead to spend each precious moment with the friends he would soon be leaving behind. Instead, he had agreed to join them for their first long vacation week on the lake. In her heart the memory seemed years ago, rather than months.

Now Kit watched as the silhouette of her beloved husband, Sean, paced back and forth in the front window. He gestured across the vacant living room toward the recently renovated sunroom and a different memory came sweeping back into consciousness. Mickey and Aiden had come up with the ridiculous scheme of using their younger sister as a cannonball. Maggie, of course, hadn't minded if it meant being invited to participate in her brothers' mischief. The fun lasted until she bounced off a wall and landed on top of the coffee table resulting in a cut that required six stitches above her left eye and wall repairs that led to the creation of a whole new sitting area.

Maggie had enjoyed all the attention that her sliced head provided on the forty-seven mile car ride to the nearest emergency room. Aiden and Mickey showered her with apologies and guilty bribes of boat rides and skiing trips. The spunky ten year old played up the suffering child act until she had secured a trip to the far end of the lake as well, where the Opinicon Hotel had a snack bar and candy counter.

Maggie had been strong and resilient then, begging to go swimming the very next day, though the doctor had prohibited it until the stitches came out.

Kit had few worries about the resolve of her family back then. After all, they were Callaghans – tight, confident, unsinkable. Maggie had been the most precocious of them all. Now she was only a shell of that steadfast tomboy. She had withdrawn from everyone including herself. At the beginning of the school year, Kit and Sean had driven her a state away to attend a private school where, they hoped, she would be able to rebuild herself. Patrick left for college and the family seemed a skeleton of its former self, a shadow of the solidarity and union it had once been. Patrick had only contacted them once since he left, to inform them that he would be visiting his roommate's home for Thanksgiving instead of returning to them. Kit was devastated but unable to argue. Sean turned his grief outward, pushing Patrick further away. How deep the jagged chasm between father and son had become. Kit shut her eyes tightly and swallowed the bitter taste of memory. She didn't think Patrick and Sean would ever regain the closeness they once shared.

Only Mickey and Aiden remained at home this year. In many ways, Mickey had begun to take Patrick's place with Sean. He was now the oldest child living home and was always there to help with Sean's projects and chores. Mickey was the light to Patrick's dark. He also had a fierce independence. He followed his own rules, returning home past curfew and sometimes not at all. Punishment was lost on him, as he seemed incapable of taking anything too seriously. Aiden, God bless him, tried everything in his power to put things back together. He never required punishment, filling his hours with schoolwork or sports. But his efforts were lost on them.

No matter how the rest of the family was still reeling, Maggie remained Kit's greatest concern. A chain of events had been set in motion through the fog of her grief and decisions made about Maggie's future, the family's future without sense or perspective. Though it tore at her heart, she had watched in silence as her baby girl disappeared through the huge double doors of the Rosemary Dylan Academy, her eyes swimming with confusion and betrayal as she looked back for reassurance from her parents, who'd had none to offer. She was just starting eighth grade, too young to be away from home.

She had completely lost the previous months, perhaps even years in a sea of sedatives and antidepressants. The decision to send her away to school had been hard for Kit and Sean. But Sean had been right. She needed the opportunity to create new memories, meet new people, and allow herself to build some semblance of normalcy. Living at home would no longer afford her that chance.

Kit sighed a visible breath of relief as Sean and the realtor emerged from the house and headed back down the path toward the dock. Every spring for the past twenty years, Kit could be seen from the calm waters on her hands and knees, laying fresh dirt along those cobblestones and planting rows of colorful impatiens and petunias from the porch steps to the dock, leading family and visitors to their beautiful cottage. She had never complained about the time and effort put into making the home and grounds warm and inviting. It had been both relaxing and gratifying to stand back and admire her efforts, as though each time she laid eyes upon it was the first.

As her husband approached, she knew how appropriate it was that their last visit to Echo Island was in the barren cold of winter. No warmth remained here now, nothing in bloom, no life. Placing a hand on her icy cheek, Kit felt the creases and lines that were invisible only a year ago. Her green eyes had dulled, and seemed to dip slightly at the corners from a pervasive frown. Even Sean, who still had the rugged good looks she had fallen in love with a lifetime ago, was beginning to show his age. His chestnut hair had gone almost completely gray. His features darkened and deepened. Time had been a burden on all of them allowing the pain to slowly bubble up from within, and force the last gasp of happiness from them all. Sean's gait was slower, lacking its once carefree swagger. She watched the stony mask shroud his eyes as he handed over the keys and felt the stinging threat of tears in her own. *God, why?* She asked the questions a dozen times a day. Sometimes pleading for answers, other times accusatory and angry. Sometimes, just because she had nothing else to say. *Why us? Why now?*

Sean wrapped his arms around her waist and solemnly led her back to the boat. No words were spoken, as they pushed off the dock and looked back upon the house on the hill knowing this was goodbye. Goodbye to their blessed life as a family. Goodbye to the sound of children running through the rooms, up and down the stairs, from the front entrance to the back screen door. Goodbye to dinners at the long wooden table on the deck in back and candlelit evenings leaning closely over a board game or deck of cards.

Somewhere in the distance, Kit thought she heard the ghostly warning call of the loon, though she knew they had moved far south by now. The crazy laugh of the tremolo was a sound Kit had often heard from the cottage windows at night. It was the only call loons used while in flight.

Kit turned away from the house for the last time and buried her face in Sean's chest as the brisk wind picked up.

Chapter One
Summer, 2003

Maggie Callaghan Stewart sat on the suede sofa in her living room, knees tight against her chest and shaking. Her deep green eyes gazed blankly ahead of her into the darkness. In the rooms above her, the three most important people in her life slept peacefully. Luke had simply rolled over when she frantically shoved the covers back and rushed from the room, her nightshirt damp and clinging to her back and hips. He hadn't heard her panting gasps for breath or the choking sobs gurgling upward from her throat.

The boys' rooms had been mercifully silent when she headed down the staircase. Knees weak and trembling, she had almost tumbled to the bottom, but her feet finally felt the cool tile of the entrance hall and she groped her way to where she sat now in empty silence. Hazy from sleep, the image from the dream returned to her.

First there was only darkness. Then, slowly, it began to lift like a black velvet curtain opening onto a stage of deep blue and she was in the midst of it all. A shadowy image floated before her, reached for her; a person without a face. It frightened her and yet, she felt a sense of comfort radiating from its core. She looked on for a moment, watching the slow, swaying rhythm of the figure. She felt a familiarity, searched for a face, a sign, that helped her understand who, and why.

In an instant, the warmth drained from her blood and she was draped in cold. She couldn't scream, couldn't breathe. She could only feel the complete chill and the frantic beat of her own heart pounding as the gentle image before her thrashed violently. Her head felt as though it might explode, the need for air and light overwhelming…

She had awoken with a gasp, sucking in air with an overwhelming need.

It was not the first time Maggie had experienced the dream. In the past few months she'd had three or four of them, always with the same theme. It left her drained, weak, and strangely curious. Why did the dream return?

Things had been hectic lately and she blamed it on stress. She worried that she did not contribute enough ever since she quit teaching when Quinn was born. Luke assured her that they would be fine with a single income after he got the partnership, but there was a loss of independence – of being able to take care of herself. She felt torn, between her passion for working with students that the rest of the world had given up on, and her need to be a full-time mom. While she loved the time she had with her sons, she still longed to be out there in the real world. Instead she filled her mind with projects she had always wanted to complete and went about accomplishing them with more self-induced pressure than any job had ever created.

It was an adventure for sure, juggling two very active boys who were up at dawn and on the move until eight, by which time she was ready to surrender the day as well. Many of those projects still taunted her. Most days it seemed that she worked all day, picking up after their messes, making meals and cleaning up after them just in time for snack, only to have the house look worse by the time Luke returned home than it did when he left that morning. Some days, she couldn't even remember spending any real time with Owen or Quinn.

Now she scanned the night-lit living room, through the front bay window onto the covered porch and beyond to the curving driveway lined with Japanese maples. Back inside, the stone-front fireplace was cold and dark. The slate mantle displayed fine crystal candleholders that winked at her, reflecting the moon. They were wedding registry gifts that had never burned a candle, never been displayed on their long dining room table surrounded by friends and family during a holiday dinner.

Maggie ground the sleep from her eyes and sighed, willing the tension from her shoulders. The house was exactly what she and Luke had always talked about, dreamed of. Before moving to the modern farmhouse shortly after Owen was born, they had barely been able to pay bills and took in several roommates during the four years that they lived in their brick townhouse on the outskirts of Hartford. It was there that she had found her passion for teaching as a classroom aide in the city. Every spare dime Luke made went to pay her tuition so that she could become a teacher. It was there, too, that they would sit with friends for "wine night" in hard, plastic chairs on a cracked, concrete patio no larger than their current bathroom. They would laugh and share stories, stare at the stars or the city lights and dream of a better life.

Now the expansive wooden deck behind their house, complete with a gazebo and hot tub was rarely used for stargazing or dreaming.The roommates had moved on when Maggie and Luke became the hard-working family of three, then four. Luke spent more evenings pouring over files and depositions at his office than he did in the comfort of his own hard earned home.

The grandfather clock began to sing its timely tune. In two hours, the house would surge to life. Luke's coffee would be perked via timer so that it was the perfect temperature and strength when he made his way down to the kitchen in a pair of old jeans he kept next to the bed. Owen would demand oatmeal, then change his mind three or four times and end up with the same cold cereal he always had. Maggie would slice up a banana for Quinn which he would eat impatiently, eager to begin a new day of exploration and climbing: around the kitchen table, down into the family room and over by the fireplace where Rhett, Maggie's Boston terrier, would settle himself for the morning routine. Luke's coffee cup would hardly be drained before he was off to the shower, taking two steps at a time up the stairs as though he could outrun the chaos of the family he had been so eager to create. Each day was a replica of the one before. For Maggie, they all tended to blur together.

The effects of the nightmare had dulled enough so that Maggie was no longer rigid with fear, but sleep was still a long way off. Slowly, she lifted herself off the couch and headed to the kitchen to work off some of her anxiety. She filled the mop bucket with steaming water and cleanser and set her sights on the tile floor. It was redundant; Luke had hired a weekly housekeeper who took care of the mopping and scrubbing details that Maggie had always complained about. Luke's good intentions were a sore topic, however, since Maggie's nightmares and anxiety had invaded their lives. She argued that he was insinuating she was incapable of maintaining the house. He would defensively explain that he knew how difficult it was to find the time with all of her other responsibilities. It always ended the same way, the housekeeper stayed on the payroll and Maggie and Luke were left feeling discredited and angry.

Sometimes she wished for the simplicity of the townhouse again, even though it had been so hard financially. At least she and Luke had struggled together then. When Owen had been born, they were young and inexperienced but it was trivial against the sparkling blue eyes of their infant son. By the time Quinn came along, Luke had been promoted to partner and their discussions revolved more around what neighborhood they should consider when moving. Few of their friends had started having children yet and interests had begun to change. When they looked into their newest child's hazel eyes to whisper, "Welcome to the world, Bryan Quinn" there was an almost imperceptible distance between them.

For as long as she could remember, Maggie wanted a close and loving family more than anything in the world. It would be the way she'd imagined her own family should have been. Holidays spent gathered around a spitting fire in the winter, or a barbecue emitting mouth-watering scents in the backyard during the summer. Laughter would bounce on the air around them and drift over to neighboring houses enticing them to join the fun. There would be none of the strained silences, disguised tensions, or averted eyes that had been the hallmark of rare Callaghan family gatherings.

As Maggie ran the mop back and forth over the same area of floor, she understood that even in this beautiful house, even without the money worries, her dreams hadn't all come true. In fact, along the way, she seemed to have let go of the most important one of all.

As expected, two and a half hours later, the Stewart house was alive with the sound of childish babble, showers running and the smells of coffee and toast wafting from the kitchen. Maggie tended to her morning chores of getting the kids up, dressed, and fed mechanically, still in a bit of a mood from her dream. Luke came down to the family room, strategically skirting the blocks that had been scattered from a bucket, and doled out his round of morning goodbye kisses to all. He reached for Maggie and noticed the distant fear behind her eyes.

"Honey, is something wrong?"

Maggie looked at the grout between the floor tiles, aching to explain her fears and portray enough urgency in the situation that Luke would want to stay home and spend the day with her and the boys. Deep inside, however, she knew that Luke would not read that much into her condition. He would brush it off as trivial, tell her to let it go and be out the door within minutes. It was a response she had grown accustomed to. Maybe, she shouldn't mention it at all and save herself the disappointment of that reality.

"I just didn't sleep very well, that's all." she finally explained.

"Yeah, you were gone when I got up." Luke said as though he had just realized it now. "What's the matter?"

"I had another nightmare." She told him and once the words had come out, she could not stop them. "It was worse this time, Luke. I saw a figure, a.... a person. I couldn't tell who it was but I was supposed to do something. I couldn't breathe and I couldn't move. It was awful." Her body tensed at the recollection and she thought maybe Luke would see how much she needed him today.

He wrapped his arms around her shoulders and held her close to him. She felt the warmth of his body against her chest, smelled the deep clean scent of him. He pulled back to look into her eyes.

"Maybe you should see somebody about these dreams, Maggie."

Maggie's eyes narrowed at the suggestion. "What do you mean 'see somebody'?"

"You know, a professional, a psychologist. It's got you all stressed out and panicky. Maybe there's something behind it. Maybe talking to someone would help you get past all of this."

"I'm talking to you about it."

He took her hands and kissed them, as he might a child who had fallen down and gotten a scrape. "I know. But it might help if it was someone on the outside, someone objective. They might see something you and I don't."

He looked at his watch and seemed suddenly in a hurry. "Look, I've got to go. It's just a suggestion." He kissed her cheek and headed to the door.

Or maybe you think I'm starting to lose it, she thought bitterly as the door closed behind him. *Maybe it's easier for you to send me off to some shrink for my troubles, so that it's not something you have to work through with me.*

She turned and headed back to the kitchen where her sons and her life awaited her.

Chapter Two

Mickey Callaghan leaned against the counter in the kitchen of his bar swallowing mouthfuls of steaming coffee and dragging on a forbidden cigarette. The previous night had been busier than usual at Mickey C's. Ever since he had signed on the local band "Irish Whiskey" to play once a week in addition to their usual weekend run, the crowds had been growing. Yet even with the fast pace of tending bar, managing the kitchen, and providing an ear for his patrons, Mickey never tired of his responsibilities as the owner of the Irish pub.

To him, it was like having a gathering of friends over every day: for good times, humor, and a bit of music and dancing. He had known the idea of a true Irish pub in his hometown in upstate New York would prove successful since the day he'd thought it up. The population of Irish was high in the area, and people loved to feel that they were experiencing the food, drink, and customs of another land. Mickey C's drew the young crowd as well, which had come as a pleasant surprise to Mickey. Those who were looking for something other than the loud nightclubs and crowded college bars somehow found Mickey C's. It allowed them to see a somewhat more sophisticated side of adult entertainment and it was Mickey's pride and joy.

His eyes scanned the darkened rooms beyond the kitchen. The wide wood planks of the barroom floor, the ash stools he'd had shipped from Dublin, softened by the trousers of men and women over many years in an authentic Irish establishment. In the high backed booths along the far wall he had watched couples begin and end blazing love affairs. He spanned the wall of cork dartboards where countless beers had been wagered, and occasionally a bit more. More living occurred in this quiet pub than many ever had the opportunity to witness, and Mickey used that as a personal and professional objective. His heart was in the bar, from the prints of lush, rolling landscapes and craggy bluffs, to the hand-etched claddaghs on the side of each bench, to the Guinness tap taken directly from Danny O'Leary's place in Killarney where he had begun his career in bartending on his first visit to the Emerald Isle ten years ago and where his dream had taken root.

He ascended the long, narrow staircase at the far end of the kitchen, returning to his living quarters. When he had purchased the building to create the pub, he still lived with his parents and was miserable. Since the space came with an unused upper level, it made sense for Mickey to renovate and move in. During the first year, the rooms above the bar were barren and drab, but as the pub gained a reputation and attracted new business, Mickey was able to invest in his personal surroundings as well. It was nothing to brag about, but it was enough for a lonely bachelor to call home. The floors were the same oak as the bar, though not as well maintained. The kitchen was small and rarely used, as Mickey took most of his meals downstairs while working. The one bedroom was spacious, located over the front of the bar with a small bathroom attached to it. The rest was a modest living area – previously two rooms until Mickey had taken a sledgehammer to the center wall and opened it all up. Skylights had been added most recently bringing light to the otherwise dim surroundings.

Against one wall was a large television, in front of which Mickey could usually be found when he wasn't in the bar itself. A black, leather sofa and matching armchair sat across from the television on the opposite wall. The oversized, square coffee table in between was another import from Ireland, costing almost as much to have it shipped as the table itself. It had been in this room that Mickey allowed himself to indulge his spending whims. A state of the art stereo enveloped one corner of the room, upon which a flaccid ivy plant that his mother had provided, silently pleaded for attention.

Mickey strode through the room, ignoring the plant and headed into the bedroom for a shower. As he sat on the bed to remove his shoes, she caught his eye, as she so often did, and the dull, familiar pain filled his chest. She was his one, critical sacrifice for the bar that he loved. Her sapphire eyes laughed at him from her place atop the Cliffs of Moher as he tugged at his Nikes. Wisps of raven hair had fallen loose from the casual ponytail she wore to dance against her ivory cheeks. Her smile was always able to warm his heart, or break it, and often accomplished both simultaneously. Many times he had thought of putting that photo in a drawer, but whenever he tried, the room lost all its light and he no longer felt at home.

He could remember his last visit to Ireland like it was yesterday. They sat in their usual booth at O'Leary's, casting shaded glances at each other over two tall mugs of ginger ale. It was the day she had broken his heart, or he had broken hers.

"It's too hard for me" she had told him, staring at the bubbles in her drink as they slowly floated to the top and burst apart. "I can't just pack up and leave my home, my education, to move across the Atlantic."

"You mean you won't." Mickey retorted sourly.

"Don't be a bastard. We're both adults. Can't we do this civilly?"

But Mickey didn't feel civil at that moment. He felt he was being torn apart by the dream of owning his own place back home and the dream of happily ever after here in Ireland. He couldn't understand why she couldn't transfer schools and he'd assured her they'd still return to Ireland often to see her family.

She couldn't understand why he couldn't find success right here at O'Leary's. He clearly loved Ireland. At times she was certain he preferred it to his own home. He certainly spent a lot of his time here.

"I love you, Mickey. Isn't that enough to make you stay?"

"Isn't it enough to make you leave?" It wasn't what he had wanted to say, it was just what came out. Couldn't she see he had the chance of a lifetime starting his own place? Even as they spoke, his new business was taking off halfway across the world.

She leaned back against the wooden bench. "There's no talking to you when you get like this. You made your decision. Regardless of how I feel. And now you use me as an excuse for why your plans aren't working out just so. You never included me in those plans, Mickey. You never once asked me if I would be a part of them. Now you act surprised that I don't want to move my whole life off to some strange place where I know no one. Well, maybe if you had stopped for one moment to ask me, it would be different. I'm not going."There. She had dug in her heels. Now she just had to wait for him to come around.

She hadn't thought he would let go. Walk away from all they had. Sure, she knew there would be arguing, probably tears too. Truth was, if he would just acknowledge that he had neglected her feelings in making this decision, she just might have followed him to the ends of the Earth.

Instead, Mickey pushed his mug aside and looked deeply at her. "I wish you the best." That was all. He stood up and walked out of the bar, out of her life. Just like that. At least she had been right about the tears, she thought as her own started to fall.

Mickey had been so certain that he wouldn't get as far as the door, he would have bet money on it. She would call his name and run to him and he would agree to almost anything. It had never crossed his mind that she would not *stop him.*

At the door to the pub he hesitated, awaiting her hand on his shoulder, or the sound of his name. He could feel the eyes of the patrons burning the back of his neck. The handle felt cold in his hand as he tugged it open.

One step out, two, three… he still waited for her to call his bluff….was still waiting…

Even now, she still lulled him to sleep at night. As time went on the voice became a little more difficult to discern. Her face never left his mind, however. No matter where he was, he could always conjure up her bright smile, her dimples when she laughed, the sadness he had seen on that last night together. As he stepped into the hot, needle spray of the shower he tried to erase the vision, for just a moment of peace.

Chapter Three

Luke draped his suit coat over the back of the leather sofa and stepped around his desk laden with files and telephone messages. As he sat, he ran a hand through his dark hair and sighed, unsure of where to begin. He rifled through some of the messages, discarding those that he wouldn't return, and placing the rest in piles of "must call" and "put off one more day". His telephone buzzed at the same moment that his door opened. Michelle Langstrom, a paralegal with the firm poked her head in the door. Luke nodded, gesturing toward the couch.

"Yes, Maureen? He spoke into the phone's speaker.

"Harris Fleishman on line two, Mr. Stewart." Replied the perky voice of his secretary. Luke rolled his eyes.

"I'm in a meeting." He told her. "Tell Harris I'll get back to him before lunch."

"Yes, sir."

Michelle leaned forward and tapped a pen against the glass table. Her blouse lay open enough to reveal the tops of her firm, tan breasts. Her honey brown locks curled and brushed against the lapel of her tailored jacket as she moved. She was sinfully attractive and could bring the machinery of the law firm to a standstill when she entered a room or strolled past a meeting. She was also bright and professional, which Luke found more useful. He could not avoid a brief scan of the figure in front of him, however.

"Michael Oxford." She stated it as though they were in the middle of a conversation. Luke placed his hands behind his head and leaned back in his chair.

"Who?"

"Michael Oxford. He started working for Digitech in '96. Assistant Director of Marketing. He was fired last summer, oddly enough, right before the suit. Rumor has it, Oxford has documentation that Digitech was funneling money."

"And where is this Oxford guy?"

Michelle wrinkled her delicate nose. "Well, that's the bad news. He was in Buffalo working for Wireless Industries until last month. His supervisor says that one day he just didn't show up for work and he hasn't been heard from since."

Luke sighed and scratched his cheek. "So how does this help us?"

"Well, we just have to find him, that's all. I know a great P.I. in upstate New York. I can..." her voice trailed off as she studied Luke's face. "You haven't had enough coffee today, have you? Stay put. We'll work through this as soon as we calibrate your caffeine levels."

Luke watched her shapely, lean legs take graceful strides toward the door. "You're not my secretary, Michelle." he contended, but she was out the door before he could complete his sentence. She returned within moments, with a large mug that she place in front of him. Immediately he drank from it, as though it would provide him with enough energy to make it through the day.

"What is it?" she asked him, propping herself on the corner of his desk causing her skirt to slide halfway up her thigh. "Your mind is not on Digitech or Oxford. So spill it."

Luke looked into Michelle's magnetic hazel eyes and then quickly down at his desk. Sighing deeply, he allowed himself to share his thoughts. "It's Maggie again. I don't know what's going on with her. She's a nervous wreck, clingy and dependent. I swear she wanted me to just drop work today to tend to her. She had another nightmare." Luke had shared this information with Michelle before. They worked together on most of his cases and she had become a sounding block for Luke, both professionally and personally. Michelle was a good listener and a practical thinker. She often found solutions when Luke couldn't. Particularly when it came to Maggie. "I suggested she see someone professionally and you'd think I asked her to make a public announcement certifying that she's nuts."

"So she refused?"

"I don't know. No. She never committed one way or the other. She couldn't get past the insensitivity of the question. But I am beginning to think it's the only way for her to get a grip. I certainly can't do it. She hasn't let me into her life since Quinn was born."

"You mean she hasn't let you into her *bed*. Metaphorically speaking."

Luke looked up, surprised. If it had been anyone else in the office, he would have ordered them out angrily, and shut himself away for the rest of the morning. Michelle was the only person he knew who could get away with it. Though the statement had caught him off guard, he actually felt a small sense of relief that she seemed to understand his frustration.

"That's a touchy subject."

"Look. I don't mean to make you feel uncomfortable. If you don't want to talk about it, I completely understand."

"No, I do. You're right. We haven't been intimate in a long time. I try to touch her and she pulls away from me like I carry an electric charge. I've been wondering if it has anything to do with the medication she was on before Quinn."

"What was the medication for?"

"I'm not really sure. She never spoke of it much. Depression, maybe. She told me she had been on it for years, and that was when we were dating. It was never really an issue, never a conversation." He felt a bit foolish as he thought back on it now. Why hadn't they had a conversation about it? "When she became pregnant with Owen she went off it, but started taking it again once he was born. I don't think she's taken it at all since Quinn was born. I remember her saying she was thinking of stopping it all together, but I just kind of brushed it off. I never thought the medication really made any difference."

"Well, maybe it really does. Can't you find out what she's taking?"

"I guess I could ask her. Or call her doctor or something. It's just been so frustrating coming home every night to someone I don't feel like I know anymore."

She touched his shoulder compassionately. "Listen, drink some more of that coffee. I'll go try to dig up Oxford for a while and then we can have a nice liquid lunch. Take your mind off your troubles. Sound good?"

Luke looked gratefully at Michelle and managed a smiled. "Sounds great."

Chapter Four

"The instinctual urge of loons to travel north and once again seek out ancestral nesting lakes is a powerful and driving force that awakens with the first hint of spring."

The breeze blew in from the west, sending ripples over the blue-gray water. It was still early in the season and a bit brisk, but it had become a habit. Sometime in May, two hunter green Adirondack chairs emerged from beneath the cottage to sit at water's edge and each October, begrudgingly, they were returned. Patrick considered it satirical that there were two; he never brought anyone here with him, never entertained visitors. Yet he had bought two chairs, and each year he pulled them both out and put them both away. He sourly mused that the empty one was for his conscience. After all, it was his conscience that he came for.

A few boats could be seen scattered upon the lake, bobbing gently among the waves. Patrick liked the quiet. Within a month, summer would arrive and the lake would be buzzing with jet-skiers and knee-boarders, fishermen, divers, families and tourists. They all flocked to Lake Opinicon in the warm weather like the loons that returned from their winter retreat, restless and anxious for a new beginning in the warm sun of their natural home.

Lake Opinicon sat nestled at the heart of the Rideau Canal in Ontario, Canada. It was a beautiful stretch of natural lakes and man-made canals running from Ottawa to Kingston connected by several lock stations. Originally built for a defensive transport route, the Rideau was never used for its conceived purpose. It opened in 1832 and became known more for its excellent fishing opportunities than its military advantage. Now cottages were prime real estate on the National Historic Site. Patrick still felt at home here. Whether it was the tranquility of the locals in the quaint neighboring towns or the excitement of vacationing tourists around the lake, there was always an air of kindness and congeniality.

For now, though, Patrick would enjoy the solitude for which he had bought the patch of land on the far northern tip of the island. Here alone he could bathe in his guilt, replay all the "what ifs", and languish in his loneliness without anyone asking unwanted questions.

It's sad, he thought, *that I can't share this with Shauna and the kids. They'd love the open air, the room to run, the glorious sunsets. It could be like it used to be...* But he could never bring them here, couldn't see himself ever telling them such a place existed. He would lose the one place in the world where he could feel the way his heart told him to.

Everywhere else he had to be what others believed him to be: strong, levelheaded, short on emotion, and long on ambition. 'Untouchable' was the term that had been used in some business circles, though he wasn't supposed to know that. And it was true when it came to Patrick professionally.

He made the connections he needed to make, nurtured the relationships that were of benefit to him, cut ties that served no purpose, and dealt ruthlessly with those who were not as skilled as he at playing the game. It had made him very wealthy and somewhat notorious, though neither truly mattered much to Patrick.

He had been playing the role for so many years he had started to believe he was actually becoming that untouchable man. That was when he'd come here and worked out a deal to buy this piece of land on the northern tip of the island. It wasn't right for him to forget where he came from, and so through some legal maneuvering, he bought the lot at full asking price, keeping Shauna and the kids in the dark. He had the cottage built and began scheduling regular "business trips" that took him away for a few days at a time. No one suspected a thing. Shauna knew he dealt with high stakes businessmen all over the country and any one of them could demand his presence on short notice. Davis, the senior partner at the firm, and Shauna's father, believed he was closing deals or setting up new business and Patrick often made a business call or two while he was away that insured he would have some billable hours or new business for his eagle-eyed father in-law when he returned.

Patrick gazed across the water at the shoreline crowded with pines standing tall as soldiers. The rocky cliffs along the southern tip of the island behind him called out. *Go there. Take a dive. Or sit here and do nothing. That's more your style, isn't it? Wait until it's too late and then wallow in self-pity because life dealt you a losing hand. History repeats itself. Here you are with another test of character. Can you live up to expectations this time? Or will you fall short once more? Don't take any responsibility for it, though.* That *would be out of character for you. It's just lousy circumstances, that's all. Always has been.*

Another voice began to argue back. *I am taking responsibility for it all. Why am I sitting here for Christ's sake? I spend every day of my life knowing that I continually screw up the lives of the people I love, don't I? I am trying to put it right. Show me how. If there is a God, just show me how…*

The fear and sorrow he would always feel got pushed deep down into his gut and churned until there was only anger. That was his way. He leaned his head back to stare up at the blue spring sky, searching for proof that he had been heard. Two Ospreys circled above him, watching with keen eyes for weak fish to surface. Fluffy white clouds floated lazily above them, moving slowly across the sky. Closing his eyes to clear the arguing inside his head, he heard the melodious tremolo of the loon. Patrick breathed in the sound as if it could fill his soul with answers.

Loons would return to the same home each year. Somehow they could always find their way. The loon was calling to find his family, to rebuild and begin life again. Soon, they would return and answer the call. Patrick found himself envious of that. If he called out, would his family answer him? The answer carried itself back to him on the notes of the loon's song. *Call Aiden.*

Chapter Five

Aiden Callaghan leaned forward, his elbows on the cold, metal desk, and looked into the eyes of the troubled teen before him. The lean youngster sported spiky blond hair with black roots and a gold anarchy symbol punctured his right nostril. His jeans were several sizes too big and hung from the middle of his hips to expose black Calvin Klein boxers. A gold chain-clad Scarface sported a cigar on his t-shirt. One foot rested on the arm of another chair showing off a pair of black, worn work boots with frayed, loose laces that had probably never been tied.

In sharp contrast, Aiden wore pressed tan pants with a light yellow oxford and tie. The natural waves in his dark hair had been carefully trained away from his face and kept under control with regularly scheduled trims. He lived a life of organization and order, and worked in one of chaos. The dichotomy suited him.

To Aiden, this was just another screwed up, needy kid. He worked with about twenty of them each year, all of them, street-smart and foul-mouthed and in desperate need of acceptance and understanding. Aiden had that gift. Where others would see a group of juvenile delinquents and turn their heads in disgust or shame or fear, Aiden reached out and connected with them. He listened, he cared and he opened himself up. And sometimes he was able to touch the lost soul deep within the hardened layers of hate.

Tommy, the one who sat before him now, silent and sullen, had come to Riverview Center for Children two months earlier on shoplifting and drug possession charges. He had a mother who worked two jobs on and off and had been rumored to prostitute herself from time to time to support her own drug habit. She had a boyfriend who wasn't able to hold down a job for longer than a few weeks. She was giving up on her son, leaving him at the mercy of the courts and the system. Aiden knew most members of society would see her as the reason kids were becoming so uncontrollable these days, but he could not place blame on a woman who was struggling so with survival herself, that she had become incapable of overseeing the survival of others. She was a victim of the same cycle that Tommy was in. The same cycle Tommy's kids would be in too if something didn't change.

They were playing a little game today, who could be silent the longest. Tommy had figured that by refusing to engage in conversation, Mr. Callaghan would give up like the others and he would be excused. Aiden, on the other hand, was prepared to spend the next four hours locked in a silent stare, if necessary. After only 23 minutes, Aiden was victorious.

"So, what's the deal, man? Can I go?"

"You haven't answered my question yet."

"Yeah, so? I ain't gonna neither."

"Then you can't go."

"Awww, man. This is bullshit. Why the fuck do I gotta come in here and sit with your punk ass three times a week?

I ain't gonna tell you what I did was wrong, or that I'm sorry and I won't do it again. So whaddayou want?"

"I don't want you to tell me you're sorry or that you were wrong." Aiden explained. "All I asked was why you feel that you don't have to do your assigned work like the rest of your class."

"Because it's bullshit!" Aiden smiled almost imperceptibly. The fish was nibbling on the worm. "I ain't gonna use any of that math shit in my life, so why am I wasting my time on it now?!"

"Tommy, I'm sure I don't have to be the one to go through the 'everybody uses math' spiel with you. I think your teachers have already covered that one."

"I know all the math I need to know."

"Are you sure?"

"Yeah, man. I know how to add and subtract and all that shit. I know it better than most of the assholes in my class." He was on the line. Now all Aiden had to do was set the hook.

"How do you know that?"

"Because the stuff they're doing in class is stupid and half of 'em can't get it right."

"And you do?"

"Yeah."

"Don't you have to answer the problems to know if you're doing them right or wrong?"

"I answer 'em in my head."

"So what's the big difference between knowing in your head and writing the answer down on paper?" He was reeling him in now and would be releasing him back into the wild in a matter of minutes.

The phone jangled noisily, disrupting the moment. Aiden angrily picked up the receiver. "What?" he barked at the receptionist showing his intense disapproval of being interrupted in the middle of a session.

"I'm so sorry, Mr. Callaghan." the young woman apologized. "Your brother is on the line and he says it's quite important. I asked if you could call him back but he refused. He said its long distance. I figured since your time with Thomas is technically finished, that maybe you would want to take the call."

His anger diffused into confusion. It had to be Patrick. Mickey was not the type to expect that the world come to a stand still at his command. What the hell could Patrick want? Aiden hadn't spoken to him or anyone else in his family in two long years. Confusion grew into curiosity.

Aiden looked across his desk to Tommy. His smug expression showed that Aiden was about to prove his theory that when it came right down to it, nobody put him first. Aiden wrestled with his interest in what his brother could possibly have to say to him, and the societal beliefs this kid held.

"Mr. Callaghan?" The receptionist's voice snapped him back to awareness. He wouldn't choose.

"Yes, put him through." he replied and then looked at Tommy's smug expression. Honesty was sometimes the most important tool in proving that you cared.

He covered the receiver. "I don't exactly speak to my brother anymore." Tommy's eyes rose slightly with interest. "It's gotta be something pretty major. Now, you can go ahead and spread nasty rumors about *my* messed up home life, but you're going to stay right here until I'm off the phone.

"Don't worry." he continued when Tommy rolled his eyes. "He likes things short and sweet. It won't take more than five minutes. Time me." He removed his hand from the phone. "Patrick?"

"Hey Aiden." He heard his brother's deep voice come through the wire. "Sorry to bug you at work. Did I get you at a bad time?"

Now Aiden rolled his eyes at Tommy and got a small smile. *Would it matter if you did?* he thought sourly. "Kind of. What's going on?"

"I need to talk to you. I've got some shit going on at work and I need to bounce a few things off someone who knows me." Aiden almost laughed aloud at the irony of his brother's perception.

"Why me?" he asked instead. "What about Shauna or Mom and Dad? Or Mickey, or Maggie?" Just about anyone made more sense than the two of them discussing something, personal or professional. Opposite poles, he thought. Patrick the stoic, follow-in-dad's-footsteps, keep-it-all-inside brother versus Aiden, the family misfit, the 'we can't fix it if we don't talk about it', outspoken, non-conformist outcast.

"Come on, Aiden. I can't go to Shauna or the others about this. You're the one who will understand and keep your mouth shut about it all."

"Seems to me the rest of you are better at that than I am." he bit back. Maybe keeping Tommy here hadn't been such a great idea.

"Nice, Aid, but the rest of us still talk to each other, at least to some extent. So you're the safe one. Besides, I need someone objective, someone who understands people. And you're trained for that, right?"

It was the first time he could remember Patrick making any reference, direct or otherwise, to Aiden's chosen profession. It certainly hadn't been a favored path for the Callaghans, but Patrick acted as though it had been downright traitorous. Tired of the conversation already, and anxious to stop the show he was putting on for Tommy, he gave in. "Alright, what is it?"

"No. Not on the phone. It's going to take a bit longer than that. Can I fly you down to New York this weekend?"

"What?! New York! Pat, I've got a job here, you know. I can't just take off whenever I feel like it."

"So, what? You don't get time off? Maybe you need to rethink your line of work."

"I have responsibilities at work."

Patrick was silent at the other end. Aiden knew it must have taken an awful lot for Pat to call him in the first place and then offer to pay for a plane ticket. And wasn't Aiden the one standing behind the idea that families should be open and honest? Not to mention, that the whole urgency of the conversation had him awfully curious about what was going on. "Fine, arrange it. It'll have to be late tomorrow, though, I've got some afternoon appointments I won't cancel."

"Great. I'll have the ticket ready for you when you board. Shauna and the kids will be glad to see you too." Aiden thought he heard the call of a loon in the distance. "Thanks, man."

"Hey, Pat? Where are you?"

"Uhh, business trip. New Orleans. Look, I gotta go, but I'll see you tomorrow."

The line went dead and Aiden slowly replaced the receiver on its cradle. Loons in New Orleans?

"So, you're going to New York City." Aiden was brought back to the situation with Tommy. "Cool. Can I come?"

"Maybe next time. Now, where were we?"

"I don't know. Nowhere."

"Right! The small step between knowing the answer in your head and writing it on paper."

"I don't need to prove I know that shit to nobody."

Aiden made a mental note to make the next topic Language Arts. "True," he replied, "but how about the idea that this one small step would keep your 'ass' out of my office?"

Tommy raised a brow and Aiden knew he had landed his catch.

Chapter Six

"Loons are extremely attentive parents.
They never leave their newly hatched
young alone."

Maggie closed the book she had been reading to Owen and Quinn and tucked Quinn in for his nap. He peered up at her through heavily lidded eyes and she bent to kiss his cheek. "Hit the sheets, kiddo." she whispered to Owen. He climbed down from the chair and trotted down the hall to his own room. Maggie followed a few steps behind to watch as he climbed into bed. He opened one eye to peek at her standing in the doorway. A small grin spread across his young face. Pride knotted and swelled within her chest and her lips spread into a gentle smile. "I love you, babe." she told him through the crack in the door and closed it softly behind her.

It was not easy raising two rambunctious boys, but it was fulfilling. Even though she was thoroughly exhausted, the joyous moments such as these overpowered the sacrifices. Owen overflowed with energy; he slept like a log, but when he was awake he gave his activities one hundred percent from start to finish. Maggie had learned the hard way that he couldn't have sugar after five o'clock if she had any hopes of getting him to settle down for the evening. Of course, with all that energy came the same amount of love.

He was her poet, her dreamer. He doled out kisses and hugs without reserve and was almost always willing to cuddle, even if it was only for ten seconds and he was off and running again.

Then there was Bryan Quinn. From the moment Quinn had come home, he tried to keep up with his big brother. At four months he was trying to crawl and he took his first steps at nine months. Quinn was more patient than Owen, though. He would spend more time trying to learn a task than Owen ever had, and he would often stick to it until he succeeded. He was more physical too. Couches, stairs, chairs, tabletops were all challenges for Quinn to tackle. He would jump off them, or climb from one to the other, until Maggie was frantic with visions of emergency rooms. She was convinced Quinn would have a stitched forehead before his second birthday. A future football player, Luke's parents mused. The way he tackled household furniture, Maggie reluctantly agreed.

Taking advantage of the blessed hour of peace naptime would bring, Maggie stretched out on the soft worn couch in the family room. Rhett circled until he found a place at her feet. The dishwasher needed to be emptied, the family room vacuumed and the garbage taken out, but it could all wait for now. Quiet was too rare a commodity to pass up this afternoon and Maggie felt drained.

As she drifted to sleep, her thoughts began to blend, one into another. She thought of Luke and his lack of interest in being home lately, which made her think of the rest of her family. Mickey, who she really should call. Patrick. Aiden, though she didn't know either of them very well. How sad that they weren't closer. Maggie drifted deeper into sleep.

She could see light above her, though she was surrounded by the dark. She reached and reached toward the brightness until it exploded around her. The darkness tried to pull her back in, but as she flailed her arms hit rock and she grasped it and heaved herself onto it. She couldn't feel the bite of its jagged edges in her flesh, or the blood that began to trickle from her knee where it had been sliced, she only thought of climbing, of reaching the top, wherever that may be. Then the ground leveled and she flung herself onto it, resting her cheek on its scratchy surface. She tried to yell for someone, anyone, but her voice clogged and it came out as only a grunt. She tried again and again desperate to make sound, but it brought only tears of frustration and pain. When she was about to give up, about to give into the darkness that still climbed toward her, she felt a hand on her back. She heard her name being yelled and she knew the voice. Oh, thank God, she knew the voice.

"Mickey!" she sobbed in a whisper. "Help. Please." She pointed into the darkness and Mickey disappeared into it.

Maggie bolted upright; her body damp with sweat and her breath coming in short, ragged gasps. Something terrible had happened to Mickey and he needed her right away. She rushed to the kitchen counter and fumbled for the telephone. It tumbled to the floor in her haste and she wrestled with the cord until she had the receiver. She knew she needed to tell Luke she was going for help. Her heart felt as though it would pound right out of her chest and the few rings before the answer on the other end of the line seemed like an eternity. She couldn't wait any longer – the memory was leaving her. The receiver clicked and the words came tumbling out.

"Tell Luke I had to go." she sputtered. "Mickey's in trouble." She hung up the phone without waiting for a response from the other end, grabbed her keys off the counter and ran out the door.

There was a certain sensation of intrigue about the bar. Bare bulbs under colored glass hoods were dimmed, heightening the air of secrecy. Most of the patrons were men in jackets and ties or women in tailored power suits, with manicured nails and freshly glossed lips. They leaned against the bar, or over a booth, with billows of smoke rising between their hushed exchanges. Most of them should not have been there at all, drinking during the workday. But this was where the important business really took place. Among the frosted mugs and martini glasses, secrets were leaked, information was passed, and deals were made. Everyone at the bar seemed to be a part of something big.

The bartender was a burly man, over six feet tall with a dark goatee. Excellent at his craft, he heard much of what took place in his establishment, but never let on, lest his clientele lose faith in him and take their money elsewhere. He had learned from experience that midday drinkers bought top shelf. So he quietly emptied ashtrays and filled orders, a white bar towel either in his hand or slung over his shoulder, a smile always at the corner of his mouth. He got his orders right the first time and rarely spoke unless spoken to. On occasion he settled a minor difference of opinion, usually favoring the stronger tipper.

At one end of the bar, Michelle crushed out a cigarette and reached for her pack. Luke swallowed down a mouthful of golden ale and shoved his glass forward to signal a refill. The bartender gave a nod, swiping the mug and opening the tap in one fluid movement. Michelle flicked her lighter and drew a long breath on the cigarette between her full lips before blowing out a thin, white curl of smoke. Luke watched it rise and spread outward above their heads. "Enough about all my troubles." He said, passing some bills across the bar and lifting his beer. "Did you get that Oxford guy?"

"Not yet." Michelle replied. She leaned in a little, aware that Luke would take notice. Their knees touched, and although she could have adjusted her position slightly to avoid the contact, she preferred where she was. Besides, she liked being close enough to see the occasional spark that lit up Luke's eyes. "I have some exciting leads, though." She sat back again, slowly and inhaled her cigarette.

It wasn't that Luke had ever let on that he was interested in Michelle. Their relationship had never turned down that road, never even stopped at the intersection to consider a direction. Michelle had learned just how far she could push Luke without making her intentions obvious and she enjoyed the game. The fact was that if she and Luke ever did discuss the possibility of a sexual relationship, it might very well ruin what she had now. *Although the sex would be phenomenal, no doubt.*

So far, Luke had been a devoted, albeit neglected, husband and father. That was one of the things Michelle loved about him. He had raised the bar on her expectations of men far enough, unfortunately, that no others seemed to measure up. He was attractive, incredibly sexy, an excellent lawyer and still a nice guy. He would have wanted her if his life had just been a little different. He *did* want her but didn't know it. And that was enough, for now.

They finished their drinks discussing where Michelle's search for the Digitech informer had led her. As they stood to leave, Michelle felt a little lightheaded. Three gin and tonics had been more than she had intended. She'd have to splash some cold water on her face when she got to the office. She couldn't allow herself to lose her edge.

"By the way, I spoke to Fleishman." Luke interrupted her thoughts and she had to clear her mind before she could respond.

"What's his problem now?"

"Actually, he wants to settle with his former employee. The harassment case. Three hundred and seventy-five K. What does that sound like to you?"

Michelle smiled slyly as they stepped outside. "Sounds to me like he did it. Did you set it up?"

"They'll be at the office tomorrow morning, nine sharp. You available?"

"I will be for this. You prepping Fleishman before the meeting?"

"You better believe it. That man has a knack for opening his mouth before his brain knows what he's going to say."

"I'd love to see that too." Luke's cell phone rang and he reached into his breast pocket to retrieve it.

"Stewart." He answered casually. He listened intently to the caller until his face grew pale and his eyes registered shock. "What? Well, what did she do with the kids? Shit." He ended the call and immediately started dialing again.

Michelle put a concerned hand under Luke's elbow. "What's wrong?"

"Don't ask." He growled as he waited while the line rang and rang. As he was about to hang up, someone picked up.

Thank God, he thought, *she's home.*

"Hello?" came the little voice over the phone. Luke couldn't help but smile at the sound.

"Hey, little buddy. How ya doin'?"

"Hi Daddy!" Owen replied enthusiastically.

"Can you get Mommy, kiddo?"

There was a silence on the end of the line. Luke could hear the television playing in the background, one of Owen's videos most likely. Maggie threw them in when she needed a little sanity. "Owen, are you there?"

"Uh-huh."

"Well, put Mommy on the phone. I need to talk to her."

"I can't find mommy, Daddy. Just me. And Quinny is sleeping." Luke's heart leapt into his throat.

"What do you mean, Owen? Is Mommy not there? Is she outside?"

"I don't know." Owen replied. "I got up and now I'm watching TV. And mommy's not here."

The blood drained from his head and he had to swallow a large lump that tightened his windpipe. "Owen, buddy. Listen to me." Luke spoke quickly, adrenaline pumping through his veins. "You just stay right there and watch your show, okay? If Quinny wakes up, you stay with him. Let him play with some of your toys or something."

"Not my action figures though. He eats 'em."

"Okay. Maybe blocks then. Stay right there, O, until Daddy comes home. I'll be right there."

"Bye Daddy." Owen hung up the phone. Luke slammed the phone shut and ran to his car. Michelle watched him go.

"I'll catch a cab." She called after him knowing he didn't hear.

Chapter Seven

"Both adults take turns sitting on the egg."

Quinn was still sleeping when Luke ran in through the garage door. Owen was curled up at one end of the couch watching cartoons. The only disaster that seemed to have occurred was the puddle of milk on the kitchen floor from Owen trying to help himself. Luke rushed to Owen's side and knelt in front of him. "Are you okay?" he asked although the little boy looked quite content.

Owen nodded and his lips formed a pout. "I spilled, Daddy." He pointed at the kitchen as tears welled in his eyes. "I got thirsty. Where's Mommy?"

Luke's fear melted away like ice on hot pavement, replaced with a sharp spiral of anger. He had to work to control his voice as he spoke to his son. "She'll be home real soon, buddy." *Goddammit,* he thought furiously. *What the hell was she thinking?* He reached for the phone on the kitchen counter and dialed his in-laws number. Maggie's mother answered on the second ring. "Kit? It's Luke. Is everything all right down there?" He didn't bother to hide his anger from her.

"Everything is fine. Luke, what's the matter?"

Luke ignored her. "Mickey is okay, then?" It would just add fuel to his fire now to hear that this whole crisis was a fabrication on Maggie's part.

"Mickey is fine. He's at the bar as far as I know. What is this all about?"

"What about Patrick? Or Aiden? Have you heard from him?"

"Luke, you're scaring me. Patrick is away on business, and no, I haven't heard a word from Aiden. Is something wrong with Maggie?"

"Your daughter gave *me* one hell of a scare today." He said accusingly. "She took off leaving my receptionist some cryptic message about needing to help Mickey. I'm at the house right now, where our *children* had been left *alone*."

"Jesus, Mary, and Joseph." Kit gasped. "Are they alright?"

"They're fine, miraculously. Any number of things could have happened here this afternoon."

Kit's legs weakened beneath her. This didn't sound like Maggie at all. "I can call Mickey, see if he called her. I don't understand it, Luke. Where would she have gone? We're over four hours away. She certainly isn't driving here. Do you think?"

"I don't know what the hell to think. She's been acting..." The door to the garage opened and Maggie stepped inside. "Never mind, Kit. She's here. We'll call you later." He hung up the phone. In one swift move he grabbed Maggie by the arm and pulled her into the dining room, away from Owen's eyes and ears. "What the hell is the matter with you?" he nearly yelled, the anger bursting out of him. Control was gone now. All of the fear and panic and rage he had felt over the past hour and had to contain, came rushing forth like a tidal wave. "Are you *insane?* You left the kids here all alone, Maggie. ALONE!" Tears slid silently down Maggie's cheeks but she remained speechless. "I don't care if your brother is in trouble, you do not leave children alone in this house!"

"My brother?" Maggie asked, confused. "What's wrong with my brother?"

Luke looked at her incredulously. "What do you mean? You said something was wrong with Mickey."

"I said what? When?"

"When you called my office." Luke rubbed his hands over his face. "Maggie, what the fuck is going on?"

Maggie covered her face with her hands as if to hide from him. She crumpled onto a chair and pulled her legs up tightly against her chest, burying her head behind her knees. Her body began to shake with sobs and she couldn't speak. Luke's anger began to fade into fear again, as he watched the woman he had so much love for break down before him. He sat next to her and tried to place an arm over her back, but she pulled from him as if his touch burned.

"Owen! Quinn!" She looked up at him panic stricken.

"They're okay." Luke replied. He suddenly felt very tired. Tired of working so hard, at the office and at home, trying to figure out his own wife who now seemed like a stranger to him. There was a time, long ago, when things had been perfect. It seemed like another lifetime now, but he could still remember the moment he had realized he was in love with her. The memory had faded some over time, but he could see them both: young and full of life and energy. It all started over a pair of ripped sweat pants and a Depeche Mode song…

Maggie agreed to stop back at his apartment after her crew race. Luke had watched her compete in every race since they met. To his surprise, he discovered that he enjoyed the thrill of a race; the charged atmosphere of avid Boston U. fans, the sophistication of the sport. He had always believed himself to be more of a contact sport enthusiast, but then, Maggie was helping to change a lot of his old beliefs. She was strong and independent, always insisting on paying half of dinner or a movie. She was gentle and thoughtful, and she was athletic and graceful, too. Her position on the crew team was the stroke, which he had learned meant that she was responsible for setting the stroke length and cadence of the sweep. He loved watching her peaceful face toughen in concentration as she moved in elegant synchronicity with her teammates. Her back glistened gold in the morning sun. The sweep cut through the water crisply, shooting forward in a rush with each drive.

They placed first in the race, extending their season for nationals. It was cause for celebration and Luke had promised to take her out on the town. Since his apartment was closest, he suggested they stop there to freshen up. He gave her a quick tour of the place and she asked if she could take a quick shower. While she was occupied, he went to work. He pulled out a white linen tablecloth and vase of red roses from the cupboard under the sink. Two wine glasses and a bottle of champagne were removed from his otherwise sparse refrigerator. It had been planned days in advance, for anyone who knew Luke, knew that he was a perfectionist in the ways of romance. And tonight, he had decided, was the night Maggie Callaghan would become his.

Many of the women Luke had dated remained good friends with him even when he was the one to end the relationship, which was most often the case. He seemed to know what women *were thinking, to predict what they wanted or needed and get it for them before they asked for it. Old girlfriends claimed they could talk to him more openly than they could with their female friends, and some just liked to keep him close should he ever have a change of heart.*

That night he was prepared to sweep Maggie off her feet with his irresistible preparations. If he was lucky, they may not even go out at all. Either way, Luke was sure Maggie would be hooked on him by the end of the evening. He flipped the stereo on low and a raspy voice flowed from the speaker filling the air…"

I want somebody to share, share the rest of my life…"

Sappy, but it would work for the mood. He heard the tap turn off down the hall and imagined her wrapping her slender body in one of his towels. He lit the candles he had borrowed from a neighbor, even though it was still midday.

"…Someone who'll stand by my side…" *He looked toward the bedroom for signs that she was almost finished. Feeling atypically nervous, he poured himself a cool glass of water and swallowed it down in large gulps. He heard the click of the door and was slightly annoyed at the spark that traveled down his spine at the thought of her. Then she stepped into the room, wearing one of his tee shirts and a pair of his sweatpants with a rip across one knee.*

"…I want somebody who'll care for me passionately…" *For a brief, uncharacteristic moment, Luke found himself unable to speak and the floor beneath him had become a floating carpet. Her hair fell in wet waves the color of burnt umber to just below her shoulders. Below that her figure gave new shape to his tee shirt, pulling it snugly at her breasts with the definition of her nipples taunting his last bit of control. The cord of the pants was cinched tightly just above her hips. Even the peek of tanned knee and bare feet made his insides swim. He felt himself tighten as he drank in the sight of her.*

Her green eyes flashed impishly as she caught sight of the champagne chilling in a bucket on the table. She raised an eyebrow at him. "I didn't bring a change of clothes. I hope it's okay that I borrowed some of your stuff." She explained when he continued to stare. He nodded dumbly and the soft clean scent of her reached him. He inhaled deeply. "And I hope you don't think you're getting out of taking me out on the town with this fabulous spread you've got here." She walked over and took a glass of champagne. She sipped at it. "Mmmm. On the other hand." She smiled mischievously as she said it, a smile that had a fistful of bees buzzing madly in his gut.

"...Someone who'll help me see things in a different light..."

He took two steps toward her and his lips crushed down on hers with an insatiable hunger. She kissed him back as fervently, her hands raking through his hair. In moments, he had her on the couch, his t-shirt that had looked so good on her discarded in a heap on the floor.

He had never been one to lose himself to emotion or loosen his grip on the controls of his heart. But there was a swirling tornado in his mind, kicking up unusual thoughts and throwing them around wildly. It was quite unfamiliar to him and yet it was a glorious high, the likes of which he had never experienced before. He had been attracted physically to Maggie for a while and enjoyed her humor more with each moment they shared together. His body and mind had wanted to heat things up, but he hadn't expected his heart to get so involved. He reached for the drawstring of the sweatpants and she tugged his shirt over his head. For a moment he just looked at her beneath him – giving herself to him, freely and confidently. His seductive plan was forgotten and he had no interest, at the moment, of regaining it.

"…And when I'm asleep, I want somebody who will put their arms around me and kiss me tenderly…"

At that moment, lost in the presence of her, Luke Devon Stewart knew he was falling in love.

The memory softened Luke's temper as he stood before Maggie now. From that moment in his apartment, none of Luke's standard moves or designs worked. Maggie proved to be different from the others: strong-willed, independent, as much the seductress as the one seduced. The combination had worked on him like a tonic.

He barely recognized the woman who sat before him now, broken and confused. "What happened?" He didn't realize he had spoken his thoughts aloud.

"I don't know. I don't remember. I put the boys down for their nap. I lay down on the couch for a moment. Then I was sitting at the lake. I had no idea how I had gotten there, I don't remember the drive at all, or leaving the house, or calling your office." She began to well up again. "My God, what's wrong with me?"

Maggie spent as much time at the lake as she could. It was where she went to think, where the family would have picnics. Luke had bought a single shell for her the Christmas after they moved and she could be seen on it at least once a week. If he had been thinking logically at the time, he would have thought to look there himself.

Luke scratched his head, confused and exhausted by the day's events. "Why don't you go lay down." He decided. He needed time to think before he could talk to her and she looked tired and confused herself. Before she woke up, he would call her parents again, to come and stay with the kids for few days and figure out a way to tell her that she had to see a psychologist.

When Maggie awoke from a peacefully dreamless sleep, it was dark outside. Her head ached, but she had finally slept, deeply and undisturbed. It took several moments for the memory of what had happed to return. *God, Luke must be furious*, she thought. But what, exactly did happen? She would never knowingly leave her children alone. The tears threatened again, stinging at her eyes, but she closed her lids tightly to ward them off. She wouldn't allow herself to continue being this weak, insecure person she was becoming. She had learned long ago that if you showed signs of weakness that those you loved would turn you away. And she had promised herself she would no longer rely on anyone being there to pick up her pieces. When had she reverted to that fragile child?

She would reassure Luke somehow, that this would never happen again. She loved her children more than anything, and would never put them in harm's way. Luke knew that in his heart, and he would forgive her. If only she could be sure herself.

She stepped gingerly down the stairs, untrusting of legs that could take her miles away without her mind knowing it. The joyful sounds of family reached her ears from the kitchen and her breath caught at the thought of her recklessness.

She pushed the ugliness from her mind and tried to put on a smile as she rounded the corner into the kitchen.

The sight before her warmed her heart. Luke sat at the kitchen table, Owen on one side of him, Quinn on the other. A book of traceable letters was open on the table before them and together Luke and Owen carefully traced the letters with a marker. Quinn had his own piece of paper and happily drew squiggles and lines.

"Daddy!" Quinn squealed, holding up his paper. Luke took it and held it in the air to examine it.

"A masterpiece, Quinn. It's wonderful! You're making letters too, aren't you, just like O?" Quinn clapped his hands together. Owen finished with an M and showed his father.

"He can't make a M." Owen told Luke matter-of-factly. "He's just a baby."

"No, he can't make an M like you can. But he is trying, right?" Owen looked at his father and exchanged knowing winks with him.

Maggie stepped forward into the room and the magic was broken. Luke turned to her, his face clouded with concern and residual anger. Owens's big blue eyes seemed to hold just a little less trust in them, a little more wariness. It broke Maggie's heart to know she caused that. Only Quinn seemed completely oblivious, smiling happily and shouting, "Mamma! Mamma! Up!"

She ignored Luke's look of pity and contempt and gave each of her sons a big hug. Gathering Owens's face in her hands, she looked down into his beautiful eyes, swallowing back the tears again. "Mommy will never leave you again, okay baby? Mommy will always be here when you wake up. From now on. I promise." One tear escaped from her control and dropped onto Owen's ivory cheek. He brushed it away and then wiped Maggie's face tenderly, with a care that seemed beyond his years.

"It's okay, Mommy. It was a accident. I have accidents too." He looked at Luke who nodded approval. Clearly, they had discussed the issue while she was sleeping. Owen went back to his letters, the incident resolved as far as he was concerned.

"I'm so sorry, Luke." she whispered to her husband, but he put a hand up to silence her.

"We'll talk about it later."

Later came after the boys had been bathed, read to and put to bed. Maggie and Luke were good at tag teaming during the bedtime routine, and often remarked at their own efficiency. Tonight the pride was absent. Luke came down the stairs shortly after Maggie. She waited for him at the kitchen table, under the glare of the chandelier, where her interrogation would take place. She avoided his eyes, uncertain of what feelings he still held about what she had done and self-doubting of his current feelings for her. There was no defense for her to present, even if she had been able to remember what caused her to rush out on her sleeping children. An apology would seem hollow, but she needed to start somewhere.

"Luke, I'm so sorry." She swallowed hard and tensed herself for her contrition.

Luke rubbed his stubbly chin with a look in his eyes that spoke volumes. He was disappointed, angry, saddened, confused, and uncertain. After a long, chilly silence he spoke, looking at his hands folded neatly on the table. "You need to see someone about this. I won't take no for an answer." Maggie nodded but remained silent. "I can get you a referral if you can't do it yourself, but it needs to be arranged by the end of the day tomorrow.

"I also called your parents. They are coming to stay here for a few days to help out with things here and see the kids."

The second comment stung. *Because he can't trust me with my own children anymore,* Maggie thought bitterly. *I will never live this down. One mistake and he's acting like we need to alert social services.* She bit her lip to contain her angry thoughts. Fighting back would serve no purpose now.

Luke continued, "I've taken tomorrow off and I'm taking the boys to the lake for the day so that you can have some time to arrange your appointment and get ready for your parents."

Maggie's head shot up in shock. "By yourselves? It's not going to happen again, Luke! It was terrible what I did, but it was a mistake. I didn't intentionally walk out on our kids! You act like I can't even be around them anymore, like I need…"

"I'm taking the only precaution I can think of, Maggie. It may not have been intentional. In my mind it's worse, because it *wasn't* within your control. Can you explain what happened? Can you tell me what you were thinking as you got in your car and drove off while our boys were inside alone? You don't *remember* if it was intentional. You don't remember any of it. Frankly that scares the hell out of me. Because a lapse of memory like that… it could happen again. It could happen anywhere. I can't put Owen and Quinn at risk like that. I won't."

"But to spend the day with them and leave me out, Luke. Why? Why can't we all go? It would be like old times."

Luke shook his head. "You need some time to yourself. And you need to find a doctor. It will be easier to do that without the boys and me around. It's just one day."

Maggie nodded and swallowed the lump in her throat, thoroughly defeated. She felt like she was losing everything. Her husband, her children, her mind. Maybe a doctor would be best. Someone to talk to. It *was* only one day as Luke said. Maybe then this nightmare would end.

Chapter Eight

The bar was relatively quiet between the dinner rush and the evening crowd. Mickey often used the time to go over inventory or update his books. He needed another shipment from his Irish supplier, but it would be too early in the morning there to call.

He could picture the rosy sun rising over the moss-covered hills. She would awaken to the smell of hot rolls and Danish. He closed his eyes to see the vision more clearly. Sliding out of bed, she would either curse or bless the hot floor beneath her bare feet each morning, depending on the season. Her home was a charming loft on the upper floor of an old carriage house. Below her was the town's nearly famous bakery "Bunns". Gwen would pull her straight hair into a high ponytail and knot it there as she made her way to the kitchen for her coveted freshly squeezed orange juice. She might sit at the circular table for a while – reading the paper or gazing out the window at the street below as it came to life. Or she might swallow the juice down quickly and rush to the shower to prepare for a busy day at university. *It must be exam time for her,* Mickey thought. *Maybe she had a late night studying and won't stir for a few hours yet. Maybe she's found a late-night study partner and isn't alone.* The thought left him with the acrid taste of jealousy.

Whatever she might be doing, her life was certainly going on without him. Danny hadn't mentioned her in his last few phone conversations and Mickey wondered if she stopped visiting the pub or if Danny was censoring his conversations. It was possible that she didn't want the reminders of her time with him, while he seemed to submerge himself in them. Had she taken down the framed photo of them at Waterfall Garden too?

It had been taken the day before he left for home from the trip when they first met. Years earlier, he had begun to travel as a way of escaping his parents and to find work after dropping out of his senior year of college. He had lived it up for two months in Mexico, found himself in Puerto Rico with no recollection of how he had gotten there, and worked briefly in Spain before deciding to visit his Irish roots.

Immediately, Mickey fell in love with his homeland. He traveled the countryside during his first few visits, enjoying the rough landscape and the plentiful bars. Eventually, he came to stay in County Kerry and decided to try and find work in a local pub. There he met Danny, and eventually, Gwen. A year sabbatical became two. After that, his visa expired and he was forced to return home.

The picture at Waterfall Garden showed none of the sadness that hid been behind their smiling eyes in the photograph, which only enhanced the memory and added to its beauty. They had taken their shoes off and rolled up their pants, to wade before the falls. It had taken Mickey three tries with the camera timer and tripod to get it right. Each time he had to reset it, Gwen would splash him on his way back to the camera and throw her head back laughing, the sound echoing around them. She was contagious and Mickey couldn't help but laugh with her. On the third try he rushed back to get in the frame, grabbing Gwen around the waist as he almost slipped into the water. They looked at each other, laughing, and the shot was taken. Afterward, they made love on the damp earth by the waterfall, slowly pouring out their feelings for one another.

Once he was home, Mickey couldn't think of much else. He didn't stay away long. When Mickey next returned to Ireland, less than a year later, he worried that he might have been forgotten by the woman who stirred his soul. Instead, he found that Gwen had the picture proudly displayed behind the sofa in her newly rented space above the bread shop. Each grateful to rediscover the feelings they had for each other, they celebrated their novel privacy and Mickey's return over a bottle of champagne. From that night on whenever Mickey was in Ireland, he stayed at Gwen's.

Mickey pushed the inventory sheets aside, thoroughly entrenched in the memories. Looking back over his relationship with Gwen, he could finally begin to understand why it had ended. For nearly seven years, Mickey dropped in and out of her life at his convenience, always taking for granted that she would be there waiting for him. And she always was. While they had never specified that their relationship would be exclusive, Mickey knew that she had dated no one else the entire time they were a couple. He could see how selfish he had been. During the years that most women were finding serious relationships and settling down to start a family, Mickey had chained her to a now and again affair with no promise of the future. How she had held on as long as she did amazed and saddened him. And why he'd never done anything about it when he had the opportunity was devastating.

Mickey pushed his chair back from the desk and stood. He strode from the storage room through the bar, aware of the exact number of bottles on the shelf offering to ease his suffering. It probably wasn't his best idea, but he needed to busy himself, so he stepped behind the bar to help out. The bartender on duty gave him a nod, only slightly curious as to why the owner had suddenly stepped in. Mickey was known to help behind the bar, on the floor, or in the kitchen, but it usually occurred when they were swamped. He grabbed himself a bottled water from the cooler, as was his habit, and started on an order.

He was surprised moments later to see his mother walk through the front door. Kit rarely visited Mickey C's and would not be caught dead in a bar at the "witching hour" as she referred to it. Mickey could tell from her expression that she was not here for a social visit. Worry lines creased her forehead and her lips formed a thin line. Mickey leaned casually over the bar as she sat down.

"Uhh, 'scuse me ma'am, but it's awful early for that tequila shot ya like so much, ain't it?" The humor was lost on her. Instead she returned it with a look of exasperation, of a woman whose days were far too dark to be lightened by cheap humor and sarcasm. Mickey leaned closer and lowered his voice. "Ma, it was a joke. What's the matter?"

Kit pinched the bridge of her nose with her thumb and forefinger trying to ward off a migraine or tears. "Oh, Mickey. Have you spoken to Maggie recently?"

"No, why?"

"Because Luke called. Apparently Maggie deserted the boys today. Luke said she believed something was wrong with you. Does that make any sense?"

"Me? I'm fine, Mom. Never better. Just look at me. Besides, I haven't even talked to Mags this week."

"I'm very worried about her, Mickey. This is not normal behavior."

Mickey knew his mother under extreme stress and anxiety. He knew because she was *always* stressed and anxious. "Look, don't you think 'deserted' is a bit harsh? I'm sure they were taken care of. How much of the story did Luke give you?"

"I don't know. She returned home while we were talking and he cut the conversation short. He spoke to your father later and asked that we come for a visit for a few days. Doesn't that seem odd?"

Mickey shrugged. "Well, do you want me to give her a call?"

Kit placed a fragile hand on her son's. "I think it wouldn't hurt. She won't open up to your father or me, but she always liked talking to you. Maybe you could get to the bottom of it."

Mickey looked at his mother's hand on his. This was the only reaching out she ever did when it came to her family – a gentle touch. "Are you worried about something in particular, mom?"

Kit pulled her hand back as though she'd been stung and stood from the barstool. "Of course, not." She defended. "Can't I just want my daughter to be happy and healthy and be a good mother to her children?"

Mickey pretended to be dodging punches. "Whoa there, champ, just asking! I'll call her. But this place is gonna be swamped in about an hour so I'll have to do it in the morning. I'll tip her off that you guys are heading out there so she can make a break for it."

Kit's defensiveness subsided a bit and she attempted a weak smile. Mickey could always be trusted to never take anything seriously. "Thank you, dear." She touched his cheek gently before her brow lowered with a new worry. "Mickey, do you really think you should be working back there?"

"Easy mom. One dysfunctional child at a time."

Chapter Nine

Aiden paid the cab driver and stepped out into the bright lights of the city. At 8:30 in the evening, New York was just waking up. The nocturnal creatures emerged from their dens, rubbing their eyes against the fabricated sunlight and stretching for the imminent hunt. Aiden felt completely out of place; a country mouse transported to the city for the first time. Looking upward, the buildings swallowed him and he was acutely aware of his place in the world. Before him loomed a modern apartment building, sprouting up from the cement like a rose amid weeds. This was what his brother came home to every night.

A doorman greeted him at the entrance and welcomed him in. Sadly, to Aiden, even the doorman appeared more sophisticated than he felt; a young, single upstate man, climbing the ladder of his own life, which wouldn't amount to a step stool here. He was directed to the "Callaghan lobby", found the chrome elevator at the end of the gleaming Italian marble and stepped inside. Depressing the button for the fifteenth floor, he realized that Pat lived almost at the top.

The ride was smooth and swift, and before he could gather his thoughts, Aiden stood before an elegant entryway. The crisp click of heels on tile announced Shauna before she became visible, and Aiden knew that he had been expected and announced the moment he had arrived. Shauna smiled warmly at the brother in-law she had met only a handful of times before and she approached him with outstretched arms, wrapping him in an affectionate hug.

"It's so good to see you." She declared in a smooth, well-trained voice.

Shauna was upper class from head to toe. When Aiden was riding snowmobiles with Patrick and building tree forts, she was being trained in dining etiquette and conversation. "Patrick will be out in just a moment. He's on the phone in the library. You know your brother, he never leaves the office."

Aiden offered a sympathetic smile. Was he the only one who realized that he and his brother might as well be strangers? *Well, except for our history,* he thought cynically. He was still unsure of what to expect. *But,* he reminded himself, *Patrick asked me here. He said he needed my help, and I agreed.*

Shauna led him through the entrance down a short hallway and into a spacious living room with a wall of windows overlooking the City. A grand piano stood quietly in one corner. Behind it, two arched bookcases held classic literature, oversized art books and law reviews. A soft suede couch in the center of the room faced a large screen entertainment center. Between them was a round glass coffee table cushioned by an Oriental Rug that Aiden was sure had cost about what he made in a year. While Aiden was still trying to adjust to his posh surroundings, six year-old Alexis wandered into the room from a high archway leading back into what must have been the bedrooms. Ready for bed, she looked like a tiny princess in a pale pink nightgown edged with lace and a matching ribbon tied in her shiny brown hair. Hanging from her hand was a worn, furry teddy bear. She peeked suspiciously at her unfamiliar uncle, and then shifted her gaze to her mother, as though for reassurance that this stranger was, in fact, welcomed into their home.

Shauna stepped in and pulled Alexis close.

"Lexy, honey, this is your Uncle Aiden. He came to visit with Daddy and to see you and Patrick and little Ashleigh. Can you say 'hi'?"

The young girl smiled shyly and whispered 'hello' to Aiden. Her eyes had widened when she heard that the stranger before her was her uncle. Aiden smiled his warmest welcoming smile and crouched down to the little girl's eye level.

"Hi, Lexy." He offered her a hug, but she wasn't quite comfortable enough to accept it just yet. It disappointed him, if only the Callaghan family could see the merit in honesty, he wouldn't be such a stranger to his siblings and their children. Hell, he'd never even met Maggie's youngest, although Mickey sent him a picture shortly after Quinn was born. Bryan Quinn… didn't every one else in the family see what Maggie was doing? Was it blindingly apparent only to him that she was walking head first into a Mack truck of pain?

Aiden closed his eyes for a brief moment, forcing the thoughts back to the attic of his mind, where they most often remained, locked up and dusty. His oldest brother had asked him for help. *Him.* Not Mickey this time, not Dad. This was what he had wanted all his life. To be needed by his brother. Deep in the secret recesses of his memory, Aiden had always wished he could *be* Patrick. Strong and mature, Patrick could always do the things that Aiden was never old enough for, never *brave* enough for. By the time Aiden reached the right age, things were so different; it didn't seem to matter any more. By then, Patrick was quiet and reclusive, and Aiden discarded any hopes of a strong bond between them. He turned to Mickey for a while, instead, an easier challenge, for a companion and confidante. But Mickey couldn't take anything seriously and so they had very little in common. Mickey was extremely social, going out most nights to parties, or with girls, Aiden was much more of an introvert. He studied hard and worked part-time jobs throughout high school and had little time for dating and drinking.

Mickey went on to college and finally Aiden was on his own, the man of the house. He found he couldn't wait to get to college himself, and set his mind on studying even harder. He never saw Maggie during those years, unless it was at Christmas. Patrick didn't come home often.

Then Mickey dropped out of college and was traveling so much, and drinking so much they wouldn't see him for a year or more at a time. When he did come home, Mickey only talked about Gwen and Ireland, as though they were his true family and home. Then he came up with that crazy idea of opening an Irish pub right here... It had all led up to the terrible events of Mickey's grand opening.

His thoughts were interrupted by Patrick entering the room like the main act of a concert. All eyes turned to him adoringly, even Aiden's against his own will. Patrick smiled and greeted his brother with a big bear hug, but Aiden saw something else too, deep in Patrick's eyes. So many years in the field had perfected his ability to read body language, and it was clear that Patrick had something weighing on his mind. He hid it well, though, even Shauna didn't seem to notice.

"Aiden, man, good to see you. Thanks for coming down all this way. Sorry I'm a little late for the reunion, I got stuck on the phone with this business exec who thinks the world needs to come to a stop whenever something goes wrong in his life." A bitter laugh escaped his lips before he caught himself and cut it short. "If only that was the way, huh, little brother?"

Aiden nodded, not sure if the question was completely rhetorical.

"Well, what are we doing standing out here? After the flight and the dirty New York streets, this guy's gotta be more than a little hungry. Shauna, let's introduce Aiden to the Callaghan kitchen, shall we?" Shauna nodded, the sweet smile never fading from her lips and Aiden suddenly found himself being shuffled down another hallway to what he was sure would be a state-of-the-art New York kitchen.

The late meal with Patrick and his family was uncomfortably quiet, but mercifully quick. Only the three adults and nine month-old Ashleigh were present and Shauna immersed herself in caring for the baby. Patrick sipped his red wine with more frequency than a casual dinner drink. He asked Aiden inane questions about his job and his life, trying to pass the time until they could retreat to his den and talk in greater depth.

Finally, Shauna shooed them away to their privacy while she cleaned up the table and got Ashleigh off to bed. Patrick led Aiden through the wide, back hallway with recessed lighting and burgundy walls. Large, expensive paintings lined one side, a beveled mirror ran the length of the hall on the other.

The hallway spilled into a professional and somber-looking den and library. Grand mahogany bookcases covered two walls, filled with hard covered books in hunter and maroon that Aiden couldn't imagine trying to read. Patrick fixed himself an oversized cordial from behind a cherry and leather wet bar and tossed Aiden a cold beer from the mini fridge. He settled himself in a stiff wingback chair and Aiden sat across from him in his professional posture. He felt out of his element in Patrick's world, and if he was supposed to be offering counseling services, he would have much preferred his cheap, paneled office and creaky swivel chair to the sophistication he was surrounded by here.

Patrick gestured to the view beyond the windows. The lights of the city glimmered beneath them, the red blinking eyes of passing traffic moved slowly and steadily among the buildings. For all its glamour and mystique, Aiden had a hard time understanding why anyone would want to live in New York. It seemed awfully high maintenance to his simpler tastes. He would rather drive his gray Accord than wait and whistle idiotically for a Checker cab, would much prefer a quick and simple stop at a McDonalds drive-thru for a quick bite to putting on airs in a restaurant where men in tails and bow-ties offered a cork for approval of the wine selections.

"It's beautiful, isn't it?" Patrick asked, watching Aiden for a reaction. Aiden shrugged and turned to face his brother again.

"I guess." He replied and paused. "So, what's going on, Pat? You didn't pay for me to come down here just to ogle at the view."

Patrick stood and walked to the window. "Did you know that I could see the towers from this room? I had an afternoon meeting there that day. I watched it happen right here where I'm standing now. I lost eight professional associates that morning."

Aiden looked at the floor, ashamed. He, of course, had known none of this about Patrick. He never even called his parents that day to make sure he was okay. He only knew from a phone message Mickey left him three days later. "I'm so sorry, Pat." He muttered.

"Look out there and try to remember it. You can't help but see the tragedy in this skyline when you remember." Aiden walked slowly to the windows. Patrick pointed to a gap between the buildings and Aiden felt his heart sink. The loneliness of it overwhelmed him, like some critical focal point had been torn out of a breathtaking landscape.

"It must have been awful." He spoke quietly.

"It was indescribable. Makes a guy think, you know?" Patrick returned to his chair and Aiden followed him. "Course, it didn't make me think enough, then. I do a lot more of that now. Too much sometimes. You ever think about something so much you end up feeling trapped by it?"

Aiden leaned slightly forward with his eyes steadily on Patrick's.

"Absolutely."

"Then you know what I'm talking about. It seems like I'm always thinking too much nowadays, but lately...lately I got one thing on my mind that won't go away." He took a long swallow of his drink. "I fucked up, Aiden. I fucked up at work and I think I'm in some deep shit."

"Explain 'fucked up' for me."

Patrick leaned forward in his chair. "Davis put me in charge of a couple of big corporations. I had to check out all the specs on them, look at their numbers, you know. The goal was to find the most vulnerable company with the most potential for profit. Then we acquire it. I was the head guy. Usually, Davis or one of his senior execs does all the groundwork and I seal the deal. I guess he was finally ready to see if I could handle it all, which got me thinking that he was starting to prepare for retirement. He doesn't have any sons. Only Shauna and Daphne, who lives in Hawaii.

"So, at first I'm thinking all I have to do is show him I can run the place and, maybe he'll hand me the reins soon.

"Well, I do my homework and one of the companies comes out looking like a prime target. In the process, though, I've been talking with the president of one of the other companies. I don't even know why Davis gave me this one, the place is a power house; no one is going to get close to it, much less take it apart. After a number of conversations with this guy, Ron Sterger, he offers me a deal. He wants to sell me his company on paper. One of the contingencies is that we keep him on at top level. Then he and I create a team to rebuild from within Davis Enterprises."

"And oust Davis?"

"Yeah. So of course, I'm thinking no deal. I'd be an idiot to pull the rug out from under Davis right before I step into his shoes. I tell Sterger that. A week later he comes at me with three instances of price fixing on stocks from Davis' acquisitions. My name is front and center as having closed each one of them. So now, I can take his deal, or go down with Davis and he'll get the company anyway."

"What exactly is price fixing?" Aiden asked.

"You get the stock of a company to drop before you acquire it. It makes the sale look necessary for survival.

After you purchase it, you buy up the stock, making the price jump, and you're a hero for reviving a dying company and saving thousands of jobs, plus you've got more money in your pocket. After a while, the prices level back out and you can take the company apart piece by piece with no one really noticing."

"And this is illegal."

"Does Martha Stewart ring a bell?"

"Okay. So then, is your name just on the papers, or were you an active part of it?"

Patrick sighed and rose from his chair to pace. "That's moot. My name is on the papers, I'm the first one who will go down. Not to mention a good number of the stocks went to me each time. It was mostly Davis. The only reason the stock came to me was to take care of Shauna. He never did trust me enough to do that myself."

Aiden watched Patrick circle the couch before he returned to the bar to fix another drink. "Isn't bringing this Sterger guy in under false pretenses illegal too?"

Patrick shook his head. "Unethical. Not illegal. But, I'd be protecting Davis, right? Who wants to spend the first five years of their retirement in prison?"

"So Davis' name is on all the documents too?"

Patrick's eyes shifted out the window and his shoulders seemed to droop. "No, it would be harder to pin anything on him. Really… I'm just trying to save my own ass. Davis has done this long enough that he knows how to keep clean." He turned back to Aiden with fierceness. "But he let me be the fall guy. There was no looking out for my ass, why shouldn't I sell the floor out from under him?"

Aiden remained quiet for a moment. He felt out of his league with the business ramifications, but could understand his brother's overall position was not good. "How do you know Sterger will stick to his deal after he's a part of your company? It doesn't sound like he's much of a straight shooter either."

"He's not, but I can't prove it yet. If I let him in a little further, I might be able to get something off him. But either way, it's easier for him to keep me around. He's got to have someone in Davis Enterprises already to have the information he does. But whoever it is, doesn't have the clout I do to pull off the takeover. That's why he involved me in the first place.

"We'd be equal partners by the end of it. Davis would hardly know it happened. By the time it all worked out, he'd probably be retired anyway and slugging down martinis in Cancun."

Aiden took a swallow of his beer and set it on the table. One question had been tugging at him since Patrick had begun the conversation. Finally, he had to ask. "Pat, you said on the phone that it had to be me you talked to. You said you couldn't talk to anyone else. But, almost anyone else would be more knowledgeable about this kind of thing then me. Why not your attorney, or…or Luke?"

The room remained silent for several moments. Aiden heard the faint voice of Celine Dion coming from the living room. When Patrick finally spoke, Aiden thought he could see a shimmer in the corner of his eye. Patrick would not look at Aiden, but searched for something beyond his shoulder instead.

"I needed it to be you. You would be honest with me about whether I'm running away all over again. I think this is another test of my character. And I failed before. I need you to tell me how to handle it 'cuz I don't trust my own judgment. I don't want to make another mistake, like the one I made before."

It dawned on Aiden what Patrick was struggling with now and it was nothing he had ever seen from Patrick before. Of course Patrick would never show this side to anyone in the family that he still had a relationship with. He felt an urge to reassure Patrick, but how? A pat on the shoulder? A hug? They would be out of place here. His feet were rooted to the ground. "Are you blaming yourself for *that*?" It was more accusation than question.

"Who else is there to blame?"

"Pat, you were a kid. You had no idea it would happen. It didn't make you who you are!"

"It sure as hell did!" Patrick sat across from Aiden again. This time he looked deep into his brother's eye as if to prove this was not up for debate. "Listen, I didn't bring you here to boost my self esteem or look into my psyche or... or whatever it is you're trained to do in the inspirational area. I don't need that. What I need is for you to look at the present facts and tell me if all I'm trying to do is cover my own ass again or if I'm making the decision responsibly."

"I think the problem is, you've somehow come to enjoy living under this cloud of guilt and hostility. You've convinced yourself you're a victim of lousy choices. No matter what I tell you, you're always going to think you screwed up."

"Dad's always been pretty goddamn clear about that, Aid. Why don't *you* ask him if I'm to blame?"

"Dad doesn't blame you, Pat. He doesn't hold you up to some impossible, unrealistic standard, like you think. You've done that all by yourself! Christ, Dad shut himself away from feeling anything! What makes you think he gives your residual pain any more thought than the rest of us? This is exactly why I couldn't be a part of this family anymore. We're all still fucked up from something that happened years ago, because no one is allowed to admit that it even happened! Does that make any sense at all?" Aiden was standing now, his arms waving angrily. Patrick returned to the bar and threw him another beer.

"Take it easy, Aiden. Don't start your soapbox shit. We've all heard it before."

If he'd been closer Aiden thought he might have punched him. "Fuck you." He retorted.

"Fuck you too. At least the rest of us still acknowledge we're a part of this family. Maybe the way we do things isn't modeled after the Cleavers or one of your Socialwork textbooks, but we try to take care of each other. Can you say the same? Do you think after two years of this silent treatment, you're gonna make us finally *see the light* and *right our wrongs*? Get over yourself."

Aiden seethed, though he knew his brother was right. He had thought the same thing himself countless times over the last two years. But whenever he considered trying to make amends, he couldn't bring himself to do it. He couldn't carry on the farce that he would be required to as a Callaghan. And if he spoke out against them all now, they'd shut him out anyway. So nothing changed. "I can't live the lie." He stated coldly.

Patrick let out a cynical laugh. "You're living the lie, bro. Just because you're not actively spinning the web, doesn't mean you're not caught in it."

Aiden's anger soared. "Give me the phone then, dammit. I'll call Maggie right now. Tell her everything. Let's get it all out right now!"

"Bullshit." Patrick returned with a sardonic grin. He tossed the portable phone across the room.

Aiden frantically dialed the number he knew by heart, though he had never actually dialed it until now. Bile rose in his throat and his stomach churned madly. When he heard the soft, gentle voice of his sister on the other end of the phone, he pushed the end button as a wave of nausea spread through him and sat down hard on the couch. It had been so long since he had spoken to her, so long since he had seen her face. Had it been worse to see her knowing she was being deceived or to not see her at all?

Patrick knew when to quit. By the look on Aiden's face, he had pushed it too far for one night. He wouldn't apologize. He'd always sucked at it, and Aiden had brought this on himself as far as he was concerned. But they were still brothers. And Aiden had handled enough for now. "Come on, Aiden." Patrick placed a hand on Aiden's shoulder. "I'll show you where you're sleeping."

CHAPTER TEN

Maggie couldn't sleep again. This time though, it was no dream that kept her eyes from closing. The late night phone call had woken her and she found herself wondering about the emptiness at the other end of the line. Was it just a wrong number? Either way, it set her mind racing again – to her day of solitary confinement as Luke and the boys shared their quality time. She'd made the stupid call for a counseling appointment. She freshened up the spare bedroom for her parents' impending visit the next day. And she sat for over an hour trying to remember.

She tried to remember what had happened during the boys' nap, when she had started losing control. Tried to remember when she and Luke had started drifting apart.

She tried to remember the last time she and Luke had made love – and that memory, at least, came back to her. It was shortly before Quinn's first birthday. God, that long ago? Luke had surprised them all by playing hooky from work and taking them to the aquarium for the day.

The afternoon passed quickly for Maggie and before long they were all back in the car, with two well-fed, exhausted, sticky boys. The aquarium had been a huge success and Maggie tried to savor each and every moment of the day. They reached their home at sunset and quietly transferred the sleeping children to their beds.

Maggie busied herself unpacking Quinn's diaper bag and rinsing sippy cups. Luke snuck up behind her and nuzzled her ear. The gesture both pleased and surprised her. "The hot tub is running." He murmured into her ear. Maggie finished rinsing out the sink, dried her hands with a dishtowel and turned to look at him. Luke took both of her hands in his, tossing the towel carelessly onto the floor and tenderly brought them to his lips.

What has gotten into you? *she wanted to ask. She couldn't think of more than a handful of times when the hot tub had been used. But she didn't say a word, was too afraid that if she did this strange but wonderful spell that had been cast over her work-obsessed husband would be broken and she would never have it again. Instead she smiled gently and allowed Luke to lead her through the French doors and onto the deck.*

Dusk settled over the yard casting shadows across the lawn. The rows of maples and evergreens bordering the yard assured them privacy so that when Luke stepped close to Maggie to undo the buttons of her blouse, she shivered only from the novelty of it, but did not resist. He slipped the liquid fabric off her shoulders and traced her neck with his lips. Her skin was soft and smooth under his hands and he thought of how long it had been.

He reached around her and unhooked her bra, letting it drop to the growing pile at their feet. Her breath caught with excitement and she reached to undo the button of his jeans. He stood for a moment, quietly drinking in the beauty of the woman before him. She had the same gentle curves she'd had at twenty, her hips only slightly more defined and, in his mind, even sexier. His thumbs brushed across her rosy nipples and he felt his stomach twist as they hardened beneath his touch. She undid the buttons of her jeans and stepped out of them, standing before him now without any walls between them.

He removed his shirt and took her hand to lead her into the steaming water. She admired his shoulders, his biceps, his lean torso. His body belied the patience he displayed and he tugged her gently to follow him. She stepped tentatively into the steeping bubbles. Tiny sparks of arousal snapped in her brain when Luke took her by the chin and turned her to see the passion in his eyes. Any doubt she felt melted away in the heat between them and she sank beside him into the water.

They settled in the bubbling waves and he took her face gently in his hands. The warmth created a thin layer of mist where it joined with the cool night air. Tenderly, he kissed her forehead, her eyelids, her awaiting lips. Their breath mixed hotly while they languished in it. He cupped her breasts in his hands, molded them with his fingers. A sigh escaped her lips, ready for him, and a chill of excitement ran down her spine. He slid his hand under her arms and pulled her onto him. Her head tipped back as his warm tongue circled one nipple and then hungrily nipped at the other. Her arms went around him and she traced a path from his tailbone to his hairline with the tip of her finger. She could feel him tighten beneath her.

Their urgent need for each other built steadily, his hands roamed her body, discovering her as if for the first time. They traced her ribcage, her abdomen, her hips and thighs before reaching the place that yearned for him most. He couldn't tell where her warmth ended and the water's began. It was a single current, sweetly entwined, that rushed over them with great sweeping motions. On the edge of ecstasy, she clutched his hips, pulled them against her, greedy for him and aching with the need to be one. He entered her and joined her ascent. Together they climbed to the crest, reaching it in the same moment and swirling hopelessly with the riptide until it washed them away.

She glistened with sweat and water while they held each other, motionless. They remained locked together as the moments passed, neither needing to say anything and both wishing to keep the feeling alive. Finally, he pulled back enough to kiss her softly. Her fingers brushed through his hair, her eyes closed in tranquility.

Maggie's eyes glistened, not from the memory itself, but the fact that it was such a distant one.

Chapter Eleven

Patrick took Aiden to lunch in Soho before his flight home. Aiden figured it was his attempt at a truce. They had not resumed the previous night's conversation that morning. Instead they sat together in the kitchen as Shauna made homemade pancakes for everyone and discussed the culture of the City. Afterward, Aiden busied himself checking and double-checking his bags, which had barely been touched.

The restaurant was upscale, but not ostentatious. Probably another conscious move on Patrick's part. They ordered sandwiches and sat in uncomfortable silence.

"Do you get out to any of the plays around here much?" Aiden attempted small talk.

"Uggh." Patrick groaned. "Shauna drags me to one every now and then. I can't stand 'em."

"Yeah. I guess I can't see you as the musical type."

Patrick snorted. "Hmmph. So...is this the only conversation that's safe for us now?"

"I think so."

"You know, Mom really misses you. You should at least touch base with her once in a while."

"Not Dad though, huh?"

"Hell, Aiden. *I* wouldn't be on speaking terms with Dad if I thought I could get away with it. Who knows what he thinks about it all...or *if* he thinks about it.

"But Mom, well. She gets real upset when you come into conversation. She feels like she's lost you now too."

Aiden felt the blow just as if it had been physical. He looked guiltily at his plate and swallowed hard. He wanted back in, but he knew nothing would be different. He'd been around this a hundred times in his head and it always ended the same. His inability to function the way the rest of them did would make him say something he would regret. Everyone would turn their anger on him and he would take it all in. He would continue to absorb the pain they radiated.

"I can't do it any more, Patrick. I can't live the way you all can."

"I know." Patrick's voice was compassionate and Aiden had to look up to make sure it was still him. Patrick saw the look on his face. "We're not living, though. We're surviving. And so are you."

This moment with Patrick was the opposite extreme of the previous night's conversation. There was brotherhood here, something he may never have felt before, and may not again. He had craved it.

He had to be cautious, though. All of the good feelings he'd had toward his family over the years had proven fleeting. Walls had been built to protect him from the pain of their dissolution. What he felt at this moment he would enjoy, but he would not fool himself into thinking it was lasting.

"It's a little less painful to survive this way." He admitted, continuing the honest display of emotions with Patrick. "Not much, maybe. But a little."

"One call to mom wouldn't have to change all that, you know. But it might make it a little less painful for her too."

"Maybe. I'll think about it."

Patrick paid the bill and hailed a taxi for Aiden. The bear hug they shared before Aiden stepped into the cab was different from the one that had greeted him upon his arrival. It was real.

"I'll be in touch." Aiden said genuinely.

"So will I."

Maggie pulled into the parking lot of a small brick building, where Dr. Jamie Cooper waited to pick apart her entire life. Her stomach knotted uneasily as she stepped out of the car and headed toward the entrance. Part of her was angry with Luke, even though she truly believed he was only trying to help. In the process, he had made her feel weak and untrustworthy. When he was home, she was overly conscious of her interactions with Owen and Quinn, as though her every movement was being scrutinized and analyzed for error. The look of love and concern in Luke's eyes had been replaced lately by suspicion. The day he had taken the boys to the beach without her had been the longest and most painful day she could remember for some time. The entire atmosphere of home had unleashed her fight or flight instinct and she feared she might run away from it all if one more thing went wrong. It was a feeling she was afraid of becoming accustomed to.

Maggie opened the door and stepped inside. The thought of spouting out all of these emotions to a total stranger only made her want to find a deep hole and crawl inside. She couldn't talk to the closest person in her life, the one who knew her better than anyone in the world, how was she supposed to open up to someone who cared or knew absolutely nothing about her?

The receptionist was an older woman, a motherly figure. Maggie could picture her around a Christmas tree surrounded by children and grandchildren, sharing old stories and laughing over eggnog and sugar cookies. She had a round face and a warm smile, and Maggie's nervousness began to dissipate. Dr. Cooper chose well in hiring her, surely knowing that such a gentle-looking woman would help put her clientele at ease. Maggie gave her name and took a seat.

The waiting area was strategically decorated as well. Oak furniture and moldings created a feeling that this was a weekend retreat rather than a doctor's office. Framed photos of gentle landscapes dotted the walls: countrysides and cornfields, sunsets and lake views created images of relaxation and release. The coffee table before her was covered with magazines from "Cottage Life" to "Redbook". There were no financial periodicals or what Maggie considered 'psychological fodder'. She absentmindedly picked up a copy of 'Ladies' Home Journal' and flipped through.

Moments later a door to the left of the reception area opened and a young, attractive woman stepped through. She had golden blond hair that hung straight to her shoulders with a breath of bangs above sky blue eyes. She wore jeans and a casual blouse that tapered at her waist, accentuating her slender build. Maggie thought she must be a client due to her casual attire, but she looked over at Maggie and spoke.

"Mrs. Stewart?" Maggie nodded and the woman moved toward her with her hand extended. "Welcome. I'm Jamie Cooper. It's very nice to meet you." Maggie stood and shook the woman's hand. This was not at all what Maggie had pictured a shrink to be. She didn't have the crisp business suit, or the glasses perched at the tip of her nose in order to peer down at Maggie in condescension. "Please, come on back to my office."

Maggie followed Dr. Cooper to the opened door and beyond. There was no couch, no oversized, overbearing desk for her to sit before while she was probed and dissected. Two overstuffed chairs rested on a round braided rug, facing each other in the center of the room with a petite end table next to each. Large windows covered the back wall and looked out over the river, softened by beige vertical blinds. On the other side of the room was a tall secretariat desk with neatly organized stacks of paper and a telephone. It seemed almost too simplified and Maggie wondered where the file drawers were or the wall clock that kept Dr. Cooper abreast of just how much time she had remaining with any particular client. Instead, Maggie couldn't even find a little desk clock in the room.

The doctor directed her toward the chairs and took a seat across from her. "Can I get you something to drink? Coffee, tea, a soft drink?" Maggie couldn't help but begin to relax in the presence of this natural woman.

"Uhh… a diet soda? I mean, if you have one."

"Sure do." Dr. Cooper replied standing and walking over to a miniature refrigerator Maggie hadn't noticed. She retrieved two cans of soda from the fridge and returned to her chair, handing one to Maggie.

"I thought we could just kind of chat today." she began. To Maggie's surprise, Dr. Cooper tucked her legs up under her as though she were settling in to catch up with an old chum. "You know, learn a little about each other. No big question and answer sessions, just easy conversation. I'll tell you whatever you want to know. Okay?" Maggie nodded but remained silent. "Okay. So, have you always lived in Connecticut?"

"No. I grew up in a small town in upstate New York. I moved to Massachusetts for high school and then went to Boston University. After school, Luke, my husband, got a job out here."

"I'm Connecticut born and bred. I've moved all over the state, lived in Massachusetts for a little while myself, then decided to come back. It gets kind of hard to breathe sometimes, in the middle of that rat race."

"Are you married?" Maggie asked nervously, afraid of asking too personal a question.

"Not anymore." Dr. Cooper replied casually. "I married my high school sweetheart in the middle of college. By the time we graduated, we had completely different life paths ahead of us. I got pregnant a few years later and he told me that this wasn't what he had planned for his future. So, he took off to Phoenix or Tucson or somewhere, and I got the papers in the mail three weeks before I had my daughter."

"Wow...I'm sorry."

"Ahh, water under the bridge, Morgan is almost six now. We're doing just fine without him."

"It must be hard to raise a child on your own." Maggie replied. "I have two sons." She was already relaxing in this woman's presence, almost sensing a liking for her she wasn't quite ready to admit to. "Owen is four and a half and Quinn is eighteen months.

"You do whatever it takes, right? It's a completely different world being a mom."

Maggie shifted uncomfortably in her seat. Her eyes began to sting as the guilt of what she had done and the anger of how she was being treated for it came rushing back to her mind. She bit her lip against the threat of tears and looked at the floor.

"Maggie?" Jamie asked with a voice of genuine concern. "Was it something I said?"

Maggie lifted her eyes to meet the worried blue ones of the woman sitting in front of her. She fought away the tears and the weakness that surged within and straightened her back shaking her head.

"Look," she began with resolve. "I was sent here largely on the order of my husband because I had a memory lapse and left my kids, our boys, home alone. I had one of my nightmares or something and I left the house with them inside sleeping. I don't even remember it happening, I don't know why I did it. I didn't want to come here. I am certain what happened will never happen again.

"But I am here now. And there have been…problems. So I might as well try this out, right?"

Dr. Cooper showed no expression on her face as she nodded "Sure". Maggie didn't know where to begin. She hadn't expected to be so forthcoming. "What *do* you remember?" she asked finally.

"I read the kids a story and put them both down for their naps. Then I went downstairs to do some chores and I sat down on the couch to take a breather. I must have fallen asleep. And then... the next thing I knew, I woke up and I was sitting at the edge of Narragansett Lake. I had no idea how

I got there, but my car was there. Part of me thought it was still a dream. I drove home and when I got there, Luke had heard about the whole thing and had rushed home frantic to be with the kids."

"How did he react when you got home?"

"He was furious. He called my parents, and they're on their way here to stay with us for a while. He stayed home, which he hasn't done in ages, to take the boys out, but I wasn't *allowed* to go with them. Like I was being *grounded* or something. Now he looks at me like I'm crazy or sick. Whenever I am with the boys, he watches me like a hawk. It's like I'm living in a prison." A single tear broke free from the iron grasp she thought she had on her emotions.

"You said something else. Something about nightmares. Have you been having nightmares regularly?"

Maggie sipped her drink and nodded, tried to regain her composure. "The same one – or variations of it. About four, maybe five times now."

"Can you tell me about them?"

Maggie looked at Jamie. She seemed like a normal person. Surely her life wasn't perfect either. Maybe Jamie would provide the listening ear that she had tried to get from Luke. She had to come as part of her sentence anyway. She might as well get something out of it.

An hour later the Stewart family minivan turned into the long, curving driveway.As she approached the garage, Maggie noticed her father's Continental parked in the turn-around. She rolled her eyes at the thought of spending the next few days with her parents. Her mother, who was a scrutinizing, critical woman to begin with, would be watching her every movement, waiting for validation that something was indeed wrong with her. Her father would remind her continually that she was still their little girl and otherwise engage in small talk with Luke and the boys.

"Mommy, who's that?" Owen asked craning his neck to see above the seat in front of him. "Is that Grammy? And Papa?"

"It sure is, babe." Maggie replied trying to sound enthusiastic about their houseguests. "I'll let you out and then you run right over there and give them big hugs, okay?" Owen nodded emphatically and released the seat belt as the car came to a stop. He was out the door by himself and running towards his grandparents before Maggie had even reached Quinn's car seat. She pulled him out of the car and reluctantly turned toward the scene. Kit stood solemnly beside Sean who was wrapped up in greeting his grandson. She peered at Maggie as though looking for some physical sign of her problems. Then she rushed to Maggie's side.

"Let me help you, dear." she offered pityingly. "I'll take the baby. You've got enough to...carry." She hesitated before finding the appropriate words. Maggie held tightly to Quinn.

"We're fine, Mom. I do this every day, you know."

Kit looked at her with injured eyes. "Well, of course, I *know*. I was just trying to help. Excuse me."

"If you're here to take over my role as a mother, you can turn right around now. I know Luke called you worried, but really, he overreacted. Luke has no idea of what goes on in this house on a daily basis. If you want to visit, that's fine, but I don't need any help, so please don't offer any."

Sean had looked up from his wrestling to hear his daughter's hostile welcome. He stepped toward the two women, prepared to defend his wife, or his daughter, whoever appeared to need it most during this common exchange of sarcasm. Kit immediately jumped to the defensive. "Well, that's just fine, then. Forgive us, your *parents*, for wanting to offer our help. Maybe we should just go."

"Kit." Sean interjected. "Let's go inside. We haven't even had a chance to say hello to each other. We've just gotten off on the wrong foot, that's all." Sean gestured toward the front door and gave Maggie a warning glance. Maggie looked away, embarrassed. She found it impossible to stand up to her father. Her mother, on the other hand, seemed to clash with her each time they met.

Biting her tongue, Maggie led them all up the walk and in the front door. Sean gazed around at the grand entryway and sparkling chandelier high above them and whistled. "You keep a nice place, Mags. That husband of yours takes good care of you." Maggie looked at her father as though he were a stranger. She had not been raised to rely on her husband for financial or emotional stability. Why had she been sent off to that fancy private school, if not to make herself an independent and capable woman? She said nothing however, and instead, led them down the hallway into the kitchen. Owen ran off to find a toy to show off to his Papa and Maggie set Quinn down on the floor while she fixed him a snack. Rhett bounded over to lavish the young toddler with kisses, sending Quinn into a fit of giggles. Kit grimaced.

"Don't let that thing lick the baby, Maggie. It's gross." She lifted Quinn and brought him directly to the sink where she began wetting a paper towel. Maggie counted to five silently and then spoke.

"Can I get you something to eat or drink?" she offered without warmth. "I know you've been on the road for quite a while, you must be hungry."

"No, no, dear." Kit spoke as she scrubbed at Quinn's face. Quinn puckered his lips against the barrage and Maggie winked at him. "We grabbed something on the way. You just relax. We can take care of ourselves, can't we Sean?"

"Sure, sure." her father replied, uncertain of how to respond to the threatening situation. "How's things, Mags? Come, sit with me. We haven't had a chance to talk in a long time."

Maggie looked at the clock on the coffee maker. She had at least an hour and a half before Luke would be home and able to entertain *his* guests himself. "Let me start on dinner, Dad, we can talk while I work."

"Nonsense, Maggie." Kit chimed in handing off Quinn to Sean. "I want to make a nice dinner for the family tonight. We stopped at the grocery store on our way in and I bought all the fixings for steak and potatoes. You just sit down with your father for a bit and I'll make myself at home in the kitchen."

She had to clench her teeth together to control the anger that seeped through her veins. Kit headed to the car to bring in the bags and Maggie turned to her father with a look of desperation.

"She's your *mother*, Mags. Just like you are to your boys. This is what she does. Can't you let her do it for one day?" The look in his eyes softened her mood slightly and she finally nodded. "Atta girl. Now sit down here and chat with your old man."

Obediently, she took a seat across from Sean and Quinn and tried to think of what to say next.

Chapter Twelve

The bar always felt sadly hollow at the end of a busy night. The chords from the band still echoed distantly from the corner of the room and when he listened intently, Mickey could still hear faint laughter in the voices of his patron ghosts. With the lights dimmed, the slow, seeping shadows were all that was left of the lively crowd. A warm yellow glow spread over the polished wood of the bar. Behind it, the glass bottles of gin, vodka, schnapps, and tequila winked at him. He swallowed hard against the temptation.

Well-meaning friends and family had laughed heartily when a young and rowdy Michael Callaghan returned from his adventures abroad with grand delusions of building his own replica tavern from the wreckage of an abandoned building. When he returned again a year later and newly sober, it was assumed that his dreams would have died alongside his recklessness. Instead, Mickey became more determined than ever to see his vision succeed. His limited visits to AA meetings were met with open hostility. One man screamed at him and told him he didn't belong and was clearly not serious about the program. Any one who wanted to continue to surround himself with the poison that ruined him, was headed down a long and deadly road.

They didn't know or understand Mickey, though. In his mind, the alcohol had not destroyed him. It was simply a means to an end. He needed to get sober to find his passion in life and make it a reality. To his pleasant surprise, he had found two: Gwen and the bar. Before that, his life had no long-term. Drinking had been his creative vehicle. He had proved them all wrong too because here he was, standing inside his own creation. Ireland in his own hometown. Laughter. Success.

Everything except Gwen. Without entirely meaning to, Mickey had designed the tavern as an almost exact replica of O'Leary's pub. He didn't know at the time that staring at a copy of the table where Gwen had broken his heart every day might eventually wear him down. Or that standing behind the same-looking bar where she had first walked into his life could weigh on him until he felt like weeping. At the time, it had just been the image in his head of the perfect bar. At the time, he had still expected Gwen to come home with him. Now, every look, every kiss, every emotion they had shared at O'Leary's, Mickey could experience nightly with only one painfully obvious missing element.

Even though he seemed to have created a life built from his painful past, he was always more comfortable and content working in the tavern than anywhere else – including O'Leary's. Though he missed it, he knew to return would bring real pain. Knowing that she could walk in any moment, looking the same as she had the last time he touched her. Here, at least, the pain was safe and comforting.

Lately though, his thoughts of Gwen had become more insistent and unrelenting. Was it because he'd been away from Ireland longer than he had ever been since he met her? Was it that the anniversary of their first meeting was closing in and Gwen had always begged him to be in Ireland at that time of year to share it together? A recent phone call to Danny reassured him that his old friend was doing well, as was the pub. Danny awaited Mickey's return. Mickey had brushed it off, saying that it was impossible for him to get away. What he really wanted to know was how Gwen was doing, but felt foolish asking. He was sure Danny would have said something if she had asked about him, but he didn't mentioned her in their conversation at all.

When they first met, Gwen reminded Mickey of his sister in many ways. He'd talked to Maggie about her often, anxious for them to meet. They had the same twinkle in their eyes as they spoke. Gwen was lighthearted toward life, like himself, but also innocent in many ways. She could close her eyes to the ugliness of the world and see only the good in others. It was the same quality that lived in Maggie. Maggie was innocence on the surface. Mickey could see that when she played with her children, when she had stood at the altar with Luke. She believed the world was a good and safe place to be. The darkness lived only deep within her, so deep that she wasn't even aware of it. Looking at Gwen, Mickey had caught a glimpse of what Maggie might have been without that deep darkness, if only things had been different.

Without realizing it, Mickey found himself behind the bar. Mysteriously, a shot glass of tequila sat before him promising to dull the pain and blur the memory. He could almost hear Gwen's voice whispering.

You've got so much ahead of you, Mickey. Don't let the liquor take it all away. There's so much love in you. So many who love you. I do. Are you going to choose that over us? Over me?

It was one of two times Gwen had seen him cry. He sobbed in her arms that night like a child. She held him until he grew silent, until he had shed all the tears that drinking had helped him shut away. Their eyes locked and he promised her. He promised *for* her. It had been three years since Mickey had last tasted alcohol.

The room was deadly silent, the distant laughter and music having finally faded back into the walls. The hollow echo mirrored Mickey's heart. There may have been love in him once, but it had been used up long since, saved now only for his beloved bar. With Gwen, there had been a reason to get up every morning, a reason to see things with clear, unfiltered eyes. There had been a reason to remember. Gwen was gone – but he had his bar. Who would really care now if he leaned on an old friend for a little while? Mickey could think of no one.

Slowly, Mickey lifted the glass of golden liquid to his lips. A second later, it swept through him with a burn he hadn't known he'd been longing for. It warmed him. The tears that glistened in his eyes were tears of release, of finally being able to soothe the ache in his heart. He reached for the bottle of painkiller and poured another dose.

Chapter Thirteen

The sky was bright and blue, with only a scattered puff of cloud to be seen for miles. Seagulls soared and swooped from above, diving swiftly to skim the clear waters. Along the shore, the sounds of gentle waves could be heard lapping against the rocks in a summer rhythm. Maggie was surrounded by childish laughter and the slightest of breezes lifted stray wisps of hair to dance against her cheekbones.

The golden sunlight warmed her face and had her shoulders turning a deep bronze. Off in the distance the motor of a speed-boat hummed. Patrick was out there with his friends, skiing and drinking probably. She heard a splash below the cliffs where she stood.

The sun dipped behind a dark cloud that hadn't existed just moments before. Lightning flashed and thunder growled. Maggie was soaking wet. Tears streamed from her face and she screamed in agony but the great booms echoing out of the ominous sky swallowed her voice. Her world had gone dark. Suddenly, there was no sky or earth and she was suspended in emptiness.

She fell deeper and deeper into the inky darkness. As she fell, the mysterious figure reached out to her again. She grasped at a hand, hoping it would stop her from falling any further. Finally, fingers clasped but they continued to fall together. She could sense they were nearing whatever might lie beneath them and intense fear gripped Maggie's throat so that she could no longer scream. She looked at the figure before her for some sign of who it was, why it was beside her, why they were falling. And in the midst of the darkness a pair of bright green eyes, wide with fear and glowing gazed back.

Maggie jerked awake drenched in her own sweat and tears. She kicked the covers off her, desperate to free herself from the bed, then raced downstairs and out the back door. Her nails dug into the deck railing as she gulped in the warm summer air, her heart thumping heavily in her chest. When at last she felt as though she could breathe again, she stepped out into the thick, damp grass of her back yard. The moon was a pearlescent sliver high above her; crickets played charmingly in the grass. It was as though she had stepped out of one world into another. Out here, in the yard, the world was calm and serene. The sweat from her body evaporated into the night air and the soft, warm breeze cooled her skin.

After several silent moments of stargazing, her breathing slowed and she felt some separation from the frightening nightmare images. She lay down among the cool soft grass and closed her eyes. She could not understand why she no longer felt safe inside the house but she was too tired to examine it now. She only knew that out here, in the calm night air, it seemed safe. Within a few moments, she had drifted off to a sleep without dreams.

Luke shifted in the bed and reached out for Maggie. Finding nothing but a crumpled pile of sheets, he sat up nervously. He listened for a hint of where she might have gone but the entire upstairs was silent with slumber. He decided to check downstairs – if Maggie had another one of those nightmares, who knew what condition she might be in or, for that matter, where? He reached the coolness of the foyer and peered left and right. The soft glow that came before dawn lit the living room just enough to display its emptiness. She wasn't in the den either. Or the kitchen, or the family room.

Luke was on the verge of waking Maggie's parents when he noticed one of the French doors to the deck was open an inch or two. With a sinking sensation in the pit of his stomach somewhere between relief and despair, he stepped barefoot toward the door, opened it a few more inches and slipped through. The gray-rose of dawn illuminated the yard just enough to make out the line of blooming trees leading to the woods beyond. He noticed the limp figure lying in the grass and a shock of fear raced from his spine out to his fingertips. He ran to where Maggie lay and placed a trembling hand upon her cool cheek. She sighed deeply in sleep and he rocked back on his knees, arching his face to the heavens in relief.

Here was his sleeping beauty, her auburn hair fanned out behind her like fiery waves upon the dew-soaked grass. Her eyes were closed peacefully and a slight smile graced her delicate lips. He couldn't remember the last time his tortured wife had looked so serene. Her silk negligee was damp and clung to every curve of her body – her soft, creamy breasts, the luscious dip of her waist, the swell of her hips. A passion that had cooled to embers sparked within again. His fingers traced her cheekbones, her jaw line, her shoulder blade.

He moved softly to lie beside her. His lips brushed her eyelids and nose until she stirred slightly. Instinct took over and his lips met hers. She was the young woman he had known in college again. He could still picture her then, her emerald eyes brimming with an almost-childlike lust for life. She had been fiercely independent then; relying on no one and yet so in need of someone to care for her. It still seemed as if it had only been yesterday and he was lost in his amazement of her.

As she awoke from her hazy sleep, he wrapped her in his arms and pulled her close. In her disorientation her hands shot up between them and she pushed against his chest, breaking them apart. For a moment he was confused, but as the present came tumbling back on him, his long-standing walls of isolation found their foundation once more. She didn't want him; hadn't for a long time.This rejection from the love of his life had become so regular, he had become numb to its bite. Suddenly, he felt like an utter fool, succumbing to his memories and opening himself to it all again. Recovering quickly, he gathered himself and stood up. His body went rigid and his eyes glazed slightly with cold resilience.

He held a hand out to help her up. She gazed upon him for a moment, her eyes searching his and then got up without his assistance. He looked away at the ground and dropped his arms to his side trying to push aside his ugly thoughts. "You gave me a scare, Mags." he told her numbly.

"I'm sorry." How many times had those words left her lips in the past month? She spoke them and he heard them and still nothing changed. The wedge was driven deeper between them with every blow to each other's hearts.

When she didn't offer any further explanation his temper flared. "Well, what the hell happened? I wake up alone and wander through the house only to find you sound asleep in the middle of the yard!"

"I had another nightmare." Maggie stuttered.

Luke waited for more but she trailed off and stood there silently, staring past his shoulder, focusing on nothing. He shifted his weight from one foot to the other tossing various remarks about in his mind and settling on none of them. Exasperated, he threw his hands up in the air. Tears welled and then trickled silently down her pale cheeks. "Christ, Maggie, when's it gonna stop?! You're a wreck! I'm digging myself a hole here trying to get a crumb, some inkling of what the hell is happening to my wife, but you give me nothing... Nothing!" The tears slowed as Maggie struggled with a response to this chastising. Luke saw the pain it was causing Maggie but he had run out of sympathy. "It's got to stop, Maggie. You take off on the kids, you use the backyard for a bedroom...Maybe that Dr. Cooper isn't doing it. Maybe you need something more...more intense. Maybe you need to..."

"Stop." Maggie put a trembling hand up to prevent what was coming next. Her mind raced with jumbled up thoughts. Nothing came together in a coherent sentence. Her body shook with cold, her shoulders glistened with dew, her lips trembled with a yearning to speak but an inability to form words. He stood before her with an expectant look on his face, waiting for something she couldn't give him. His gaze seemed to burn into her, blaming her. It was too much for her weary mind. She bolted past him and fled into the house.

She stumbled into the kitchen out of breath, shaking and damp. Luke was only a few steps behind. To both their surprise, Sean stood at the sink, staring at them. "What in God's name is going on here?" he demanded. Then as Maggie looked up at him, he saw the look in his daughter's eyes, a look he remembered from long ago and rushed to her side. "Maggie, your skin is like ice! What's the matter? Luke, what happened?"

Though it was just dawn, Luke felt like he had been awake for days. "She had a nightmare, Sean." he explained, tired of sounding like a broken record. He retrieved a blanket from the couch in the family room and draped it over Maggie's shoulders. "She's okay, I think. She fell asleep in the yard."

"The yard?! How'd she get there? What kind of nightmare?"

Maggie allowed them to talk as though she was not even there. The conversation buzzed around her like a pesky mosquito – present, but largely ignored. She retreated from the discussion, found a kitchen chair and sank into it. What was happening to her? Where was the strong woman she had worked so hard to become?

"I told you, I don't know, Sean!" Luke was speaking angrily. "She doesn't talk to me any more. You're her father – maybe she'll fill you in."

"What is going on in here?" Kit walked into the kitchen in slippered feet and a terry robe. "You'll wake the boys with all this racket." She surveyed the scene before her with disdain, glancing from Luke to Sean and then noticed Maggie, trying to disappear into the corner. She stood frozen, unable to comfort her daughter as she knew a mother should. She had missed that opportunity long before now. Instead, Kit questioned the men with her eyes and Luke repeated the story once more.

Kit busied herself starting the coffee as she searched her mind for a way to help her child. Moments later, both Luke and Sean accepted a cup in silence. When Maggie and Kit's mugs were filled, Kit sat across from her daughter and reached out to take both her hands. "Maggie, honey, I think you need to go back on the medication. None of these crazy nightmares and things were happening until you stopped taking it."

Maggie's eyes cleared a bit as she looked at her mother. She could feel her father's concerned stare, could sense Luke's embarrassment of her. Upstairs, she knew her sons still slept – her two great accomplishments in the world. What had become of their mother? Her eyes stung from sleep and tears. Her body was weak from strain. Kit's grasp on her hands tightened. Maggie looked quickly at Sean and Luke then back to Kit. She was scared. "Does that make me crazy?"

"No, Maggie, of course not!" Sean interjected immediately, but Maggie had finally found her voice.

"I mean, if the only way I can be normal is when I'm medicated, doesn't that make me sick? And then, what am I? What kind of person am I in my children's eyes, in Luke's eyes?"

Luke stepped towards her for reassurance but she held him off with her hand once more. "No. I have been off that stuff for years. It's not causing my nightmares and I'm not crazy. I'm not going back on it now." She heard a thump from above and knew that Owen would be downstairs shortly. She needed to put an end to this and put things back the way they were before. "I had a nightmare. That's all. I went outside for some fresh air and fell asleep. That doesn't make me crazy."

Owen shuffled into the kitchen, his hair tousled from sleep. He saw Maggie and smiled that magnetic smile that always clarified her purpose in life. "Hi mommy." he chirped. She went to him and wrapped them both in the blanket. His warmth soothed her soul.

"Hey baby." she nuzzled his neck. "What would you like for breakfast this morning?" And with that, Maggie made clear that the conversation was over.

Chapter Fourteen

Aiden finished dictating a progress report and packed up his things. It was a beautiful day, not one to be spent entirely indoors. He looked forward to sitting on the rooftop of his apartment and sinking his teeth into a good psychological thriller. Maybe he'd even grab some steaks for grilling on the way home and treat himself to a homemade margarita.

Colleen, a friendly, cheerful colleague, knocked once and opened his door as he came around his desk. She was one of the rare ones in this field, who never looked like the burn-out would destroy her. She was a devoted case manager who somehow seemed able to separate her work from her personal life. Secretly, Aiden admired her a bit. She had it all figured out, while he felt lost in the game.

She noticed he was on his way out and decided to walk with him. "There's a bunch of us going to 'The Waterfalls' tonight if you'd like to come along."

'The Waterfalls' was a popular nightclub on the other side of town. It packed a crowd, usually of twenty-something singles looking for romance. It had never been a scene Aiden considered himself a part of – even when he was twenty-something.

"I think I'll pass but thanks."

"You know, Aiden." Colleen began in a therapeutic tone. She placed a gentle hand on his elbow. "Some of the staff here consider you a little... well, stand-offish. Not me, of course!" she added with a nudge. "I know inside that cool exterior is a fun-loving night owl just waiting to spread his wings. Maybe if you loosened up a little and came to one of our get-togethers once in a while, you'd find that life can actually be fun."

"They think I'm 'stand-offish' and don't have any fun?" Aiden asked sarcastically. Colleen shrugged her shoulders. "So, I intimidate people a little then. Hmmm." He pretended the idea impressed him, which, perhaps it did just a bit.

"Come on, Aiden. Everyone needs some friends. Especially in this business."

"Are you saying that I don't have any friends now?"

"I'm *saying*, what do you have planned for tonight that could be so much more important than a few strategic hours with your co-workers? We're starting to take it personally, you know."

Aiden's blue eyes flashed with mischief. "So you *are* included then." He had to admit there was an attraction there, for him at least, and that it had been a while since he'd been out with anyone – whether one-on-one or in a group. She was right, too. It wouldn't hurt to have some people from work on his side. "I'll have you know that I had quite a busy and exciting night all planned out. But, alright. You've twisted my arm. I'll go."

"Great! Eight o'clock. We'll meet you there." She turned with a smile as she bounced off toward her car. "Don't back out. I'm looking forward to it."

Aiden's eyes followed her movements smiling. *Me too,* he thought, slightly surprised at himself.

Patrick paced the floor of the den like a caged bear. He wanted to be angry with Aiden for not telling him what he needed to hear, but knew he should have expected exactly what Aiden said. His brother was stubborn, pig-headed, and, unfortunately this time, very good at what he did. Patrick knew deep down, he was right too. The problem was he didn't have time to delve into the depths of his own psyche. He had more immediate problems. If he defended Davis it opened his firm up to the SEC vultures, not to mention the media. They would both get buried, his career would be destroyed. If he sold Davis out he could lose his family, his world, his reputation. He had built his house of straw and now a strong wind was blowing.

The ringing of his cellular phone jolted him from his thoughts. He strode to the bar irritated, and flipped it open. "Callaghan, here."

"Sir, Ron Sterger is on the line." His secretary's purely professional voice came over the line. "He says its urgent he speak with you right away. I informed him that you were unavailable, but he insisted that you take the call. Shall I transfer the call or tell him I can't reach you?"

"Get a number where I can reach him, Paula, and tell him I'll call him in ten minutes." Patrick snapped the phone shut. Sterger was breathing down his neck and he had no idea what to tell him. Patrick grabbed his briefcase and headed out the door. He refused to deal with this mess within the walls of his home. He had worked too hard to shield Shauna and the kids from the ugliness of his career to let it all fall apart now.

He had barely stepped onto the elevator when his phone rang again. Certain it was Paula, he answered it quickly.

"Mr. Callaghan?" a gruff voice asked and continued before Patrick could respond. "This is Peter Sylvan from the Securities Exchange Commission. We spoke briefly a few weeks ago and I've left several messages for you since, but you don't return my calls." He scolded. "I need to meet with you, Mr. Callaghan, and it needs to be soon."

Patrick's stomach churned. He did not like the condescending tone in the caller's voice or being made to feel like a schoolboy who had been caught passing a note. It didn't fit his controlled demeanor and he wouldn't allow it.

"Well, Mr....uh."

"Sylvan." Came the irritated reply.

"Yes, Sylvan. I'd be more than happy to meet with you. You just need to make an appointment with my secretary. She knows my schedule better than I do." He added with a false laugh. "Call my office and set it up."

"Well, Mr. Callaghan, I think if we just met for a drink or something this could be handled quickly. I don't think there's a need for a lot of formalities."

"I am a busy man, Mr. Sylvan. I don't get much spare time. An appointment really would be best. Give Paula a call, she'll take care of it for you." He flipped his phone closed before Peter had a chance to respond. Two close calls. But how much longer could he play this game of dodgeball before one snuck up on him and knocked him out?

Chapter Fifteen

Maggie sat again in the beige chair of Dr. Cooper's office. Dr. Cooper was perched in her usual spot, directly across from Maggie, looking casual and comfortable in white capris and a wide-striped Polo shirt. Her shiny blond hair was pulled back into a low ponytail, making her look more sorority girl than therapist. Maggie found herself slightly envious but admired her genuine friendliness. She wondered if they had met under different circumstances, would they have established a friendship? Or was it just a typical reaction for patients to wish their therapists could care about them outside the walls of their office?

They talked in detail about Maggie's parents who had finally left that morning. She shared with Jamie how difficult their visit had been. "Tell me about the rest of your family. You have three brothers, correct?"

Maggie nodded, shifted her eyes briefly toward the floor. There was a moment of silence before she shrugged. "There isn't much to tell. We aren't close."

Jamie raised an eyebrow, taking in the reaction. "Tell me a little about each of them."

"Well, first is Patrick. He's the oldest, six years ahead of me. We were never very close – probably because of the age gap. He's married now and lives in New York City with his wife and three kids. He's a businessman, but I don't truly understand what it is that he does. Something about buying failing companies and restructuring them. It's his father in-law's business.

"I rarely see them. In fact, I've never even met the baby. The last time we got together was for Quinn's baptism." Her voice gradually softened as she spoke until it was almost a whisper.

Guilt seeped in through her pores allowing a sudden chill to enter. Patrick and she had hardly even spoken to each other in almost a year. Just the usual call at Christmas. Even that had been pretty stiff, as usual, and punctuated with uneasy lapses in the conversation. It was always the same when she spoke to Patrick. *Why?* She wondered. *Were we always so distant? Did we always have so little in common? Was it more Patrick or me?* She couldn't remember a time when they had been close. Certainly she had tried though, right? *It had to be him. He's cold with everyone, it's as much a part of his personality as...*

"What about the others?" Dr. Cooper interrupted.

"Mickey is next." She relaxed visibly, eager to put that concern behind her. "We're closest. I talk to him the most, but we don't get to see each other much.

"He owns a bar in upstate New York. He eats, sleeps and breathes his work. Literally, he lives right above the bar. Oh, *and* he's a recovering alcoholic."

Surprise registered on Dr. Cooper's face and Maggie let a sarcastic laugh escape. "I know. My parents didn't think it was a very good idea either, but his heart was already in his work when he got sober. He built the place pretty much from rubble. He's very committed to it. It's designed to look just like this tavern in Ireland that he worked in for a while.

He spent a lot of time there over the years. Anyway, he says working among the drinking helps remind him why he quit. He seems pretty smart about it all now."

"Why do you think you feel closest to Mickey?" Dr. Cooper asked.

Maggie thought for a moment. "He's the most 'real'. He is who he is and doesn't make excuses for it. And he's genuine." Maggie bit her lip as she considered each of her siblings in turn. "Pat has always been distant and Aiden doesn't want to have anything to do with us at all. You know, Mickey was the only one who bothered to visit me the whole time I was at Dylan."

"You went to Dylan?"

Maggie nodded while memories of her time at the Rosemary Dylan Academy flashed through her mind. "My parents sent me there for high school. I guess they wanted more than a public school education for me." She shrugged it off with indifference, but the doctor shifted in her seat and leaned in closer.

"Did you want to go?"

"I don't know." Maggie's eyes remained on her feet. "I guess I never really cared."

"What about your school friends?"

"I…I don't think I had many friends before Dylan." Maggie admitted. "See I've always had a kind of memory issue. I was on medication that was supposed to help. But I can't remember much before Dylan. And then, when I took off on the kids, I… well, I'm worried that maybe my memory issues are back.

"I used to talk to my roommates at Dylan," she continued, "and they would go on and on about things they used to do at home, friends, family gatherings. I realized that I couldn't really share in that. I mean, I had vague recollections, more like feelings about when I was little, but no stories. I think that's why when Mickey would come to visit I got so excited. It helped me look more normal. Does that *sound* normal, Dr Cooper?"

"Call me Jamie, Maggie, please." She took a long sip of her bottled water and smiled warmly at Maggie. "What's normal for any of us? It does seem unusual. What was the medication you took?"

"Clona… clonaze-something. Anyway, I stopped when I got pregnant with Quinn. My parents wanted me to go back on it. Now Luke does too. But I don't want to. I don't like being constantly dependent on some drug. And the entire time I took it, I don't think it helped my memory at all. What do you think?"

Clonazepam? That was an anti-anxiety medication. Jamie thought. *Why would it be used to aid memory?* "I don't think I know enough about you to make that choice." Jamie said as she made a mental note then changed the subject. "Tell me about Aiden."

Maggie nodded and swallowed hard.

"Aiden."

A sigh escaped her lips as she thought of her handsome, stubborn middle brother. "He's two years older than me. He cut himself off from the family a couple of years ago. I know he's still living in Syracuse and I know he's a social worker, but that's about it." Tears welled in Maggie's eyes as she reopened the wound of loss she hadn't examined in ages. "I haven't heard from him in such a long time." She swiped at a tear that had dislodged from the corner of her eye and journeyed slowly down her cheek. "I think I need to stop talking about them."

"Okay." Jamie patted her arm sympathetically. "You've wandered through a lot of difficult thoughts today. Let's take a rest from it all for now." She folded her hands in her lap and looked at Maggie earnestly. "Before you go, I wanted to ask your thoughts on something. I've been thinking that we could try some hypnosis."

Maggie gasped but Jamie continued on. "Now, I know some people consider hypnosis to be less than scientific, but I've used it in a few cases with significant results. Your difficulties with remembering are a concern. Those memories, though, are likely to be stored in your subconscious. Under hypnosis, the subconscious is allowed a voice. We may be able to get to the bottom of your difficulties lately."

Tiny moths began to dance against Maggie's rib cage. Hypnosis? Wasn't that something used on psychotics and multiple personality cases? She admitted she didn't understand psychology in great detail, but her understanding of hypnosis was to uncover cases of child abuse and hidden pasts. What did that have to do with running out on her children or recurrent nightmares?

Jamie spoke again, as though she were able to read Maggie's thoughts. "If nothing else, we may be able to determine what truly happened the day you raced out of the house. That memory is lodged somewhere in your subconscious too, it just needs a chance to float up to the surface."

"Would I...remember what I say?" Maggie questioned nervously.

"Absolutely. This isn't like what you see on the talk shows these days, Maggie, it's much more controlled. You will remain conscious the entire time. It's simply a deep relaxation, a state that we rarely allow ourselves to experience without assistance. You will be able to control how long you are under hypnosis and you will be able to 'wake up'," she signaled quotations with her hands, "any time you choose."

Maggie remained silent, uncertain of what to say about the idea. For the first time since Maggie had met Jamie the fear of being mentally dissected returned.

"Listen," Jamie continued, "You don't need to decide right now. Go home and think about it for a while. Talk it over with Luke and let me know what you decide. It's completely up to you."

Maggie cleared her throat and attempted a smile, relief washing over her features. "Okay." She let out a deep breath. "Thank you, Doc...uh Jamie. I'll see you next week?"

"Absolutely." Jamie placed a gentle hand on Maggie's shoulder. "Don't let yourself get swallowed up by all of this, Maggie. You're a strong woman whose faced challenges before and hurdled them. This will resolve itself and you will have your life back."

Maggie bit her upper lip. She thought of the distance between her and Luke, the angst between herself and her parents, her insecurity with her own children. She looked further at the lost relationship with her own brothers. Strength was one characteristic she felt she lost somewhere along the way. That Jamie could see it gave her some hope.

Contrary to Jamie's suggestion, she wouldn't discuss the concept of hypnosis with Luke, she would make the decision alone. Luke had certainly lost faith in Maggie's strength, she could not continue to lean on him and be so...needy. And hypnosis sounded so...severe. Luke would certainly believe she was a basket case if she shared that suggestion with him.

Nodding an ambiguous agreement at Jamie, she left the office in silence to consider her choices, and her fate. Jamie watched her as she left.

Maggie went to Dylan, she thought. *Girls usually went there for greater reasons than a stellar education. And why would Maggie be given Clonazepam for memory problems? Or is that simply what she believed?*

Chapter Sixteen

Aiden had to admit he was having a good time at "The Waterfalls". He had more in common with some of his colleagues than he would have expected and his interest in Colleen had doubled since he arrived. One moment she was sharing a story of camping with her college roommates and sharing dinner with a young bear. The next, she was tearing it up on the dance floor with her girlfriends. He watched her closely.

After about an hour though, he'd had enough of the loud music and yelling to be heard. While he enjoyed the company, he was ready to spend some time with just Colleen. When she returned from the dance floor this time, he signaled to her and leaned in close.

"How about trying someplace else?" he suggested casually. Her brown eyes twinkled when she smiled back at him.

"I know a great place! C'mon, I'll drive." She added grabbing her purse. They said a few quick good byes and made their exit.

In the car, Colleen gave Aiden's arm a squeeze. "So... it wasn't that bad was it?"

Aiden grinned genuinely. "Nah, it was okay. Do they all think I'm still too 'stand-offish'?"

Colleen laughed. "Actually, no one really thought that. It was just the only way I could think of to get you out.

Everyone loves you at work. They just want to see you outside of work once in a while."

"Well, I'm glad I went. It was nice. Thank you for the invitation, really. I have to admit though, that place isn't really my usual scene."

"I'm with you." Colleen agreed. "It is a bit noisy. You'll love the next place, though. It's much more casual and the food is great."

Aiden stole a sideways glance at his companion while he continued to face straight ahead. Colleen appeared completely at ease with herself. There was a quiet confidence, one that didn't require outward show. It matched how he thought of her professionally, but now he realized that it suited her personally as well.

"I'm glad you agreed to leave with me." He added, more seriously this time. "...and not that guy who kept trying to rub up on you on the dance floor."

Colleen threw her head back with laughter but her flushed face gave away some small hint of embarrassment. "Oh my God, you saw him? I thought, hoped, it was just my imagination." She paused and glanced over at Aiden, locking eyes for a brief moment. "Me too." It was almost a whisper. Aiden felt the most pleasant tug at his heart.

She pulled into a parking spot and turned off the engine. "Here we are."

Aiden stepped out to see the large wooden signed boasting a claddagh symbol and the name "Mickey C's" engraved in green script and the liquid feelings he'd been starting to enjoy vaporized. He hadn't been paying attention to where Colleen was taking him. Anger and embarrassment welled up within his chest – he couldn't go inside. He looked anxiously at Colleen.

"You know," he suggested. "I've got a great roof." Colleen gave him a quizzical look.

"Huh?"

"My roof. You can walk right out on it and sit out there under the stars. It's a gorgeous view."

"Aiden, are you trying to get me to go back to your place?" she teased.

"Well, yeah. I mean, no. Not in that way. I just..." He sighed and ran his fingers through his dark hair trying to organize the jumble of thoughts in his head. "I just thought it might be a little more peaceful." *A lot more peaceful than walking in there*, he added to himself.

"Let's save that for the next time I get you to come out of your office and step into the real world." She replied lightly, unaware of how rigid his body had become. Her arm snaked through his. "Tonight let's just get to know each other over a mug of Irish whiskey."

You don't know what you might learn, he thought as they began walking toward the door. *Unbelievable that I have managed to avoid this family for years and in the span of two weeks, I will have run into both of my brothers. Must be the luck of the Irish. Hey, maybe Maggie's in there too.*

They opened the door onto a warm and friendly haven. Several regulars were perched at one end of the bar smoking fat cigars and commenting on the golf highlights being shown on the small television set attached to the corner wall. Young couples performed their dance of romance; a casual touch of the hand, a well-placed laugh. Some larger groups converged around booths eating and gesturing wildly while others encircled a tense game of pool. It was clear that Mickey's place was doing well. It was just as Aiden remembered it, from the opening night celebration, the last time he had set foot here.

Aiden's eyes darted to the bar where Mickey moved smoothly from end-to-end building ales and pouring shots. He had a relaxed manner as he laughed with customers and spoke to his waitresses. He looked at home, and for a moment Aiden felt the familiar and deep pang of longing for the family he had turned away.

It brought him back to that last night.

It was the kind of day that family reunions were made for. The parks and lakes were brimming with swimmers and sunbathers. The scent of barbecued chicken filled the air. High above, the sky was a solid ceiling of pale blue broken only by the warm orb of the golden sun. A day such as this caused most people to avoid being stuck indoors, but as Aiden entered the thick oak doors to his brother's new venture, he realized there were a number of them who didn't seem to mind being inside after all. Those that still preferred the fresh air could enjoy it on a comfortable outdoor deck attached at the back of the large, open dining room.

A group of young men played the guitar, violin, wooden flute and drums on a small but adequate stage between the bar area and booths. The playful tunes added a charming air to the establishment. Young and old alike were enjoying the opening.

Months before, it had still been just a wreck of a building on the outskirts of a struggling town. Within the crumbling walls Mickey had been able to envision a quaint tavern, a warm and inviting shelter from the harsh realities of life beyond its doors.

A place where people could step inside and feel as though they had entered another country, another world even. He had pictured a slice of Ireland, scooped up out of the vast green rolling hills of its island home and transplanted it here, for all to enjoy. Some had called him foolish, a dreamer, a risk. But Mickey had pushed on despite the warnings that his little ideas were doomed to fail and break him both financially and emotionally.

Aiden admitted that Mickey had outdone himself. While he had always been the most easy-going, honest Callaghan of them all, he'd had a way of avoiding the tough stuff. Perhaps that had changed too, now that he had something he could truly call his own.

Patrick stood stoically at one end of the bar, a protective arm around the shoulder of his pregnant wife. It was a surprise that Patrick had come at all, he entrenched himself so deeply in his life in New York City. It lifted Aiden to see him supporting Mickey, and he thought, for a brief, unprotected moment, that maybe the Callaghans could salvage a shred of the family they'd been so many years ago. Maybe we'll come through the other side of this after all, *he pondered. With that thought, he eagerly joined the rest of the family in congratulating Mickey.*

The opening turned out to be a huge success. As the crowd began to thin out, the Callaghan's all gathered around the bar to have one last drink and toast to Mickey. Mickey built a tall Guinness from the tap for each member of the family and responsibly grabbed two bottled waters for himself and Shauna. Patrick and Maggie had probably had a bit too much: Patrick because he was uncomfortable and Maggie because she was enjoying a rare adults-only night out. No matter, the mood was high and the moment was rare.

Aiden had been certain that the rain cloud over the Callaghan's was finally clearing. Even Sean and Patrick seemed to be getting along. "To life after death." He raised a glass to toast.

The cold, hard glare of his father burned into him. Patrick stiffened noticeably. Mickey stopped wiping the bar and looked at him incredulously.

"You've got some goddamn nerve." Sean seethed through clenched teeth.

"I didn't..."Aiden stuttered. "I just meant... we all seemed so..."

"Aiden, please." Kit appealed.

"Did you come here just to start something again?" Mickey accused him through clenched jaws..

Aiden felt suddenly attacked. He had simply been trying to acknowledge the progress it seemed they were finally making. Had it all been in his mind? "No! And what the hell is that supposed to mean? I was making a toast!"

"Bullshit." Patrick slurred slightly. "You had a motive coming here tonight. Just like you always do."

The defenses shifted back into place. "Don't everyone suddenly jump down my throat just because I'm the most psychologically healthy one here."

"Oh, cut the shit, Aiden." Patrick retorted. "We're all sick of your psychological analysis of us. We do just fine until you open your mouth."

"Fuck you."Aiden snapped.

"Stop it! All of you!" Kit begged, her voice rising nervously, hands shaking. "I am asking you all to drop this now. Maggie is here...home…which is so rare…and precious. And it is Mickey's big night. Do we have to fight?"

"I'm going to the bathroom." Maggie announced with disgust. "I don't know why this family can't have one single night

together without an argument." She disappeared into the back of the restaurant.

Sean turned to Aiden, the hard glare still in his eyes.

"Aiden, this is completely uncalled for and out of line. If you can't respect the family's wishes, I think you should leave."

Aiden blinked at his father in mild disbelief, a burning sensation building in his throat. "The family's *wishes? They're certainly not mine and last I knew I was still considered part of this family. You're wishes, Mickey?" his gazed shifted toward his brother. "You in on this?"*

Mickey remained silent.

"No. But you'll just go with the flow right? Make no waves, skate through life. And what about Maggie? Are they her *wishes? Oh, that's right – she doesn't get a vote. 'The family's wishes'. That's the biggest bunch of bullshit I've ever heard!" The few remaining patrons had begun to glance with interest at the family squabble.*

"Aiden, I have asked you to leave."

He felt the slap of his father's words as surely as if they had been physical. Looking at each member of his family in turn, he felt only disdain. Even Luke, who was unenlightened regarding the profound fissure that ran down the Callaghan line, appeared disappointed in his behavior. His love and concern had been lost on them all. And he had been foolish enough to think for a minute that this might change. Idiot. *He returned the same cold glare that had shattered those hopes.*

"I don't think you get to make that decision, Dad. Your kids are adults now. And its Mickey's bar." They both looked to Mickey, whose eyes darted from one to the other with uncertainty. Tough decisions, choosing sides had never been his strength. He settled on Sean a moment too long, and Aiden

watched the change come over him, as though sedated by his father's thoughts.

"Aiden, you need to leave. I don't need this kind of scene in my bar."

Maggie returned to find the situation worse than when she had left it.

"That's fine." Aiden slammed his drink down on the bar, splashing the ale across the polished wood. He looked back once on his way out to find his family's eyes on him accusingly. It was an image that would burn in his memory and tear at his heart.

All but Maggie who appeared saddened and confused. The way he would remember her from that moment. Pity for his sister engulfed him, overriding the anger that preceded it. In that moment, he wanted desperately for her to understand that he trusted her, that it was not her fault. "Maggie," he began and Sean immediately stepped forward to stop him. "Mags, when you need me, I'll be here." He let the door close softly behind him.

"Aiden?" Colleen tugged at his sleeve. "Are we just going to stand in the doorway all night?" She pulled him toward the bar, his feet reluctantly coming unstuck from the floor.

They sat on polished stools halfway down the bar. Mickey worked the far end and made his way toward them slowly, tending to orders as he moved. "What can I get..." he looked up and lost his voice as his eyes met Aiden's for the first time since that night. The whole bar seemed to go silent during the eternity that took place before either man spoke. "Aiden." Mickey finally managed.

"Mickey." He wasn't certain if he saw relief or regret on Mickey's face.

Colleen sensed the tension and cleared her throat. "I guess you two know each other." It worked. Both pairs of matching green eyes looked in her direction. She sucked in her breath as the similarities became obvious.

"Hi." Mickey stretched out a hand in an attempt to resume his typical demeanor. "Mickey Callaghan. This handsome punk's brother." The emphasis had been on punk, though Aiden caught the sarcastic humor that came with it.

"Wow. So the 'C' is for…" she began wagging a finger at the Mickey C's sign behind the bar. The two men nodded simultaneously and Mickey flashed his devastatingly charming smile.

"Aiden, why didn't you tell me this was your brother's place?" Aiden was at a loss for words. He was both ashamed and relieved with the way Mickey had glossed over the strain between them. Somewhere deep inside, hidden beneath layers of anger and bitterness, Aiden was glad to be here. Seeing Mickey now, hearing his voice brought those feelings to the surface.

"Well, you know," he finally managed. "I didn't want to use his celebrity just to get you to like me." He looked at Mickey who rolled his eyes.

"So, what can I get you two?"

Mickey looked much the same to Aiden, save for the dark circles under his eyes. They were minimized, of course, by his infectious smile and cavalier demeanor. Had there not been such a bridge between them, Aiden would have liked to ask if everything was all right but instead, he simply requested two Harps. Maybe it was just the lighting.

ꕥ

They stayed for over two hours, enjoying the food and drink. Colleen beat Aiden in a friendly game of darts and they even joined in on a dance that many of the patrons seemed very familiar with. Although Aiden kept his main focus on Colleen, he found himself watching Mickey from time to time. His brother knew many of his customers by name and often had conversations with them as though they were old friends. He was also seen as quite a catch for the ladies – Aiden had seen some young and single woman hit on him at least a half a dozen times throughout the evening.

The friendly, lover-boy smile was always there, naturally, never forced. Aiden was thinking how much better Mickey seemed to be doing for himself than either he or Patrick were.

As Aiden and Colleen finished their food, two Irish coffees were brought to their table. "Courtesy of Mickey C" the waitress told them with a wink and a smile. Aiden looked toward the bar to acknowledge his brother's kindness. Mickey was involved in a conversation with another bartender who seemed to be having a problem with one of the patrons. Mickey spoke to the bartender, who nodded and headed back to approach the situation, probably with some new tactic Mickey had recommended. It seemed, at that moment, their job choices were not all that different from one another.

Aiden was interested in how Mickey's advice worked out with the bartender and his young, drunk and angry customer. If he hadn't been, he might have glimpsed the quick flick of Mickey's wrist as he downed a shot – his fifth that evening.

Chapter Seventeen

Maggie eventually agreed to test the hypnosis idea. However reluctant, she determined that if it could possibly uncover why she ran out on her children or bring an end to her nightmares (which had continued on a regular basis) she had to be willing to try. There was a soothing sort of quality to Jamie's voice, as Maggie relaxed her tense muscles and grew heavy in the soft chair. The weight of her thoughts started to lift, as Jamie's voice seemed to come from farther and farther away. She heard Jamie ask her to think back to an easier time in her life, to remember something good or happy. She felt too tired to look back on her life, to evaluate its worth, yet, despite her resistance, she began seeing herself in college.

She was at a Young Professionals Convention with her good friend and roommate, Chloe Stevens. They roamed the large room filled with booths offering information about their companies and attempting to entice their guests to consider their firms after graduation. She hadn't wanted to go. She had been considering changing her major from Business Management to Education lately. Chloe had insisted, though. Ever cerebral, Chloe jumped at the chance to get additional course credit for spending a day amidst a bunch of greedy suits. Since her boyfriend, Steve was at crew practice that morning and she had the day off, Maggie had reluctantly agreed.

They snuck out for a few moments for some fresh air. Several Boston University classmates lingered around the gazebo, talking and smoking. Chloe and Maggie found a small table and rested their aching feet. Above them, the spring sky was bright and full of cotton ball clouds, below them the river snaked its way through the city sparkling like diamonds. It was a day that Maggie should be spending on the water herself, rowing in rhythm with her crew mates, listening to the splash of the water as the oars sliced through it and the coxswain yelled out the paces. Further down the river, she knew Steve was doing just that in his own team's scull, maybe thinking of her as she was of him.

A shadow blocked her from the warm sunlight. She gazed up into the face of a tall and handsome man. His eyes were the color of a Cancun sea and they gleamed as he looked into her emerald ones. He smiled crookedly, and Maggie, instinctively, smiled back. "Got a light?" he asked smoothly, his voice spreading like molasses over Maggie's body. She shook her head, but Chloe handed him one. He cocked his head and lit the end of his cigarette, then returned the lighter to its owner and thanked her. Maggie waited for him to walk away, looked forward to it almost, as her body's immediate reaction to him left her a little unsettled, but Chloe spoke up and invited him to stay.

He took a seat between the two girls and extended his hand. "I'm Luke Stewart." He introduced himself casually. As Maggie took his hand, fire shot up her arm.

"This is Maggie." Chloe inserted, when Maggie had difficulty finding words. Chloe introduced herself as well, and soon they were engaged in conversation. Luke was in law school at Boston, and planned to finish in December, a semester earlier

than scheduled. Maggie made note of this as a sign of ambition. The more he spoke, the more intrigued Maggie became. He had a natural confidence about him, the kind that people couldn't help but be attracted to. But unlike so many of the other guys she knew, it didn't seem to come with an over inflated ego. Sure but not cocky. And his eyes. When they caught hers, it took her breath away.

Several minutes later, Chloe excused herself to return to the convention. Maggie had no interest in roaming from table to table, trying to appear interested in what the companies had to offer. She could have sat at the table talking to Luke for the rest of the afternoon. But Luke seemed to realize he had been gone too long and began to excuse himself as well. A wave of unexpected fear swept through Maggie at the thought that she may never see him again.

"There are a couple of firms here, that I wanted to get in front of before I skipped out." He explained as he rose from the table. Maggie nodded her understanding and grudgingly stood. "I've got to get my face out there, if I hope to get a job after law school. It was great chatting with you, though. And thanks for the light."

Maggie nodded and smiled, unable to find something intelligent to say. Luke started to turn away and walk towards the double doors that would lead him back to the convention and out of Maggie's life. "Hey, Luke?" She heard herself speak, but was not quite sure of what she would say next. He turned and raised an eyebrow at her. "Yeah?"

"Uh, good luck. You know, on the job front and graduating early and everything." She could kick herself for how juvenile she sounded. But Luke took a few steps back her way, a crooked smile on his face.

"Can I see you sometime?"

Maggie's heart beat so loudly she was sure he would hear it. "Yeah. I think I would like that."

"Could I get your number or something?" His eyes never left hers as he asked. She quickly found a napkin and he offered her a pen. She scribbled her phone number and name and her fingers brushed his as she handed it to him. "Maybe we could get together this weekend. I'll give you a call."

She watched as he walked back into the convention center, hoping he really would call and knowing that she would be desperately anticipating it for the remainder of the week. She never realized that she hadn't thought of Steve once since Luke had arrived.

"Go back a little farther now Maggie." Jamie's voice told her. "What was it like for you before college? How was high school? Think back on a time, when maybe things weren't going so well for you. Where are you now?"

"I'm at Dylan." Maggie replied somberly. "I just got there. Mom and Dad dropped me off. They took me to meet Ms. Merrill and then just left me with her."

"Are you mad about that?"

"I shouldn't be. This is supposed to be the best opportunity for me. Not many girls get accepted here and the ones that do are usually very successful later on."

"Is that how *you* feel, or is that something you were told?" Jamie questioned.

"That's what *everyone* keeps saying. But, I don't really want to be at this stupid school. Why are they making me go here? I want to be at home." Tears began to form under Maggie's closed lids. "I don't want to cry in front of people

I don't know and I don't understand what I did to make everyone so mad."

"Who's mad?" Jamie asked.

"Everyone. Mom and Dad. Patrick and Aiden. Everybody argues around me. That's why they're making me go so far away. They're all mad at me. But I don't even know what I did!"

"Maybe they're not really mad at you, Maggie. Maybe they just thought you would have a better education here. Does that sound possible?"

"That's just what they said. I know it's not the real reason. Ms. Merrill is going to take me to my new room. She says that I have a roommate and that her name is Jenna. I've never had a roommate before. She probably won't like me either. I just know I'm gonna hate it here. Oh, crap!"

"What's the matter, Maggie?"

"I can't stop the tears." Tears streamed down Maggie's adult face as she recalled the fear and sorrow of herself as a twelve year-old girl.

"It's okay, Maggie." Jamie soothed. "It's okay to cry. I'm sure Ms. Merrill understands."

"Nooo." Maggie moaned. "Not here. Not in front of Jenna. I promised myself. Please...not here." Maggie covered her face with her hands and began to sob.

"Maggie," Jamie spoke more harshly now, discarding the soothing voice for one of authority. "When I count to three, you will be fully conscious. You will remember everything, and you will feel awake and refreshed. One.....two.....three."

Maggie opened her eyes, blinking at the sunlight that streamed through the large window. Jamie sat across from her, right where she had been before. She smiled gently, waiting for Maggie to react. Maggie returned her smile weakly and wiped the tears from her eyes.

"Wow." Maggie said finally. "That seemed so real, like I was really there again."

Jamie nodded. "It's all back there in your subconscious." She explained. "It just needs the right forum to surface again. With all of the daily stresses and responsibilities in a person's life, there isn't time to return to any previous points in your journey. You remember pieces, important events or feelings. It's as though you must step outside of your current self. When you give yourself the opportunity to do that, your entire existence becomes accessible."

"So what did it all mean? I mean, what does it have to do with me now, or my nightmares?"

"Maybe nothing. But we've only explored a very short period of your life. We have to continue digging and remembering. The explanation for everything that you are right now, including those nightmares, can be found by looking at how you got here. The answers are in there somewhere. We just need to be patient."

"So we're not done with this?" Jamie shook her head. Maggie released a sigh. " I hope this doesn't mean I'm going to cry like a child every time I come here."

"Maggie?" Jamie asked leaning forward in her chair. "Do you still believe that you were sent to Dylan because your family was mad at you?"

Maggie was silent for a moment. Her eyes still gleamed from the recent tears. Jamie noticed a small quiver in her lip before she spoke. "No, I don't think so. I don't regret going to Dylan any more. The first year was rough, but it got a lot better. I think I was just mad that the decision was made without me. Leaving home at twelve, well, it made me stronger. It allowed me to stand on my own two feet. But it still seems like I was awful young for that. I was never once asked how I felt about it."

"So, you're still mad at your family, then?"

Maggie looked at Jamie. "My family is Luke, Owen and Quinn. No, I'm not mad at them."

"You know that's not who I meant."

"Mad at my parents? I'm over being mad at my parents. I think what I have for them is more an absence of feeling." Maggie responded. "Speaking of parents, I have to go or Luke is likely to bring them back here for good. I'll see you Monday."

Chapter Eighteen

Patrick drummed his fingers on the top of his desk and looked at the clock for the third time in two minutes. His time had come; there was nowhere to run any more. Peter Sylvan had made the appointment at his own recommendation and would be in his office any minute.

Patrick had met with Sterger earlier in the day. It had not gone well. Sterger was like an owl deadlocked on the sight of a mouse. He was ready and willing to go for Patrick's jugular if need be. Patrick was quite certain he had sent the SEC to his door as one more scare tactic.

Paula buzzed in over the intercom to inform him of Mr. Sylvan's arrival. "Show him in."

He clenched and unclenched his fists to release the nervous energy. The door opened and Paula announced Sylvan. Patrick stood and reached across his desk to politely shake hands, but it was returned with only a cold formality. They each took a seat across from one another and Peter folded his arms in front of him.

"I won't waste your time or mine with a lot of small talk, Mr. Callaghan." Sylvan began gruffly. "There have been accusations made. Serious accusations." He emphasized the word in case Patrick had misconstrued his purpose for being there. "Allegations of stock market fraud. Price fixing.

It has been brought to the attention of the SEC and we are considering opening a formal investigation of the matter."

Patrick felt tiny beads of sweat prickling the hair on the back of his neck, but kept his expression calm and neutral. He waited to hear his terms. He studied the smug-looking man before him with loathing. He looked the type who would have sailed through business school, who got the internship of a lifetime dropped right into his lap due, no doubt, to extensive family connections. It would have kicked off a career with enormous potential. He'd soared up the corporate ladder with neither a skinned knee nor a bruised ego. He never scraped or clawed against the competition. He never had to strategize every single step he took or practice conversations with every corporate head around the country before a mirror as though reading from a script until the lines flowed perfectly. He never brown-nosed or kissed the ass of his own father in-law for years just to make a tiny advancement in his profession. He would never need to rub elbows with everyone he was told might 'benefit the firm' or 'had a lot to offer' or 'might just come in handy down the road'. Instead, *his* elbows were rubbed, his ass kissed.

Now, this excuse for a lawyer perched in Patrick's leather chair and preached to him the integrity of business ethics. He wanted to reach across his mahogany desk and wrap his thick fingers around that crane-like neck to shake all the presumptuous superiority from his stringy body and leave him in a heap on the floor.

'...and it is our duty," Sylvan continued in a self-righteous monologue that could have been orated before a state bar swearing-in, "as representatives of the law, that we conduct ourselves in ways that condemn illegal behavior." He paused there for emphasis and Patrick wondered whether he was expecting a full confession on the spot. When Patrick didn't move so much as an eyebrow, he began again.

"It has been documented that all interactions regarding this matter have been conducted under your supervision."

Patrick calmly picked up a sterling silver pen and wrote a note. He intended to look as though he might be gathering evidence for a possible slander suit, but what he actually wrote was simply "Bastard".

"Mr. Sylvan," he began clearing his throat and leaning into his desk. "I counsel my clients on a wide variety of matters. If they acted upon all of them I'd be the highest paid partner around. I follow the rules of stock brokerage. Now, I am unaware of these documents you are referring to, so I am sure you will understand when I tell you that until they are made available for my review, this meeting is over."

"I'm not a police officer, Mr. Callaghan." Sylvan stated with a cold, piercing glare. "I am not here to draw up charges. I have been sent to rectify matters before it reaches that level."

Patrick pushed himself away from the desk and rose, circling around to rest against one corner. "Like I said, Mr. Sylvan, this meeting is over."

Peter Sylvan reached down to grasp the red leather Gucci briefcase at his feet. A look somewhere between pity and disgust crossed over his face. Pausing at the door of the office, he snorted his disapproval. "Matters will only get worse from here, Mr. Callaghan."

As he strode from the prestigious and serious room, Patrick turned to look out the window behind his desk. "They already have, Mr. Sylvan."

Mickey showered and dressed quickly with a beer in one hand. Sean had called with more of a demand that he come for dinner than a request. Sean so rarely insisted on anything that Mickey knew better than to refuse. He sped across town to the old white colonial that had once been home. He parked the Jeep in the turn around, withdrew the key and sighed deeply before jogging to the front door, wishing he'd been able to get one more drink in him before coming.

Kit was already in the foyer to greet him as he stepped inside. Enticing smells wafted through the hall from the kitchen in the back and he breathed it in.

"Smells great as always, Mom." He told her wrapping her in a warm embrace. She patted him gently on the back then pulled away to study his face.

"Is everything alright, honey? You look awfully tired."

Mickey pried his mother's hands from his face and held them at his waist. "Everything's good, Mom." The worry lines along the top of her nose that were permanently etched into her features, deepened as she continued to search his face. She still knew when something was wrong with one of her children. Knowing Mickey would say no more, she finally patted his hand.

"Okay, then. Come try my sauce." She led him down the hall and into the kitchen for a sample. Sean was hidden deep in the fridge searching for a forbidden snack before the main course.

"Hey, Dad." Mickey greeted him and Kit closed the refrigerator door, shooting him a look of warning.

"Mickey, good to see you." They shook hands briefly. Mickey accepted the wooden spoon of spaghetti sauce and tasted it. Kit smiled at his thumbs up.

"So, what's going on?" he asked them, leaning against the counter. "It sounded pretty important that I come over."

"We've been away for a week, dear and we wanted to catch up, that's all." Kit replied emphatically. Mickey didn't buy a word of it. Kit and Sean Callaghan went on extensive vacations at least twice a year and never needed to 'catch up' when they returned. But it had always been Kit's preference to exchange friendly conversation before getting to the heart of the matter. When the time was right, they would discuss it. "Can't two people miss their son?" she added.

"Sure. You do know where the bar is though, don't you?" he teased. "In fact, even Aiden found it the other night."

Sean simply grunted but Kit spun around on her heel to face Mickey anxiously. "Aiden came to see you? Mickey, that's wonderful!"

"Well, he didn't exactly come to see me. He was with a girl." Tears brimmed in his mother's eyes. She clasped her hands together at the news.

"Oh. That's fabulous! How is he doing, Mickey, tell me everything!"

"We didn't really get a chance to chat, Mom." Mickey shrugged. "I was working and he was on a date."

"Mickey! You haven't seen your brother in years. You couldn't sit down for twenty minutes and catch up?"

"There wasn't time. I think Aiden was caught off-guard. I don't think he knew he was coming to my place until they were already there. And he didn't know the girl that well. They were still covering all the formalities and getting to know each other. It wasn't the place to drudge up bad blood."

Kit waved a dishtowel in the air as if to fan away a mosquito. "There's no bad *blood* in the family. It was all just a misunderstanding." Sean grunted again. "Oh, go on, you old fool. Hold it against him for the rest of your life. We raised our children to have minds of their own. But when they don't agree with your take on things, they're automatically wrong."

"Kit, I won't discuss it. Aiden made his choice about this family. Let him live with it. Now is dinner ready or not?"

Kit mumbled something under her breath as she began to bring the food to the table.

Mickey was on his second helping of pasta, when Kit folded her hands neatly under her chin and peered across the table at him. "Aren't you even curious to hear about our trip?"

"Of course." Mickey mumbled through his spaghetti. "How's my precious godson?"

"Quinn and Owen are both fine. Quinn is growing so fast and Owen has a very strong will. They're both awfully attached to Maggie."

"Well, of course they are, Kit." Sean piped up.

"I didn't mean anything by it, Sean. I think she's a very devoted mother."

"So things went well, then?" Mickey interjected quickly.

Kit wiped her face. "She's having terrible nightmares, Mickey, and we're very concerned. We told you that Luke called us because she abandoned the children."

"'Abandoned'? Mom, come on." Mickey stated in defense of his sister. "She doesn't even remember doing it."

"Which is cause enough for her to go back on her medication! I think this whole discussion is unnecessary, Sean. We need to just put our foot down!"

"Do you hear yourself, Kit?" Sean leaned in. "She is not a child anymore! We can't send her to her room if she doesn't do what we say. Maggie is a grown woman who can make her own decisions. If you continue to push like this, you'll only drive her further away."

Mickey smiled almost imperceptibly in response to his father's words. *Maybe Aiden has taught us all something about the psyche after all.*

"She is *not* capable of making her own decisions, that's my point. Maggie is a fragile, confused girl and somebody needs to take charge of this and see to her well-being. If no one else will stand up to the task then I will!"

"Mom, slow down. Maggie is not fragile. She is a strong woman with a husband and two well-balanced children. If she is confused, it is of no fault of her own. She's been misled..."

"She's been protected." Sean corrected.

She's been lied to, Mickey thought but dared not say. "I'm not sure why I'm here. This sounds like a disagreement between the two of you."

"It's not a disagreement, honey." Kit shook her head sadly. "Between anyone. Your father and I both agree that Maggie listens to you. She trusts you. If you suggested that she try the medication again, she might do it."

Mickey pulled back from the table. "Wait a minute. I can't tell Maggie what to do. First you insist I call her, now this. Dad's right – she's an adult now. She and Luke are the only ones who can make that kind of decision."

"But Mickey, Luke doesn't even know the whole story. He doesn't understand what's at stake!"

Mickey looked out the kitchen window to the lawn behind the house. He could remember the forts that had been built out there and the snow tunnels. He could still see his brothers and Maggie stomping through mud puddles and chasing rabbits. But Maggie couldn't. Her memory had been stolen from her. And the medication his mother spoke of had been the tool used to do it. He looked back at his mother with a somber expression. "Maybe he *should* know. Maybe it's time that Maggie know too."

His mother's look of horror assured him that she couldn't let that happen.

Chapter Nineteen

Jamie studied Maggie closely as she entered the room and took her usual seat sensing more unease than usual. "I've remembered some more." Maggie admitted quietly. Her eyes focused somewhere over Jamie's shoulder. "Not much, but some." Jamie wanted to congratulate her, but sensed it was premature.

"Can you tell me what it was?"

"When I was pretty little, seven or eight, I think, this stray cat started hanging around our house. Mickey and Aiden used to sneak food into their fort and the cat would slip in some time during the night and eat it.

"For a while, it wouldn't go near any of us. I used to lean up against one of the trees in the backyard and call and call. 'Here kitty-kitty-kitty', for hours just trying to get him to come closer. Then I thought that maybe it was because it didn't have a name to answer to, so I called him 'Hushpad' after this cat in a book I had read who used to steal food all the time."

"Quite creative for a seven year-old."

"Finally, one day, Hushpad slowly made his way over to me and I got to pet him. I knew at that moment he would always belong to me. Suddenly, he would follow me everywhere and his fear of people disappeared. He would walk right through my mother's legs and into the house if he knew I was in there. If I cried for some reason, he could find me no matter where I was.

"Well, one day he disappeared. He had run away, or maybe got caught or killed, I don't know. I was crushed. I couldn't stop crying, I even made myself sick. And do you know who took care of me?" Her eyes connected with Jamie's for the first time during the story and they glistened with sorrow and loss. Jamie shook her head slightly.

"Aiden. He put up posters all over town. He combed the streets everyday after school. He hugged me and rocked me to sleep every night that Hushpad didn't come home. He even made up some story about a place where all cats go if they die and wait for their owners. And he told me," her voice softened.

"He told me I could never lose *him*. We could remember Hushpad together because we would never be apart." A tear broke away from the corner of her eye and slid gently down her cheek. "Why am I only remembering this now? How could he care so much then, and not care at all now?"

"Maybe he does care, Maggie." Jamie soothed. "In his own way. Age can complicate things so. Maybe he doesn't know how to express how much he cares anymore." Maggie shook her head and wiped her face with the back of her hand.

"If that was the case, he never would have done what he did. He never would have ruined Mickey's big opening. He would have shown up to the kids' baptisms! He *said* he would be there for me." Maggie became thoughtful for a moment, her damp eyes narrowing in remembrance. "He said it that night too – at Mickey's opening. After the whole scene he created, Mickey kicked him out. And at the door he told me he would be there for me. He said, when I needed him…"

Jamie reached for Maggie's hand, feeling a friendly connection with her beyond a professional need to help. "Couldn't you contact Aiden?" she asked feeling a small drop of hope coming from the woman before her. "I'm sure he misses you too. Maybe he regrets detaching himself from the family, but doesn't know how to find his way back to you."

Maggie's cool green eyes hardened, her jaw clenched and unclenched in a long practiced bitterness. "No." she answered defiantly. "I'm not the one who cut him off. I didn't walk away. He was very clear about his feelings for me, for all of us."

"I think he hurt Mickey most..." she continued after a moment. Her eyes softened as she thought of her other brother, darkening into a deep forest of green. "It was his special moment and Aiden ruined that for him. Mickey always wanted, depended on his family being close. He was always at his best when he was surrounded by people he loved. I think that's why he drank so much. That night Aiden destroyed it."

The sharp piercing of the phone woke Mickey from his foggy sleep. He rolled over, tangled in the disheveled sheets and reached blindly at the intrusive noise.

"What?" he growled into the receiver when he finally got it to his ear.

"Now, that don't sound like the young Callaghan I know!"

Mickey sat up straight in bed at the sound of Danny's voice, pulling the phone off the nightstand and sending an empty shot glass and tumbler of water crashing to the floor. "Shit! Danny is that you?" he asked.

"Aye, it sure is. We've been missing you around these parts, so I'd thought I'd bug ya some more. Everything all right over there?"

Mickey tried to shake out the dense cobwebs in his aching head, only succeeding in making it throb more. "Yeah, yeah. I just dropped something." He suddenly wished desperately for a sip of the cool water that spread slowly over his floorboards, or better yet, some of what had been in the shot glass that lay in pieces. Had Danny said 'we'?

"Well then, when's yer next holiday?"

"I don't think it's in the cards, Dan."

"Look," Danny lowered his voice some as though not wanting to be overheard. "I know yer last visit wasn't the best, but I think it's time you come back. Visit yer old friends, settle some unfinished business, ya know. God, we're like yer family over 'ere."

Mickey longed to ask about Gwen, wanted to know if she was the unfinished business Danny spoke of. His friend's reference to his last visit had been the closest they had come to talking about Gwen in months. He clenched his teeth together tightly to fight back the questions that ached to betray him. "I run a business, Danny. I can't just pick up and leave anymore. You should understand that better than anyone."

"Ya can't let yer business be your life."

"Look who's talking! In all the time I've known you have you ever once left that goddamn bar to come here? You all think there's nothing beyond your shores, that life can't exist beyond your door. You want to see me? You miss me so much? You come here for once!"

The other end of the phone was silent for a moment. Danny was not used to this angry, bitter Mickey. Even over the last months, during their phone calls, knowing he was heart broken, Mickey had tried to sound light. Tried to prove nothing had changed. It hadn't fooled Danny, but he began to wonder now how much damage it had done to Mickey. "Well, now I just might, with a warm invitation like that."

Mickey ached for something off the top shelf of the bar. He ached that he had yelled at his best friend. He ached that he couldn't ask about Gwen. Danny was like a brother to him, closer than his own, by far. Danny and Gwen had been the ones at Mickey's side as he fought sobriety and eventually won…well at least then. He was afraid of letting Danny down. And if Danny ever told Gwen… "Forget it. You're busy, I'm busy. Uhh, I got someone at the door. I gotta go. I'll call you soon." Mickey hung up the phone and buried his aching head under his pillow.

Danny put the phone on its cradle and turned back to the bar. He knew Mickey too well and didn't like the sound of him at all. The man Danny had just spoken to was anyone but the person he knew. Whatever was going on, Mickey didn't want Danny, or moreover, Gwen to know anything about it. Which could only mean one of two things. He had found someone new or he was drinking again. Danny was certain that the man he had just spoken to was not someone recently bitten by love.

He peered down the bar to the tables where Gwen was delivering stacked sandwiches and stew to a group of locals.

She smiled and spoke easily with them, and they shared a comfortable camaraderie. It broke Danny's heart to see her, to think of first before and then after Mickey walked into her life. Gwen was a typically stubborn Irishwoman and Danny had never given up his efforts to help her swallow her pride and see reason. Gwen and Mickey were his family, and absolutely meant for one another.

He had always prided himself on being an excellent judge of character, but made it a practice not to get involved in the personal lives of others. After all, a good bartender listened and understood everything that went on in the lives of his patrons, but never interfered with fate. When Gwen and Mickey had gone their separate ways Danny assumed it would last a month or so, and things would return to the way they had been before. He figured Mickey would return to the bar, apologize for all his shortcomings, turn on the charm, and the rest would be history. After all, he had never seen Gwen so completely happy as she was when Mickey Callaghan was in the room.

Danny had been wrong this time. Dead wrong. It was over a year now, and Mickey had not returned to their beloved town. And Gwen… well, Gwen had been through a lifetime of heartbreak, sorrow, and more in that time. She left her studies and began waitressing for Danny full-time. He knew she could have gotten any of a hundred better paying, less exhausting jobs, but Danny had a feeling that her career move had been quite intentional, just in case a lonely, dark-haired American wandered back in someday.

He had continued to keep quiet about the whole thing, waiting for nature to take its course.

Maybe this one time, though, nature needed a little help. It was long past time his two closest friends found their way back to each other. Giving a sharp whistle, he caught Gwen's attention and signaled her over to the bar.

"You rang, boss?" she teased and hoisted herself onto a stool. Danny's serious expression wiped the smiled from her face.

"Gwenny, I'm worried about Mickey."

He noticed the immediate flush that spread over her cheeks at the mere mention of his name. "In fact," he continued, "I think he might be drinking again."

"What?" she gasped.

"Don't you think this charade has gone on long enough?"

That got her fur up. "What are you suggesting, Danny O'Leary? Certainly not that I am to blame if Mickey's fallen off the wagon!"

Danny placed a calming hand on hers. "Gwen, I'm not blaming you. I just think that you've been moping about and Mickey is moping about and..."

"I am *not* moping about! You know exactly what I do with every minute of my day. There is no *time* for moping." she seethed, but Danny remained undeterred.

"...and perhaps the two are connected." He completed his sentence.

Gwen opened her mouth to argue, then snapped it shut again. There were no words of defense though she'd never admit it aloud to him.

"Listen, the bar is well staffed for the next week or two. Maybe a bit of a holiday is just what you need."

Her eyes narrowed suspiciously. "Just what are you getting at, O'Leary?"

Danny busied himself wiping down the gleaming bar. "Nothing 'tall, Miss Gwen. I just think a trip might be nice for ya."

"You're out of your mind! Me go runnin' to him? He's the one who walked out of here. He walked out on me. On us!" Gwen's dark lashes trapped the large tear.

"Put aside yer pride, Gwen. For Mickey. No one's keeping score! See some of the world while you do a good deed and put yer life back together. I hear the states are mighty pretty this time of year."

"Well, then. You be sure to take some photos."

"Will that do it, Gwen?" He threw the bar rag down, the humor evaporating from his voice without a trace. It worked. His tone made Gwen take notice. "If I take you there – will that do it? Because by God, if I have to drag you onto a plane, I'm just about crazy enough to do it. I've tried not to meddle, but you two are about the biggest idiots a man could know. Now. Get your things together and I will order the tickets. We're going!"

Gwen's mouth hung open at Danny's demands. "And get that darling baby girl of yours ready. It's about time she meet her Da."

Chapter Twenty

The country roads wound their way between rocky hills and through overgrown farmland on the way to the ferry dock. The sun was slowly sinking, casting a warm splash of pink and blue into the summer sky. The window of the Mercedes was rolled down sending warm scents of fresh cut grass and lavender through it. Patrick breathed it in deeply trying to release the tension that had followed him all the way from the office.

He had been a coward. After Sylvan left the office a new wave of fear spread through him. Thoughts of being fired by Davis were followed shortly by thoughts of Shauna filing for divorce and full custody of the children. Then he would be torn away from Lexy, Patrick and Ashleigh.

It had been too much to swallow, so he had fled. A coward. It should come as no surprise to him that he had been weak. Hadn't he proven himself a coward many times before? This time should be no different. He was racing back to his haven – the little cottage on Opinicon – his for exactly this reason. He raced toward its warm embrace. It accepted him as he was.

Still, it was different this time. He never needed the cottage so desperately before – never used it as a hideaway from anything more than himself. Certainly not as a refuge from the law – was that what he was doing? Shauna had sensed it this time too.The tone in her voice as he explained the last minute change in plans showed that Patrick would not get away with his lies much longer. Of course, Shauna was too well-mannered to blow up at him over the phone. She would wait patiently until he returned home to engage in a much more civilized argument.

He turned the wide corner and came upon the docks. The area had been significantly modernized since his childhood, though it retained much of its retrospective charm. A few novelty shops dotted the sides of the street. There was a pizza parlor and a café. Old-fashioned street lamps gave it the look of a Venetian alleyway or port in its glory day. The ferry master, Jack Barnes' boy, once with only a flatbed boat, now had a grand whitewashed dock with carved wooden banisters.

A large arched sign above the entrance announced "Echo Island Ferries" etched in deep green lettering. Kit and Pat had done more for this small farm town than they knew when they sold their piece of Echo Island to Jack and Edna Barnes. The inn that had once been their summer home was now the focal point of the area. Loyal guests from near and far had spread the word about the beautiful surroundings and warm hospitality until Jack and Edna had needed to extend their season a full month on each end.

Patrick pulled into a vacant parking space and turned off the engine. He knew the ferry schedule by heart and had fifteen minutes before its next trip to the island, so he grabbed his duffel bag and briefcase and headed toward the café. He changed from his office attire into jeans and a t-shirt in the restroom and then ordered a chocolate milkshake at one of the plastic patio tables facing the lake. Already he could feel himself relax. He had no problem escaping the profile of big-city business when he came here. It wasn't how people knew him, wouldn't be expected. There were no presumptions of how his life was being lived, no eagle eyes watching each move to be certain his reputation remained in tact. Occasionally, he received a look of pity or sympathy from a fellow passenger on the ferry and he knew his story had been told again. Other than that, he was simply the quiet young gentleman with the little cottage on the north side of the island who kept to himself.

As he sipped his favorite childhood drink the image of Sylvan returned, still fresh and buzzing in his head. How eager Sylvan was to watch Patrick crawl gnawed at him. At this moment he was probably organizing the incriminating documents and stacking the deck in his favor. A feeling of unease swam circles in Patrick's stomach and he ran a nervous hand through his thick hair a few times as if to push the thoughts from his mind. He knew he was cornered and was reminded of the chess games Mickey and Aiden used to play avidly. He rarely joined in on a competition, partly because he knew both of his brothers were better players than he was. But he knew enough of the game to understand that he was in 'check' now. It might just take their knowledge of the game to get him out of it.

Michelle strode down the hallway of the office, almost giddy. Her tight black skirt accentuated her firm buttocks as her hips swayed with her gait. Her long salon-tanned legs were smooth and shapely, accentuated by strappy sandals and a high, thin heel. The white blouse she wore was one button short of professional apparel, but no one at work had complained about her fashion sense yet, and if one were to *really* look, they would catch a tantalizing glimpse of her powder-pink lace demi cup.

The manila file clutched in her right hand was the perfect excuse into Luke's office this afternoon. Hard work and determination had paid off for her again, and it was apparent in her sparkling eyes. She opened the door without knocking as was her usual habit and found Luke dictating a letter for his secretary. His dark hair was lightly sprinkled with gray and she had the fleeting urge to run her hands through it playfully. She pushed the thought aside and regained her composure as he looked up and smiled. She waved the file above her head like a trophy, and, brushing her honey locks away from her face, propped herself up on the edge of his desk, providing him with an excellent view of inner thigh.

"I got him!" She announced proudly tossing the file in front of him. "Oxford. I found him and he's willing to talk about it as long as we meet him somewhere obscure."

Luke peered at her with weary eyes. "That's great, Michelle. Really. Where'd you find him?"

"Chicago." She answered. The buoyant joy in her face slackened. "What's the matter? You should be as over the top about this as I am. The whole case could be riding on his depo. Instead you look like your cat just died."

Luke rose from his seat and turned to peer out the window at the city below. He could remember his years in law school or clerking, storming the bars with buddies just blocks from where he stood now. His biggest concern then was whether one date knew about the other, and maybe what would be on the upcoming final. It wasn't so many years ago and yet it seemed like ages. He hadn't enjoyed a night on the town since... he couldn't even remember.

His thoughts shifted to home. Maggie was withdrawn and solemn. She avoided eye contact with him and was vague about her sessions with Dr. Cooper. Dinner each night was filled only with the clink of the silver and the boys' random babble. Owen seemed to sense something was wrong, and was regressing to a clingy, whining toddler, which had begun to grate on Luke's already raw nerves.

For some time now, work had become his escape. Lately, however, his senior partners seemed to be stacking his caseload intentionally, with no regard for his situation or sanity. Now he dreaded being at work as well as home. He felt trapped, like an animal in a hole, scratching and clawing at the dirt in futile hopes of reaching the light. Gazing over the bustling streets, he saw the light he was digging for. He didn't think, thinking right now would cause him to be the responsible, predictable man who had gotten him here in the first place. Instead, he turned to Michelle and threw on a lopsided grin.

"You're right." He stated as he steered her toward the door, "We should be celebrating. Let's go. Drinks are on me."

Chapter Twenty-one

Maggie relaxed against the back of the chair, eyes closed, breathing steadily. Jamie's voice was a whisper sending her deeper and deeper into her own mind. Darkness enveloped her, a comforting and welcome shroud. Jamie was asking the darkness to part like a curtain and shed some light onto Maggie's past. As the lights slowly rose, she could see people before her...talking. Her focus grew clearer and she could begin to make out faces.

Dad paced restlessly back and forth across the living room. Mom sat off to the side in an armchair sobbing, her face buried behind her hands. Mickey and Aiden were on the couch, faces aimed at the floor, they were crying too. Patrick stood at the doorway, looking as though he might run out through it at any moment and disappear.

She was sitting on someone's lap, with arms wrapped around her comfortingly. She couldn't see who it was, didn't turn to look, but she felt safe, must have known who it was. She looked on at the scene before her, seeing, hearing, but not understanding what was happening.

"They were your responsibility, Patty." Her father bellowed angrily. "How goddamn hard is it to watch after your younger brother and sister for one afternoon?" Patrick seemed to sink further into the doorjamb, withering at his father's anger. Kit stifled

a moan. "It was your irresponsibility, your childish ways that..." Maggie's eyes widened slightly. Her father swore.

"Stop it, Sean!!" her mother shouted hoarsely through her tears. "It's not Pat's fault. It's nobody's fault. It was just an accident, a horrible…horrible..." her voice trailed off as the racking sobs returned. "We have to leave. We have to get out of here now. This isn't good for anybody. Sean, take us home. Please"

Her father's angry eyes remained on Patrick. "Dad," Patrick choked while his eyes pleaded. "I'm so sorry. If I could take it back, Dad, please… don't… hate me." He looked at Maggie as though she were a china doll dangling from a shelf, that might fall at any moment and shatter into a thousand irreparable pieces. Patrick, who had always been untouchable to her, whom she had always tried to impress, to make proud, to gain attention from. So strong and handsome and sure. He seemed broken now.

"Patrick?" she tried to speak but it came out as a whispered squeak.. He flinched at the sound of her voice and turned his head further away from her view. What had she done? Why was everyone so upset? Why wouldn't Patrick look at her? She looked to Aiden and Mickey, sitting silently on opposite ends of the couch. Aiden's head was bent so low it was almost between his knees, his hands at his ears. Mickey looked up and saw Maggie. There was such sadness in his eyes, great depths of it that made Maggie suck in her breath. At the sound, her mother rushed over and knelt in front of her, gathering her small face in her hands.

"Maggie, baby, are you okay? How do you feel honey?"

"Mom?" was all Maggie could manage but at least this time the word had actually formed on her lips.. Her mother's face blurred before her again. She tried to focus on the glistening tears that streamed from her mom's eyes and reached out to touch one. "Mom?" Her mother sank to the floor before Maggie,

weeping desperately. Her father rushed to her, lifting her and returning her to her seat.

"Take us home, Sean!" She begged him. "I can't stay here another minute. Get the family together and take them home." Her voice trailed again as Dad nodded, holding Mom close to his chest.

"We're going, Kit. Right now. Kids," he began, standing tall and taking charge, "get down to the docks quickly and call for the ferry master. Get whatever things you need, we'll get the rest later. Patrick, I expect you to be in charge of getting your brothers to the boat. Get. It. Done."

Maggie saw Patrick wince in pain at the tone and accusation in his father's words, but he went to the couch to gather Mickey and Aiden and head upstairs to pack. Fear began to grip Maggie as the stranger holding her stood and she clung to the warm body that smelled of lavender and lemon pledge.

"NO!" she screamed violently, her eyes closed tightly, her body trembled. "We can't leave him here! No!!"

Maggie startled upright to find herself sitting in the wing-back chair while Jamie looked on, wide-eyed. Reality flooded her mind, the psychiatrist's office, her panic attacks, and nightmares. She felt drained by her memory; the thoughts and images of it that lingered on, swimming through her mind.

"Maggie, that was huge!" Jamie cheered. "Your memories were clearer than any yet. How do you feel?"

Maggie felt such a mixture of emotions that she couldn't respond. Should she be proud of her breakthrough or cry for the terrified version of herself she had seen? Should she breathe in relief or gasp in fear?

"I'm not sure." Maggie finally whispered, replaying the fresh memory over again. "That place. It wasn't home. We had a summer home. A cottage.

"Jamie, they were all…we were all…broken. What happened?"

"You are doing extremely well. I think those answer are yet to come. We may want to take a break for today. Does that sound alright?"

"I have to tell Luke. I…I think I should call…Aiden now."

Jamie rose and reached out to place a gentle hand on Maggie's arm. "Now that you've opened up your mind to the past, the memories may start coming more quickly. You've shown that you're ready for them. If you find that it becomes overwhelming, will you call me?"

Even as she gathered her things together to leave, images of a cottage where she once spent her summers flickered like frames of film in her head. She could see the gravel roads and the sparkling water. She could remember the loons and blue herons, and finding frogs in the bay or turtles sunning themselves on logs along the shore. They had stayed on an island. She could remember being ferried over to it, all huddled together on a small barge with suitcases and groceries.

"Maggie, will you call me?" Jamie repeated.

"Yes, yes. I really need to find Luke. Thank you, Dr. Cooper." She turned and bustled out the door, anxious to share the possibility of uncovering all of her nightmares with Luke. And uncertain of what she might find once she did.

Chapter Twenty-two

The café was buzzing with businesspeople in suits and college students in jeans, talking on cellular phones, tapping at their laptops, or engaged in lively discussions at a table with friends and colleagues. The counter kept a constant flow of high-octane coffee and baguettes available to its patrons. Luke and Michelle sat in one corner of the room, by the large front window with the word *Tivoli* etched across the middle. They were both silent for the moment, Luke, leaning back against the wrought iron chair and Michelle, absent-mindedly stirring her coffee with a spoon.

Luke looked upon the woman who continually listened to his problems without ever complaining for the past year. She had watched him make partner, tipped him off on important cases, organized his depositions, found legal loopholes when needed and constantly advocated for him to the senior suits. And more recently, she had become a confidante and companion. Allowing him to escape from a reality that could become too much to bear at times. She was always in his corner, always fighting for him, never asking anything in return.

She was beautiful too. Her honey hair curled in springy spirals that danced against her shoulders when she spoke or moved. Her eyes were an intriguing mix of light and dark. Many times, the only thing that calmed Luke recently, were those gentle eyes. Certainly she could be spending her time with some guy who spent six days a week in a gym, or drove a Ferrari, or flew her to Paris for a weekend. Instead, she seemed content to spend an hour a day across from Luke as he poured his heart onto the table. He spoke of Maggie, Owen and Quinn, his troubles at home, his stresses at the office, how difficult his life was. She just listened and commiserated, never judging and seemingly never tiring of him.

Realizing she had been stirring her coffee for several moments, Michelle tapped the spoon gently against the side of the mug and set it down. She looked at Luke, tilting her head slightly and offering a warm smile. "What is it?" she asked him. "You're a million miles away."

Luke looked at the caring, beautiful woman across the table from him. "Why do you listen to me, day in, day out? Don't you get tired of the same complaints over and over again? Don't you want to be spending your lunchtime having fun with your girlfriends, or with a young, energetic guy? You've got to be sick of listening to me gripe all the time."

Michelle averted her eyes from Luke's and uncharacteristically bit her lip. After a lengthy silence, she looked directly at him with a serious expression.

" No. I don't get sick of listening to you. I don't want to hang out with my girlfriends or with some young guy, as you put it. To be honest, I don't have many girlfriends. And... I am not really interested in any one... romantically. You are the only one who makes me feel needed."

She raised a hand to silence him when he opened his mouth to speak.

"Please, don't say something kind and sympathetic. I know what my odds are with you and I'm not going to ask you to do anything that would compromise who you are. " She hesitated, and then continued. "I'm not telling you this so that you feel bad, or pity me, or anything. You asked why I listen to you every day.

"I enjoy every moment I have with you, Luke. Whether it's about work or kids or even Maggie. I like it *too* much, and maybe it's unrealistic of me to feel the way I do. But I do."

Luke swallowed hard and took a moment to digest the information he had just heard. Michelle, a young, vivacious, attractive woman was interested in him: a slave to the office, married man and father of two who had not experienced intimacy in months. The honesty of her words quickened his pulse and aroused his desire. His own wife rejected him sexually, and yet, somehow, this young woman sat directly in front of him, basically telling him how she wanted him. The irony of it almost made him laugh.

His head began to swim with unneeded images of he and Michelle together. He could see them making love on a table right in the middle of the café, or on his leather couch back at the office. He could see Michelle standing before him nude, the swell of her breasts and hips, her narrow waist – wanting *him*. How long had it been since he had been wanted? He could almost feel those soft curls against his neck and chest, almost taste her soft pink lips...

"Maybe, we should get back to the office." Michelle interrupted his thoughts. "You've got court in an hour and a half and I've got all those doctor's request forms to send out."

Luke nodded, standing carefully and adjusting his suit coat. This new understanding of Michelle and the realization of his own attraction were more apparent then he had expected and brought a barely visible grin to his lips. Where his mind had previously been a million miles away, as she had said, it was now just down the street at the Radisson. He held the door open for her as they headed back toward the office building, where he hoped to be able to regain some of his composure before being expected at the courthouse. His view as he walked to catch up to her, however, seemed to indicate that it would not be an easy task.

Michelle maintained a steady pace all the way back to the office. Her mind reeled at the realization that she had actually told Luke how she felt. For months, her feelings for him had steadily grown, her need to spend time with him became a kind of addiction. Now, everything in her universe had tilted out of control; reality and fantasy had become intermingled because of the words she had promised herself she would never say to him. She was sure her cheeks were flushed, her whole body felt like slow-flowing lava, weakening her muscles and draining her strength.

He hadn't said a word since she opened her big mouth. He was probably thinking of a way to get a new paralegal to work with, right now.

She reached the double doors to the office building several steps ahead of Luke and headed straight for the elevator. Maybe there was a big enough gap between them that he'd have to take a different lift.

"Michelle, wait up!" he called and she sighed, holding the "Open Door" button impatiently. She tried to brace herself for the "it just wouldn't work" speech she was no doubt about to hear.

Luke got to the elevator, out of breath from trying to keep up. He looked down into her eyes. "Christ, would you just slow down a minute?" he asked exasperated. She stood, lips slightly parted, her tongue tracing her teeth.

"Luke, you don't need to say it. I already know…"

Before he realized the full extent of what he was doing, Luke took her face into his hands and lunged hungrily for her mouth. She responded immediately, meeting his eager tongue with her own. He crushed her against the back of the elevator consumed by greedy passion – his for what he had needed for so long, hers for *who* she needed. Her fingers raked through his hair as she'd so often imagined doing. His hands pressed against the back wall, trapping her so that his body could press more firmly against hers as the elevator door slowly closed.

Chapter Twenty-three

"The average dive takes less than a minute."

Maggie hadn't been able to think clearly since she'd left Jamie's office. Pieces of the scene she had remembered while she was under fell together with more memories of the past. Her father had been so angry, her mother so tormented.

In her relaxed state, she had only seen the living room, but now she remembered it all. She knew that a hallway ran behind the fireplace leading to a large, open kitchen filled with cupboards. An open hearth stood beside the door that led out onto the back porch. She could almost smell the cooking that used to waft through the house from the large double oven. She remembered her room, which had been at the top of the stairs. She had wanted it to be pretty – pink and white, but her mother repeatedly assured her that was impractical for the cottage. It was like a dream she was having while awake, hazy and strange.

She was surprised when she found herself at one of the doors to Luke's office building. She had been walking in circles downtown for almost half an hour, lost in thought, while Jamie's office was only two blocks from Luke's. She realized she was anxious to talk to Luke about what was happening. If she was starting to remember things that happened years ago she would certainly get to the bottom of the events on the day she left the boys. And then Luke would see it wasn't her fault. They could start to rebuild their relationship.

What was it that had her father so angry that day? She thought as she pushed through the revolving glass door. She tried hard to remember every detail she could about the memory. *It was Patrick he was mad at. But why? What did Patrick do? And when had all of this happened?*

She turned the corner, her heels making a clicking sound against the cold marble floor that bounced off the walls and ceiling high above her. One of the elevator doors was still open and she quickened her pace to catch it.

Her first thought as she saw the couple passionately embraced, was how badly she wanted that back with Luke again. But the gold band flashed against the steel of the elevator wall and she could see the three small diamonds set diagonally across the front. She looked at the back of Luke's head, his dark hair sprinkled slightly with gray…and long thin fingers raking through it. Shock rocketed through her. The door closed on the awful scene before her and she staggered back a few steps holding her stomach, which had begun to turn. She was certain she was about to scream. Or vomit. Or both.

The walls around her seemed to close in, the ceiling fanned out in a crazy spiral and her world began to spin. As the edges of her view darkened, she felt someone at her arm, but she could not hear them or speak to them. Her legs weakened and the darkness overtook her.

She awoke surrounded by strangers peering down at her and flushed with embarrassment. The sun beat through one of the tall glass windows like a spotlight on her humiliation. She put a hand up to ward off any further assistance, assuring her onlookers that she was fine.

Slowly the memory, *oh, why did it have to work so well now?* came back to her. Bile rose in her throat.

On weak legs, she rushed out of the building and fled the two blocks to her car, fighting the demon memories that followed on her heels. Visions of the scene in the elevator pecked at her incessantly and she squeezed her eyes shut to ward them off. Eventually she got the car started and squealed out of her parking spot.

She had to stop once, to pull the car over to the side of the road and throw up. Her hands shook against the wheel and tears streamed from her face, but she held tight, determined to reach her children alive.

She tried desperately to make sense of it all, to guess at when it all started. Was it when she started suffering from nightmares, or maybe since right after she'd had Quinn; she hadn't been very interested in sex since then and Luke never protested. Had it gone on even longer, or was this maybe the first time? She discarded that idea quickly, certain that she would not be unlucky enough to catch her husband kissing another woman the very first time he ever did it.

Perhaps, though, this was why he had wanted her to seek professional help so badly. Maybe he wanted her to think she was losing it...no, Luke wasn't that malevolent. Was he? He had become increasingly impatient with her over the last several weeks, months even. Suddenly the late nights working on cases, the frequent Saturday trips to the office because he forgot something, all seemed to make too much sense. And with the realization that an affair had been so obvious, came another wave of emotions.

How stupid she had been! How utterly pitiful he had made her look. While she left her job to stay at home, raise *their* children, make *his* meals and wash *his* shirts, he was finding intimacy in the arms of another woman. A woman who, by the look of her, had never cooked a well-rounded meal in all of her short little existence. It was a textbook case of the husband cheating on his wife, told so many times in so calculated a manner that even made-for-TV-movies had to add twists to the plot for excitement.

Who was this man she was married to? What had happened to the Luke she knew? Had she pushed him away by obsessing over the nightmares? Had he stopped being attracted to her? Was family life not as exciting as he had hoped? The tears dripped from her chin to stain her linen jacket. She blinked long and hard to clear her vision. Just when she had finally thought she could see an end to her nightmares, the panic attacks, the memory lapses. Just when she had begun to uncover pieces of her life that she had lost somewhere along the way. This news was going to make Luke and her stronger, bring them closer together. Why had this happened now?

She finally reached the babysitter's driveway on two wheels and made a quick attempt to straighten her face. Later, she would not remember what she had said to Mrs. Dixon, or how she had explained the tears that wouldn't stop flowing. She scooped the children up as quickly as possible and drove straight home. She left the boys in the car with a DVD playing while she ran inside.

With the children occupied, Maggie flew up the staircase and into her bedroom. She tugged at the large suitcase that was stored under the bed until it came loose, nearly knocking her over. Quickly recovering, she ran to the large walk-in closet and began tearing at her clothing, yanking it off the hangers without reason. She threw an armful of shirts and jeans into the suitcase, then rushed to the dresser and began wrenching open drawers. Next she ran into the bathroom, grabbing at shampoo and brushes and makeup, whatever she could think of that she would need for the next few days. She never stopped to think where she was going, what she would do, she just knew she had to leave. She dropped her bags at the top of the stairs and hurried into Owen's room to gather his things. Finally she grabbed clothing from Quinn's room, stuffing it into the same suitcase as his brothers. Nothing was folded, but it would have to do.

She carried everything downstairs at once and brought it immediately to the back of the car. She checked on the boys, happily watching Playhouse Disney, and went back in to fill a backpack with snacks and drinks and books and toys.

It dawned on her that she could stay with Mickey. He would know what to do next, he would make sense of this mess and help her think about it logically and sensibly. With everything she could think of she returned to the car. She was much calmer now, felt in control, now that she had a kind of plan. She backed out of the driveway with dry eyes.

Chapter Twenty-four

Luke was grateful for the privacy of his office. He closed the door softly behind him and wiped his face in a vain attempt to erase the kiss from his lips. His body had betrayed him with a vibrancy that had been dormant within him too long, but his heart cried out with regret for his one weak moment.

A mixture of feelings washed over him as he fell into the nearest chair. Visions of Maggie and Michelle, Owen and Quinn battered his mind. Unable to shake them, he stood again and rifled through his desk for some work to distract him. Before he found it, Michelle stepped into the room, knocking gently beforehand, to warn him.

"Luke..." she put a hand up to prevent him from spewing the apologetic man-talk that was likely to come from his mouth and quietly closed the door.

"Please, don't say anything. There is nothing for you to be sorry for. I knew your state of mind and I think I tried to capitalize on it. For that, *I'm* sorry. I am not sorry that it happened, but I know that we need to put it behind us. I need you to forget it, so that it doesn't compromise what we have here."

"Michelle, you're..."

"Don't say I'm a great girl, but...or I'm very sweet, but blah, blah, blah. That's not what I need or want. The truth is, I'm not any of those things. I wanted this to happen and I think I manipulated things so that it might. I wish that I hadn't, because I would much rather you did believe those things of me. What I want from you now...what I *need* is for you to tell me we can move on from this and continue a professional relationship. *Please*."

Luke's was confused. She was letting him off the hook for the kiss. But she also thought they could continue to see each other on a daily basis like nothing ever happened. Could they do that? He could feel his body threatening to betray him again as she stood feet from him. Could he be honest with Maggie and still work with Michelle? Would he be honest with Maggie at all? A sharp pain throbbed at the bridge of his nose. He couldn't concentrate.

"I...I can't think around you right now." He told her finally. Checking his pocket for keys, he walked briskly past her to the door, catching the scent of her as he went and realizing that he could never trust his body around her again. She grabbed his arm before he could escape.

"Please, Luke, just tell me I still have a job here." She begged him.

He looked into her eyes, then looked away quickly. He pulled himself from her fiery touch afraid he would succumb to his hungry desires once more. "You were here before me, Michelle. Your job is secure."

"Luke!" she called after him, but he was gone.

Summer was official on the lake. The jet skis seemed to have multiplied since the year before. The fish must have revived too after a number of years, because Patrick could not remember ever seeing more rowboats stuffed to the brim with rods and nets and tackle.

The mood on the island was of celebration; spirits were high with the prospect of long sunny days and cool star-filled nights away from the realities of life. Though he smiled warmly at his neighbors and their guests when he passed by, he could not bring himself to share in their revelry. In fact, it made him feel even more desperate – more crazed than before.

For the past two days he had taken refuge from the smiling vacationers, hiding within his own house with the curtains drawn, the lights off. He had not changed, showered or shaved in almost 48 hours and his diet consisted almost solely of vodka. As his drunken haze thickened he felt as though he could slip beyond the boundaries of reality and escape to the madness that beckoned him.

He had called Shauna only once in the time he had been gone. She was as close to hysterical as he'd ever heard her, worried about where he was, what was wrong, why he was being so secretive. He didn't even bother with a business trip story this time, he simply told her he needed time to think. Her sobs pierced his heart, but he hung up the phone without a good-bye, too drained to reassure her. His voice mail at the office was filled with urgent calls from Detective Ludstrom, stressing the severity of the situation and the need for Patrick to return his calls immediately. He was at the end of the long rope he'd been given. He paced about the darkened living room, bristling with restless anxiety and yet no solutions came to him. The only idea that he had come up with was the cliffs.

As the thought settled into his liquor-soaked mind again, he realized he needed help. One more day alone, on this island, and he just might do it. Though he hated to make the call again, afraid of the response he might hear, he finally picked up the receiver and dialed Aiden.

"Hello?" Like a blessing, Aiden answered on the third ring.

"Aiden. It's Patrick." His voice was thick and raspy with a desperate edge to it.

"Pat, are you okay?" Aiden asked with alarm. After their last confrontation, he wasn't sure he'd hear from his brother again, though he found himself relieved by it.

"No. Not okay. I think I'm losing my mind. Please, Aid. I wouldn't ask again if I didn't think it was absolutely necessary. I need you to come up here."

"Up here?" Aiden repeated, confused. New York was southeast. Patrick would never refer to it the way he just had. "Patrick, tell me what's happening."

"I think it's over Aiden. The whole thing. Work. My marriage. I…I can't do this on the phone. I need your help Aiden. I'm sorry. I'll beg if I have to."

"Okay, okay. I'll get on a plane. You're at home?"

"No. Just take 81 North, man."

"Patrick, where are you?"

"I'm at the island."

Aiden almost choked. "The what?"

"The island, Aiden. I'm on Echo Island."

Chapter Twenty-five

The pub was alive with music and chatter. Mickey moved swiftly mixing drinks and sliding chilled mugs of ale down the polished bar. The occasional swallows he gulped down himself went unnoticed in the swirl of activity. He felt on his game – carrying on casual conversations with patrons looking for a sympathetic ear or a word of advice, monitoring the probable blood alcohol levels of his regulars and keeping an eye on the band and his waitresses. This was how he had always imagined his bar would be, and the cool burn of tequila as it coated his throat only made him feel more alive, the sights and sounds more vibrant.

Twice during the evening he had gotten offers from women. The first had tried small talk that built until she found something they had in common – an appreciation for country music. Then she dropped the bomb, offering him an evening of prime rib and line dancing, which he declined graciously. The other had a few more drinks under her belt and cut right through the formalities. She asked him immediately what time he got off work. The assumption that he was a mere bartender angered him and his response was somewhat less civilized than the one previous. He toasted her hasty departure with a double shot of vodka.

As the evening progressed, the band played more ballads and Mickey's sway became only slightly more pronounced.

He was growing weary, the frozen smile became more forced and a dull ache pounded at his temples. He longed for the moment when he could lock the door and settle in to a late night, just him and the bottle.

He swiped three empty mugs from the bar and clumsily lost his hold of them in their journey toward the sink. They crashed to the floor, glass spilling everywhere, sparkling like tiny jewels around his feet. He cursed under his breath at his own foolishness. Then, bending to retrieve the dustpan, smacked his forehead on one of the metal coolers. "Sonofabitch!" he sneered with a mixture of pain and embarrassment. When he was able to regain his control, his quick sweeps successfully retrieved the fragments of shattered glass and corralled them into the pan.

"It doesn't look to me like things are as great as you'd have us believe."

A tingling sensation ran the length of Mickey's spine as the smooth Irish brogue brushed over him like a cool wind. He stood slowly, afraid to look past the bar into the eyes he could already picture so clearly in his mind. Even without hearing it in a year, he would know that voice anywhere.

When he finally did turn, the bar spun and faded before him as he found himself staring straight into the eyes of Guinevere Fitzgerald.

Aiden paced nervously in front of his desk. What the hell was Patrick doing on Echo Island and why was he so anxious to go join him? He had allowed his memories of the place to fade – forced them to, in a way. Holding onto them only embittered him more toward a family that found it better to lock away sorrow than to face the pain and begin to heal.

Something deep inside him wanted to go. He couldn't help but wonder what the island looked like now, or what he might think as he stepped over the mossy rocks again. Even with their harsh words in New York, Patrick had come to him again. Aiden knew that his troubles were bigger than past mistakes, even if, psychologically, they had been borne there.

It dawned on him just how much each of his siblings still suffered from the decisions made during the summer of '86. Mickey faced a long road of sobriety ahead. Maggie suffered great gaps in her own memory. He was estranged from his own family and seemed unable to connect enough with anyone to consider building his own. Patrick, in some ways, suffered the worst repercussions of all. For years he had struggled with his own guilt and self-loathing, building a world around him that seemed destined to continually reinforce his own darkest fears about himself. And their parents. Had it been fair for them to have to make such difficult decisions in their time of greatest grief ?

It had always been easy for Aiden to place the blame on them, and certainly they did deserve some. After all, they were the adults. They were the ones Aiden and his siblings had relied on at the time to guide them out of the darkness. But what had it been like for them?

A knock at the door temporarily released him from his thoughts. To his surprise Tommy poked his head through the door. "Mr. C, you got a minute?"

Aiden nodded and gestured for Tommy to come in. He sat in his usual place, leaning forward with his elbows on the arms of the chair. Aiden followed his lead and took a seat behind his desk. "To what do I owe this unexpected visit?" He could see that Tommy was bothered by something.

"I'm going home for the weekend." Tommy replied simply, as though that told the whole story. Aiden knew what home meant for Tommy. A strung-out mother, her abusive boyfriend and a lost soul of a sister. Not to mention the tough group of thugs he called his friends.

"You're worried about it." Aiden thought of his own feelings about going home.

Tommy rubbed an imaginary spot on the floor with the toe of his shoe. "Well, yeah."

"What specifically is bothering you?"

"It's not like this place, man. In here, it's all about me, you know? People teachin' me and counselin' me and givin' me work jobs to get experience and shit. I ain't got time for all that at home. I gotta worry about everyone else there. It's all about them."

"Who?"

"My mom, and my sister. 'Asshole' treats mom like shit, she just takes it. When I'm there I gotta do something about it. I ain't gonna let nobody disrespect my mom in front of me. So then I get in a fight or do something stupid so she don't have to put up with his shit no more, and I'm back in lock-up and it just starts all over again." Aiden understood the overwhelming feeling of needing to protect a member of your own family. But he had failed at it. Would Tommy fair better?

Tommy continued. "Then there's Abby, my sister. You know, she's real smart. Way smarter than me. And she could really be somebody, ya know? She could, like, do something with herself. But what sorta shot does she got at a real school? My mom can't even get a meal on the table, how's she gonna put my sister through school?"

He was silent for a moment but Aiden expected there was more. "I gotta be a different person there, ya see? I wanna be all that shit you guys try to feed us, but it ain't like that out there. I gotta take care of my peeps, ya know? My family." He corrected himself.

Aiden was amazed at the difference in Tommy, his honesty and insight. At that moment, no one could tell him that he couldn't be part of making a difference in a child's life. He chose his words carefully, their meaning had to be clear.

"You need to strike a balance, Tommy. You said it wasn't about you at home, but it is. You need to take care of your mother and sister. I believe that – and I understand it. Your choice is in how you do it. You can do it the way you've been trying, land yourself in jail every six months or so, or worse. But are you taking care of them when you're in jail? Or, you can take care of them by taking care of you. Take the steps, face the tougher choices. Make enough out of yourself to provide for those who need you."

"Yeah, yeah. Make something of myself. But that'll take years. What about now?" Tommy asked, his expression pleading for a solution to his life. "What happens in the time it takes me to do all that?"

"You tell them you love them. You let them know you are trying. You focus on you. And praying a little probably wouldn't hurt either. Will it be easy? Hell, no. It'll probably be the toughest thing you ever do. When you want to hit your mom's boyfriend and have to talk yourself out of it – that will be incredibly hard. But remember, your mom makes her own choices. And you make yours."

They sat in silence for a while, contemplating their next move. There was a comfort and companionship held within the room and it seemed neither one wanted to break it. For Tommy, it was the realization that he had some of the most difficult moments in life still ahead of him. For Aiden, it was learning to appreciate that however much you can teach a child, they almost always teach you more.

Finally, Tommy stood to leave and Aiden closed his eyes briefly, waiting for the fragile moment to crack. "Mr. C?" Tommy turned at the door and Aiden looked at him expectantly. "You alright, man."

Aiden smiled a wide, genuine smile. "Thanks. And uhh, Tommy… I have to go home this weekend too."

"You worried about it?"

"I am."

"Tough choices, man." Tommy said shaking his head as he left the room.

He wasn't gone for more than a minute when there was a quiet knock on Aiden's door. He looked up to see Colleen smiling brightly.

"Shit!" Aiden exclaimed and then immediately apologized for cursing. "Tonight was the roof thing…the steak… the stars!"

The smile slid from Colleen's eyes but remained in place. "You're backing out."

"No! Well, kind of…I just promised my brother I'd go see him."

"Mickey?" Her face brightened again at what she saw as a minor change of plans.

"No. Different brother."

Aiden knew that anything thing he had with Colleen was in a very tentative and fragile early stage. He could probably explain his way out of it and get a rain check, but what was he risking by doing it?

Aiden threw his hands up. "Colleen. I'm not any good at this."

Confusion clouded her eyes. "At what? Breaking a date?"

He circled around his desk to be closer to her. "Well, that too. But I mean, the dating thing. I...haven't done it much and I... I don't know how to be that guy who might be even remotely appealing to you without coming off sounding like a total jerk."

Colleen smiled gently at him. "Aiden, you don't have to be any certain kind of guy. Just be you. That *is* what's appealing to me."

"Really?"

"Really. Now if you have to break our date, just cut to the chase."

"I promised him I'd go."

"Then you need to go."

"You won't think I'm a jerk?"

"No."

"And you'll let me make it up to you?"

"You *better* make it up to me."

"So...I'm going to kiss you now."

"That would be a good place to start."

Aiden leaned in slowly, wrapping his hand around the back of her neck to pull her into him. His lips brushed hers gently first, and then settled in more deeply. Heat ran from his head down through his body. He couldn't believe he was about to give this up for Patrick.

After several rushed heartbeats, Colleen pulled away to look up at him, the smile back in her eyes. "I hope you're not gone too long. I may need some more of that soon."

Chapter Twenty-six

The sight was almost enough to render him sober. His heart jumped into his throat while he drank in the sight of her like a man lost upon an arid desert for years. Her raven hair fell lightly around her shoulders framing her high cheekbones, kissed by the sunlight to a gentle bronze. Her eyes, offset by rays of auburn shooting through the blue.The sharp, delicate bridge of her nose had just a dusting of light freckles and her cotton candy lips turned up in one corner with sarcasm as she watched him look her over.

He wasn't the only one in the bar whose attention had been turned by her appearance. Gwen had natural beauty. It required no pruning before a mirror or hours in a salon chair. It was as simple as her presence and something she was quite unaware of. It was the way she fit comfortably into her worn jeans, the way her blouse clung and draped in all the right places. It was the graceful movement of her slender fingers tapping with controlled nervousness on the edge of the bar. Several pairs of eyes shifted their attention to focus on her, and waited, as she did, for a response.

It took a moment to find his voice and steady his nerves before he whispered, "Gwen". It was the word she had tried to deny that she needed to hear. From that voice.

The random drinks that had gone unnoticed by patrons and employees alike, could not get by the woman who knew him better than anyone. "Well, Mickey, it looks like I got here just in time."

Mickey searched her eyes for the love he was certain he had lost.

"You have no idea." He replied.

Gwen quickly, though temporarily, took over control of the bar. "Who's the manager?" she firmly asked Mickey, who hadn't taken his eyes off her yet, as though she may return to just a photograph if he did.

"Gwen, I'm the manager."

"Not tonight, you're not. Who's in charge when you're not?

"John. Down there at the end of the bar." He gestured, still staring.

"Fine. John! Mickey is done here for the night. You've got everything under control right?"

John approached the pair, confused. "Who's she?" he asked Mickey.

"The one that got away." He replied.

"That's enough, you drunken fool. I wasn't a fish on a line. But right now," she said, turning to John, "I am this man's sense of reason, so I am in charge. I'm telling you he's got to take the rest of the night off. So, is everything covered here?" John nodded, dumbly, still confused. "Great. Now, does this bloke still live upstairs?" Again, John nodded. "Fine. Mickey, out from behind that bar and let's go."

Without a word, he obeyed her direction and led her to his apartment over the bar.

Once inside, he turned to envelope her in a long hug, overwhelmed by his relief at seeing her. She coldly pushed him away and directed him to the couch. Looking deeply wounded, he sat.

"You're off the wagon."

"You're *here*."

"I'm about to turn around and catch the first plane back home, if you don't start explaining yourself to me. How long have you been relapsing?"

Mickey felt the courage from the alcohol drain right out of his body when she threatened to leave. He felt sober instantly. "A couple weeks." He replied finally, dragging his hands over his face. "But Gwen, it was temporary."

"Temporary, eh? A couple of weeks sounds like it's becoming mighty comfortable again. So when will it stop?"

"Right now. I'm done. Swear it."

Gwen set her duffel bag and shoulder sack down and sat on the large table in front of him. "And what if I wasn't here confronting you right now? How long would it have gone on for then?"

Mickey anguished over his answer. How badly he wanted to reach out, to touch her hair, trace her face with his fingertips, press his lips ever so softly to hers. He almost couldn't bear the sight of her without being able to hold her, and at the same time couldn't completely trust himself to believe she was real. Even the thought of alcohol lost its glory.

He tore his eyes from hers, looking at the floor in defeat. "I don't know. I mean it didn't matter. Not nearly as much, anyway. No one cared. No one even noticed I was drinking. All it took was one look at you, and I don't need it." He looked up at her again. "I just can't keep doing this without you, Gwen. I've only been miserable. Tell me it's not too late for us. Please."

Gwen dropped her guard for a moment, her eyes softening at his words. Then, just as quickly, the mask of firm disappointment returned. "We won't talk about this now. Not with God knows how much booze in you. You need to show me you mean it, Mickey. If you're not for real about getting sober again, I am out of here."

"I mean it, Gwen. I'm sober right now, honest. Seeing you knocked the drunk right out of me." He smiled to break the tension, but she didn't take the bait. "How did you know that I needed you?" he finally asked.

"Who says I came here because you needed me?"

"Then why?"

"You said no one even noticed. But that wasn't true. Danny noticed immediately and he couldn't even *see* you.

"But like I said, we won't have this discussion right now. You're going to sleep and we'll talk tomorrow."

"You're staying here?"

"No. I've got a hotel room for the night."

"But we've always stayed with each other. Ever since we first got back together."

"Mickey," Gwen said slowly, but without pity. "We're not together." She stood up to leave but Mickey grabbed her hand.

"This isn't a dream, right? You'll be back tomorrow?"

She could no longer resist the longing in his deep green eyes. Though she maintained a safe (however, difficult) distance, her cheeks flushed and her eyes shone. "I promise." She vowed and turned before she was lost to him again.

Chapter Twenty-seven

"It also appears that young birds, once they've reached adulthood, frequently return to the lakes of their birth."

Stark pavement stretched out before her as she drove blindingly on. The lush, green fields and mammoth boulders carved out to make room for the highway were lost on Maggie. She could see only the image of her husband, wrapped in the arms of another woman, sharing a passionate kiss, the kind she hadn't felt herself in… in ages. In the edge of woods ahead of her off the passenger's side, hid a mother deer and her fawn just before the clearing, watching the busy vehicles whiz by. Had she noticed them, Maggie may have been reminded of the beauty or the simplicity of life, may have thought to slow down and appreciate the gifts that she had. But she was unaware of their presence.

Owen and Quinn had both fallen asleep in the back seat, tired from the unexpected excitement of an unscheduled trip and the idea of seeing Uncle Mickey, or "Silly Mickey" as Owen called him. Owen had asked at least a half dozen times if Daddy was coming on the trip too. It killed Maggie to bite back the ugly words and the flood of tears that needed release, but she gripped the steering wheel tightly and controlled her voice telling Owen that Daddy had a lot of work to do, but they would call him from their uncle's place to say 'hi'.

Thinking to herself, Maggie decided she might wait a day until she called. She could think of nothing to say right now that didn't stab at her heart when she thought of actually speaking it. After a night talking things over with Mickey and being away from him, maybe then she would be able to confront him. Perhaps, though a night without her to answer to was something Luke looked forward too. No – she couldn't even imagine that. It crossed her mind, that a night of not knowing where she or the boys were, might just strike enough panic in him, to make him regret the mistake he had made.

The thought of Luke's terror, when he realized that his unstable wife had disappeared again – with his children this time – caused her to feel pity for him, and the irony of it released the emotions she had been holding in. For the first time since she had arrived home, she allowed the tears to overcome her. The highway blurred and she blinked to clear her vision.

Unable to think with a level head, the thoughts flew at her randomly, often overlapping, becoming tangled in her mind. She used Jamie's calming techniques, breathing slowly and steadily. She tried to empty the thoughts of Luke from her mind and began to focus instead, on remembering more from her past.

She could picture the warm glow emanating from the trimmed Douglas fir. Beneath it, boxes were adorned in colorful metallic paper and oversized bows. Kit flitted in and out of the room, nervously filling cracker trays and refreshing drinks. Maggie surveyed the room skeptically and found no holiday cheer at all. Aiden and Mickey were hunched over a chess game without a word between them. Patrick was on the leather sofa reading the paper with a surly expression on his face. She knew he hadn't wanted to come home for the holidays. Mickey had filled her in on a conversation he'd overheard between Patrick and Dad that had apparently changed Patrick's plans. Sean was in the kitchen now, reportedly slaving away on the turkey. Hiding was more like it, *Maggie thought. He hadn't sat down with the family since she'd come home two days before.*

Mickey claimed 'Check', breaking the silence momentarily. Aiden cursed under his breath, bringing a smile to Maggie's lips. Aiden was extremely competitive and hated losing. He quickly maneuvered his king to safety and the silence resumed She closed the novel she was reading for her English class and reached for a stick of celery.

"So, Patty, you got any preppie girlfriends down there in Notre Dame?" she asked mischievously.

Mickey peered at Patrick over the chessboard to see his reaction. Patrick's eyes never shifted from the paper. "No." he grumbled.

"Well, maybe if you took your nose out of the financial columns once in a while, you'd get some action." Though Patrick didn't flinch in the slightest, the color of his neck slowly changed to pink. She enjoyed the effect. "Aiden has two of them. Maybe he could share. Right, Aid?"

"Mags, shut up." Aiden warned.

"Oh that's right. Aiden doesn't date. Mickey's the girl- juggler. Do they know about each other, Mickey? You can tell us. This is what family gatherings are for right? Catching up?"

"Hmmph." Aiden grumbled. "Yeah, this is some great family get-together, ain't it Mickey?"

Mickey put his hands up, keeping his eyes on the chessboard. "Leave me out of it. I'm completely neutral and I'm outta here after dinner. I'm not embarrassed to admit that I thoroughly enjoy the opposite sex."

"Nice." Patrick snarled. "You have a date on Christmas?"

"Hey, I'm the only one who still has to live here in case you forgot. Excuse me for wanting to get out once in a while."

"Maggie, stick to your own business and stay out of ours." Patrick snapped.

"Leave her alone, Pat." Mickey defended.

"Or what? She gets a little kick out of causing trouble and then everyone tiptoes around her so she won't get upset. She's a little princess and I'm sick of it."

"I am not a princess!" she argued back.

"Yeah, whatever, Mags."

Kit stepped into the room at that moment to break up the argument. "Everybody stop." She urged. "It's Christmas, for goodness' sake. Patrick, you know better."

"Right. My fault." He sneered standing up and snapping his paper closed. He strode out of the room without another word.

"Can we all act like it's the giving season and stop this childishness?"

She remembered another Christmas. One much further back.

The Christmas tree that came into view this time was far less elegant than the one previous. Cotton ball snowmen and paper plate Santas dangled precariously from its limbs. Strings of popcorn and paper chains seemed to have no sense of order to them. The leather sofa was replaced by a worn, checkered couch and most of the cushions were on the floor. No one sat reading the paper and there was no chess game. Joyful music drifted out of an old record player in the corner.

Presents were strewn about the floor randomly. Patrick proudly displayed a new skateboard while Aiden searched under the tree for his name. "Here, Maggie. This one is for you." Came a small voice and she quickly ripped at the holly-and-wreaths paper. Inside was a shiny, plastic purse; purple with a large daisy clasp front. It was just what she had told Santa about. "Mommy, look!" she squealed with delight running into her mother's open arms. "Santa remembered!"

"It's very pretty, Maggie." Her mother agreed, turning the purse around in her hands to admire it properly.

"It's girlie.*" One of her brothers stated in disgust. Maggie made a face and stuck her tongue out at him.*

"I like it, Maggie." Said another.

"Thank you." She turned to her brother with a smile and their laughter filled the air.

Things had *not* always been dark and moody at the Callaghan house. She had always remembered the holidays during her time at Dylan or college. It was only these warmer, gentler Christmases that had been swiped from her mind. Why? What had happened to go from the family she could now see they had once been to the family she remembered? Did it have something to do with the cottage? She had only just remembered that too. Was there a connection? There was something else about the two Christmas memories. Something just beyond her reach that seemed important.

The road sign on the highway ahead advertised exits for both Syracuse and the Thousand Islands, depending on your choice of direction. Maggie slowed and pulled off to the side of the road, just in front of the large green sign for Route 81. The boys slept on and Maggie stared up at the words ahead of her.

The realization came slowly that she did not have to head toward Mickey's. She could look for the answers herself. She put the car back into drive and headed north, not west toward her hometown and Mickey's where she had intended to go. She didn't trust her memory enough yet to get her all the way there, but she knew for certain that she had to try. Lake Opinicon sounded like exactly where she needed to be.

Chapter Twenty-eight

Patrick was at the dock waiting when the ferry arrived with Aiden. He shifted his weight from one leg to another impatiently as the passengers stepped off the boat, then greeted his brother with a strong hug. Aiden was surprised by the gesture but returned it genuinely.

"How does it feel?" Patrick asked him spreading his arms wide. Aiden scanned the familiar yet forgotten surroundings, breathing the air deeply.

"Better than I expected." He finally said, hoping he didn't sound too analytical.

"It brings peace, Aiden. I swear it does. I can remember things that I'm not allowed to remember anywhere else. Problem is I can't forget things from out there anymore." He gestured beyond the boundaries of the shoreline.

"Do you think it was right, what Mom and Dad did?" Aiden asked after a few moments of silence. They were walking up the cobblestone path now, facing the house. Aiden stepped across one stone and recalled skinning his knee in a race to keep up with Patrick and Mickey.

Patrick sighed deeply. "You just *have* to talk about it don't you? No – I don't think it was right. But I went along with it, didn't I? We all did. We were young. We still believed that what our parents told us to do was best. You went along with it too, Aiden. Your method may have been a little different than the rest of us, but you kept quiet just the same."

"I regret it every day of my life. I counsel kids every day to do something I can't do myself. I'm a hypocrite, Pat." They turned at the top of the hill and Aiden stopped to stare at the house he hadn't laid eyes on in seventeen years.

"You're only human, Aiden. If you're anything like the rest of us, you did what you had to do because you were *told* to. We were still kids. And now... well, now the truth would be harder than the lie."

Aiden acknowledged the truth of Patrick's words in silence. It was the first time he could remember any member of the family talking so openly about it with him. Maybe this island that had brought so much pain really could bring peace now. Maybe he could finally learn to accept things as they were.

"Edna will fall over when she sees you." Patrick changed the subject.

"My God, I haven't thought about her in forever. And Jack? Now that you mention it, I didn't see him manning the ferry."

"Jack passed away the winter before last." Patrick explained. "That was his son on the ferry – Robert. He kind of took over for his father during the last few years, but I don't think it's what he wants to do with his life."

"I'm so sorry to hear about Jack. And Edna's keeping the place up all by herself?"

"She hires a lot of help. But yeah, she's running the joint."

Aiden studied the manicured paths, the gardens. Guests of the inn sat in lawn chairs, boarded boats or canoes, or walked along some of the many paths throughout the island.

"Do you find it all too touristy now?" He asked as they started down a dirt path away from the house.

Patrick laughed sarcastically. "What the hell do you think *we* were?"

Aiden blanched. "We were vacationers, though. Practically residents. This isn't the same thing."

Patrick stopped on the trail and faced Aiden with a grin. "You still see it through fourteen year-old eyes. We thought we were residents, but to the locals, then and now, we're all tourists. Jack and Edna deserve this place, they made it worthy of... happiness again. And they're from the area. No one looks at them with anything but respect and dignity for bringing some honor and prosperity to this area."

He was right. The feelings Aiden was having came from that teenage boy who still lived deep inside him, though he had been silenced long ago. Every step he took brought on another glimpse of his youth. He wasn't seeing anything as an adult and it embarrassed him.

Patrick sensed this and reassured him gently. "It's alright, Aid. When I first stepped into my cottage I felt like I was eighteen again with my very own place out of view from Mom and Dad. I could drink there, or swear out loud. It took me two days of acting like an idiot before I remembered I was a grown man with a job and wife."

Aiden laughed at the image, but was secretly relieved by his brother's confession. Patrick turned back to the trail and continued on. "In fact, my cottage is right on top of the spot where we made that little fire with the stolen matches."

"That *little* fire?" Aiden laughed. "When we didn't realize that the pine needles that carpet this whole island were flammable?"

Patrick nodded. "And Maggie decided to play town crier and rat us out to Dad."

The memory was a sliver of sunshine through the thunderclouds of his remorse. He missed Maggie so. Even after she had changed so much, had lost all of her own childhood memories – all of the good things they had shared – he felt that somehow he should be able to watch over her and take care of her.

"How is Maggie?"

"I'm not really sure. I talked to Mickey about a week ago. Mom's concerned about some nightmares she's been having. She wants Maggie to go back on her meds."

"She's off her meds?" Aiden wondered what impact that might have on her.

"I guess." Patrick shrugged. "Well, here it is." Aiden looked up the trail to see the cottage Patrick had built to return to Echo Island.

After a late dinner, Patrick and Aiden set out with some flashlights and a cooler of beer to walk the perimeter of the island. They talked of what had changed and what remained the same. They discussed Aiden's career and Patrick's family, each at length, without delving into the reverse for either. Finally, they reached the tall rock cliffs on the southern shore, the furthest point from Patrick's place. They sat together with the cooler between them. The moon and stars provided enough light for the lake below them to glisten and sparkle. The trees on the main shoreline stood as tall shadows, embracing them within their dark water-world.

Patrick reached for a beer, handed one to Aiden. For several moments they simply sat in silence.

"Patrick," Aiden finally began cautiously. "Your phone call frankly scared the shit out of me. Then I get here and so far you've been a great host and we've shared some good memories...which, don't get me wrong – I appreciate remembering that we have some good memories. But, what the hell is going on?"

Patrick took a long swig from his bottle and reached into the cooler for another. "I think I underestimated you, Aiden. I think I always have. Twice in the last two months I've called you and both times, you came running." He took another swallow to steel himself to what he was about to say next. What he was about to become very accustomed to saying. "I'm really sorry about that."

Aiden let the statement sink in. This was a different person he was sitting next to. Here they sat on the treacherous cliffs of Echo Island. Never in a million years would Aiden have seen himself back here, much less with Patrick. And now...he was apologizing to him.

"I think maybe you were right. I think we all hid behind the opportunity to lie. Not just to Maggie but to ourselves. I dunno... I let Dad blame me and I took all that into myself and now...I can't even breathe. I've been so afraid of making the wrong move that I never considered just doing the right thing.

"I'm getting out, Aiden."

"Out?"

"Of the business. This morning I went into town and sent out some emails. By now Davis has read my resignation, effective immediately and is on the phone with his daughter, ripping me a new one."

"You left the business? Last I knew that wasn't one of the two choices you were trying to make."

Patrick grinned beneath the lip of the bottle. "I know. Ironic isn't it?

"After I called you, I drank myself into a stupor. Good thing too 'cuz if I hadn't passed out I might have done something rash. But when I woke up, I took a kayak ride. I went all the way to the far end of the lake. I remembered our boys only camping trip. And I remembered something I let myself forget in all these lies."

Patrick downed the last of his beer and stared down into the waters. Aiden thought, maybe, that tears were threatening.

"That night, sitting out at the fire, we were watching the burning coals fade out, full from burnt marshmallows and bologna sandwiches. You know what I was told?"

Aiden shook his head in silence.

"I was told that I was cooler than Dad. That taking all you guys out to camp was the coolest thing anyone had ever done and that it would be a favorite memory for all of time." Patrick looked at Aiden and his eyes glistened. "It wasn't so much that Dad went down a notch, but that someone could see me as being even close. It was the best I've ever felt about myself. And in all these lies…in all of this loss…I lost the memory of that moment.

"So why did it come back to me now? When I am feeling at just about my lowest point ever? I think it was a message. I think…" he broke off.

Aiden reached into the cooler now and twisted off two more beers, handing one to Patrick in unspoken understanding and acknowledgement.

"So what happens now?"

Patrick looked down to where the cliff met the cobalt water and the moss-covered rocks just beneath the surface. "I wait for Shauna to call me, confused and upset that this has happened. I listen to her go on about how she doesn't even know who I am any more. I go back and turn myself into Sylvan and Ludstrom." He took a deep pull on his beer and swallowed it down hard, as though trying to swallow back a bitter resolve in his mouth.

"I hope that with my clean track record, I don't do time. I hope that Shauna doesn't divorce me. But if I do...if she does...I will at least have faced it. I will, maybe, at last stop running."

"Can I do anything? Help?"

"You have, Aiden. More than you know. But yeah, there are a couple things you could do for me. First, hang here with me another day. I want a chance at a few more good memories here. And...be around when this all comes down. Even if it's just by phone."

Aiden smiled in the darkness, even though a tightness fought at his throat. "You got it, bro."

Chapter Twenty-nine

Gwen returned to the hotel room where Danny and Mara awaited her. She took her daughter into her arms and covered her face with feathery kisses. "Mum's back, sweetie." She cooed.

"And how's the Da?" Danny asked.

"Oh, Danny." Gwen sighed and collapsed onto the bed, holding Mara in one arm while she tugged off her boots."Just seeing him, I could get all wrapped up in this again! It took every ounce of my composure not to climb right over that bar. What have you done bringing us here?" She looked into Mara's face as she spoke, seeing Mickey's eyes gazing back at her with unconditional love. Mara reached out to gently pat her mother's face and Gwen was sure that her daughter could understand her dilemma. "And you're right." She continued. "He's drinking again. A right mess he made of his mugs. I took him straight out of the bar to his room."

"And then what?" Danny smiled devilishly.

" Don't be dirty. I left him there. He swears he'll straighten out again now that I'm here. He wants me back."

"Well, then. Happy endings must be my specialty!"

Gwen gave him a sideways glance. "I told him we'd talk in the morning. I said nothing about Mara, or you. Danny, I'm terrified! I know that it's wrong to keep Mara from him. But

I don't know if I can trust him. What if he can't stop? What if he can't stop and I'm too in love again to care?"

"Gwen. Stop with the 'what ifs' before you make yourself dizzy. You will talk to him tomorrow and then we'll see. You'll know in your heart what to do."

Gwen lay back on the bed and held Mara to her. "Okay. So you don't mind holing up here with sweet pea just a wee bit longer?"

Danny sighed wistfully. "I finally make it across the ocean and all I get to see is the inside of this hovel."

Gwen scoffed. "It's hardly a hovel. You've got cable and pay-per-view, and room service! Best of all you had your goddaughter all to yourself for two whole hours!"

"An offer I couldn't refuse, I admit. But I would like to see some of the outdoors as well. And this bar that's supposedly a genuine replica of the world renowned O'Leary's, I'd like to see that too. Oh yeah, and that old friend of mine. Wouldn't mind setting eyes on him again, so I can rattle some sense into his skull."

Gwen stood and hugged Danny tight with her one free arm. "I'll talk to him in the morning and then I promise, we'll get you out to see America. You are the absolute best, you know that?"

"I do."

The phone shattered Mickey's dream. In it, he had chased after Gwen only to have her disappear again and again.

He cursed the darkness beneath the window blinds for not being the dawn that would bring the real Gwen back to him. If she hadn't been a dream too. He reached blindly for the phone that continued to chirp at him incessantly.

"'Lo?" his voice was gruff with sleep.

"Mickey?"

"Yeah. Who's this?"

"It's Luke. Maggie's gone again. She's got the kids this time. Is she with you?"

Mickey sat up, coming fully awake with the desperation in Luke's voice.

"No. I haven't heard from her."

"Jesus Christ!" Luke yelled into the phone. "I'm losing my fucking mind, here, Mickey! She's gonna get herself killed."

"Luke, calm down. We'll find her. Who else have you called?"

"Just you and a few of her friends. No one's seen her. I didn't want to freak her parents out again…yet. I went to the lake. I drove all over town. I went into the city. I'm calling the cops."

"How long has she been gone?" Mickey tried to keep his voice calm for Luke.

"I don't know! I got home late. She wasn't here. She could have left this morning for all I know!"

"Okay. Just breathe for a sec. Did she have any plans all day?"

"No!…I don't know…yeah. She had an appointment with her therapist. She was going to drop the boys off at the babysitter first. I'll call them!" The new lead had Luke's voice shaking with fragile hope.

"Luke, what time is it?"

"What? Oh…it's….wow…it's 3:30 in the morning."

"Okay. Can you wait a couple hours to call these people? I'll do some calling around myself as soon as the sun's up. But other people might not be as receptive to 3 am phone calls as me. And, frankly, you sound like a lunatic right now."

Mickey heard Luke's voice break on the other end of the phone. His breathing was hitched and uneven. "I screwed up, Mickey. And now she's gone."

"*You* screwed up? What are you talking about, Luke? Did you guys have a fight or something?"

"No." Mickey was certain Luke was crying now. "There's no way she could know…but…"

"But *what*, Luke?"

"I…I kissed another woman today. At work. But there's no way Maggie knows. I just…this is what I deserve."

Mickey felt his neck and ears grow hot. "You did *what*?!"

"It was a mistake!" Luke defended quickly, and then lapsed back into his pool of guilt and shame. "I fucked up. But I stopped it. And I'll leave the firm…I'll never see her again…whatever it takes. I just need to get Maggie and the boys back."

Mickey thought for a moment, letting the anger simmer. "Did anyone see you?" he growled.

"No! I mean, they couldn't…I don't think so. It happened in the elevator."

"Was there anyone else in it?"

"No."

"Okay." Mickey sighed deeply. His emotions couldn't take much more of this roller coaster night. He thought briefly about the bottles in the bar beneath him then quickly shoved the thought from his head. "Just *sit* there for a few hours." *Wallow in it a while,* he wanted to add. "No calls until seven, got it?" He didn't wait for a response. "I'll call mom and dad at seven and you can bet they'll have an APB out on her by 7:02. Let me know if you hear anything and I'll do the same. Understand?"

"Yeah."

"And, Luke?"

"Yeah?"

"If you *ever* screw around on Maggie again, I'll drive down there myself and kill you."

Chapter Thirty

"Loons are so perfectly designed for an
aquatic life they have been called
'feathered fish'."

How Maggie wished Jamie were with her now. After waiting through the early morning hours in the car, the sound of the ferryboat engine, the smell of lake water mingling with fresh pine, even the cool breeze on her face all brought back a flood of childhood memories. She could recall the feel of the rocks and pine needles beneath her bare feet, the cool splash as she first entered the water on a hot summer day.

She remembered *swimming*. For as long as Maggie had previously been able to remember, she'd held a bizarre love-hate relationship with water. She admired the beauty of it, revered its ability to calm and sooth, and was deathly afraid of being submerged within it.

When she was at BU, some friends had convinced her to go out for the crew team. When she got into the shell, and began the rhythmic rowing motion, she found a new love. She followed the stroke calls of the coxswain, and yet was completely in her own world. Cutting across the water, with the sun on her face and the wind riding over her shoulders was the most peace she'd ever found.

After the team's first win, there was a traditional "dumping" of the boat. Several of the guys who had been watching waded out into the river and tipped the entire team into the water. As soon as she was submerged, Maggie was hit with complete panic. In her terror, she inhaled a mouthful of water and had to be dragged to shore.

The experience had been humiliating and Maggie almost quit the team. After several conversations with her teammates and coach, it was agreed that Maggie should stay. The dumping tradition was abandoned and Maggie did her training on foot or from within the shell only. She never swam with the team and she never went more than waist deep into the water again.

But these memories were telling her something different.

Now, she realized, she had once been a swimmer – a decent one. Sean built a diving platform one year, a short way from the dock and taught her perfect diving form. Knees bent, fingers together, arms against her ears. She would practice for hours to get it right. Sean occasionally brought a lawn chair down to the water's edge to coach. "Atta girl, Mags!" "Bend those knees!" "Point to where you're going!"

In fact, she used to ski and kneeboard all over the lake. Patrick usually drove while the others all took turns. First Mickey, a show-off on trick skis or even barefoot. Patrick would throw his head back and laugh as he maneuvered the boat from side to side, or hit some passing yacht waves head-on.

He used to laugh a lot, Maggie thought.

Aiden was never a natural at water sports, but he always tried his best. His intense, competitive nature had him venturing outside the wake, knees knocking together so that it seemed he was almost sitting upon the water. He would eventually get across, a smile of proud accomplishment spreading over his face. In his excitement, his balance would shift, and he usually found himself face down with a mouthful of lake water. Patrick would turn the boat around to pick him up and give him a good-natured slap on the back as he was pulled into the boat. Occasionally he would sulk. And then it was Maggie's turn.

Maggie was a die-hard tomboy as a child. Growing up surrounded by boys, she set difficult goals for herself in order to be perceived as an equal by her siblings. If Mickey could get up on one ski, then she had to be able to do it too. If Patrick could do a flip off the diving board by himself, then she had to learn. She never recognized her brothers' admiration of her at the time, how they doted over their proud, spunky little sister. *Ohhh*, she gasped audibly. *How close we used to be.*

The ferry approached the dock and Maggie looked up the hill upon the stone house, aglow in the early morning with a twinkle of lights that danced in the like fireflies. Her breath caught in her throat and she pulled Owen closer to her. It was all so familiar to her now, though she had not set eyes upon it in nearly twenty years, had not even remembered its existence until her own memory drove her to it.

As if on cue to welcome the new visitors, a pair of loons poked their heads from around a smaller island, floating gently along the water's edge. One called out to her. The sound was enough to fill Maggie's heart with both the joy of coming home and the emptiness of not knowing what home was. Their lonely sound echoed over the lake, one asking *where*? And from further down the lake another answering *here*.

The upper section of the house was painted eggshell white. Five small windows peaked out from the eaves. The third one had been hers. The main level must have been renovated, or very well cared for over the years. The large rounded stones surrounding the main entrance were polished to a gentle shine. Natural oak columns blended the magnificent building into its habitat. Towering oaks and scratchy pines grew up from behind and around it, embracing the home she had once known.

Ground lights led a path from the dock upward, surrounded by colorful irises and lilies. The walkway was still cobblestone – Kit had done that herself, one by one. An oak sign at the bottom of the path announced that the house was now called "Echoes – The Barnes' Inn". It saddened Maggie to see it, though she was not sure why.

"Mommy, are we staying there?" Owen tugged on her shirt and pointed at the house. Most of the passengers had already disembarked and were making their way up the hill.

"Yes, honey." She replied taking his little hand in hers. She perched Quinn more securely on her hip and made her way to the ramp, a slight, uneasy feeling settling over her, as though she was slipping into another time.

She approached the front desk timidly, children in tow. The interior had only traces of its former existence – the grand stone front fireplace, the glossy hardwood floor, the bare wood curving staircase. A large greeting area had replaced their family room, with modern furnishings scattered about and watercolor prints done by local artists dotting the pine walls between each large window and offered for sale. The porch along the north side had been enclosed, and offered a resting place for tired guests, or a meeting place for those seeking company.

Maggie was curious to examine the rooms out of view: the kitchen that she knew was behind the large fireplace, the bedrooms upstairs, to walk through and touch what remained of a past she had allowed herself to forget. In her mind, she could see a heavy rectangular table and high backed chairs where they ate. She could place the sink and double oven and especially the pantry where her mother hid sweets. She was certain it would all look different now.

"Welcome to Echoes." An older-looking woman from behind the desk greeted them with a warm smile. Her chocolate eyes twinkled from behind wire-rimmed spectacles.

"I...don't have a reservation." Maggie apologized, suddenly realizing this unplanned trip might have more obstacles than her memory.

"Oh, dear." The woman knitted her brow and worry lines appeared on her forehead as she consulted her books. Rarely did one simply wander across dirt roads and slow-moving ferries to an isolated island without having secured a place to stay. "I don't think we have a thing available. The weekends are dreadfully busy."

"Oh." Maggie distractedly peered at the staircase, aching to see the rooms beyond it. Quinn began to fuss and she lifted him quickly into her arms, finally understanding that she had nowhere to stay. "Oh." She repeated and looked at the woman rather embarrassed. The woman behind the desk peered back at Maggie as though trying to read her thoughts.

"Is everything alright, dear?"

"Yes…I… I mean…well…no." *What are you doing here?* The voice inside chastised. *You look just like the crazy woman Luke believed you to be.* She peered at the kind woman before her and the tentative excitement over recognizing a small window of her past deflated. "I'm sorry. How foolish to not even reserve a room. It was, kind of, an unplanned trip. I used to come here. When I was younger."

The woman lowered her glasses and studied Maggie for a long, awkward moment. "When you were younger?" She finally asked, breaking the awkward silence, though it was more a thought than a question. "Well, I've lived in this area all my life. Do I know you? You seem somehow familiar to me."

Maggie looked into the woman's deep brown eyes, the face worn from years of difficult work that somehow remained softened with cheer and warmth. There *was* a familiarity between them, a comfort almost. Maggie sensed that she would be safe with the woman. Then the scent of lavender and lemon pledge returned to her so forcefully that she could have been knocked over by it.

A lump formed at the back of her throat and she was afraid she would be unable to reply. Why had all of these memories been erased? Why had she locked up so much of her past? Had the others done it too? Were they aware that she had? She began to tremble before the woman she realized had once held her in safety. She had once been cared for lovingly by her and now didn't know her at all.

"I'm Maggie…Stewart. Maggie *Callaghan* Stewart?" She whispered it like it was a question, as though this familiar stranger might be able to tell her if it were true.

The woman's eyelids fluttered in shock and she looked, momentarily, as though she might faint.

"My heavens," she finally managed, placing a wrinkled hand on her heart. "Oh! My dear, sweet child." She rushed around the desk and enveloped Maggie in her arms. "Just look at you! My God, you're a grown woman now with your own precious ones!" She cupped Owen and Quinn's face in her hands admiring them in turn. Then she turned back to Maggie and did the same. "Please come into the kitchen and sit with me. What a journey you've had!"

Maggie wanted to wrap herself in the warmth of this stranger's sudden hospitality, but she hesitated. "I'm sorry." She began, stumbling on her words. "I know that I knew you, that you… helped take care of me. But I don't…I can't remember your name."

"I'm Edna Barnes, dear. My husband Jack and I bought this place from your parents when they sold it. And yes, I did take care of you… and your brothers for many years. Since you were just tots, like your boys here."

Another wave of embarrassment swept through Maggie. How utterly thoughtless she must appear, not to remember a woman who was clearly an important part of her life at one time. A part of her life that she was only now beginning to piece together.

Edna sensed her discomfort and patted her shoulder gently.

"Why did they sell it?" Maggie asked in a whisper. Edna shifted her gaze briefly to the floor before taking Maggie by the arm.

"Let's go in the kitchen and sit."

The double oven remained where it had been in her memory. A combination of feelings from her surroundings and the kind hospitality of Edna Barnes brought a fresh stream of tired tears to Maggie's eyes. Edna brought juice and doughnuts over for the boys and a steaming mug of tea for Maggie. She saw the tears and reached sympathetically for a hand with both of hers.

Edna had heard that Maggie had been hospitalized for a time after the Callaghans last left the island all those years ago. Had she been brainwashed there? Clearly, Maggie had little recognition of her, and she was once practically a member of the family each summer. It wasn't that she was hurt by it, nearly twenty years had passed and her life had been so changed by the events of that summer. It was more a curiosity – if Maggie didn't remember her, what *did* she remember?

"Maggie, you know we can find a place for you to stay while you're here. But, pardon me if I sound nosy, did you try Patrick first?"

Maggie looked up from pouring Quinn's juice into a sippy cup. "Patrick?" she repeated. "Try him for what?"

Edna realized too late she had put her foot in her mouth. She often wondered about Patrick Callaghan and the little stone cottage on the northern tip of the island. Why he always came alone, spent his time cooped up in the cottage. While he had always been friendly and helpful whenever they crossed paths, he never spoke of his family, even though he wore a wedding band. At least, that had been true until yesterday, when Edna could have sworn she saw him with another man walking through the garden paths behind the house. In fact if she hadn't known better, she would have thought it was Mickey or Aiden, but she brushed it off at the time. And now, here was Maggie…

"His cottage, on the northern end of the island." Edna explained. Maggie's green eyes widened with surprise. "You didn't know about his place here?"

"Ms. Barnes. I didn't know about…I mean I didn't remember here at all until yesterday. You're saying Patrick comes here often?"

"Yes, dear. All the time. In fact, he's here now. Actually, I even thought one of your brothers might be with him."

Well, that answered one question – maybe more. They had not forgotten this place. Only her. So what did that mean?

Maggie shook her head as though sweeping away the thoughts that would not fit in. "Mickey? Aiden? No. That's impossible."

Edna did not wish to argue. Maggie already appeared so lost and confused. "Well, no matter. We'll make up a room for you here. I even have a crib available for the little one. Maybe later you could pay your brother a visit."

Maggie hugged her boys more tightly to her. They were the one thing in the universe that she was sure of at the moment. "You must think I'm very rude." She apologized again. "This is Owen. He's four and a half. And this little guy is Bryan Quinn. We call him Quinn." She hesitated.

Bryan Quinn. Bryan …. There had been another.

"Maggie, you're pale as a ghost."

"I'm…" she stumbled over the words. "I'm very tired."

"Come on. Let me show you where we can put you."

Maggie wasn't certain she could bear any more memories just yet. Her stomach recoiled at the mere thought of going upstairs.

"Edna?" she appealed, "I can't…go up…not yet. Do you have anything…down here? This is all… very difficult."

Edna thought for a moment then winked. "We have my old room. Off the back entrance. It's small, but I think we can make something of it."

Maggie wanted to hug her for being so understanding, but didn't have the strength. She offered a grateful smile instead. "Thank you."

Out on the lake, as the sun continued to rise above the island, a loon called out to its mate and heard only herself as a reply.

Chapter Thirty-one

Promptly at seven, Luke began making his calls. The boys had been at the babysitter's that afternoon. Maggie was quite upset when she came and got them, but Mrs. Dixon had not felt it was her place to ask questions. Luke's stomach turned over at that news.

During his time banned from the phone, he had wandered through the house. In their bedroom, dressers had been left open and clothes were scattered across the floor. He looked under the bed to find the suitcase gone. His stomach had turned over then too. This didn't look like a nightmare Maggie had been running from.

At quarter to nine, he was able to get a hold of someone in Dr. Cooper's office. Yes – the reluctant voice told him – Maggie had made her appointment. Had something happened there to set her off? He found himself hoping that was the case.

His panic was enough that whoever answered the phone at the doctor's office agreed to call Dr. Cooper and have her contact him. She finally did at ten after nine.

Dr. Cooper listened as Luke unrolled the horrid events of the past twelve hours and eventually was willing to share with him that Maggie had remembered a summer home. She said that Maggie left quickly to share the news with him and that she seemed relieved and excited about it. He asked her what time that might have been and the response shook him.

His world came crashing down around him. Could his timing have been *that bad*? He hung up on the nice doctor and fell to his knees.

Mickey awoke early, his first thought that he had been dreaming again. His head throbbed and concentration was a task. He went over the events of the previous night several times in his mind before reaching the strong conclusion that they had all actually occurred. Which meant several things: he was done with drinking once more, he had a second chance with Gwen, and his sister was missing.

He rose slowly and poured a tall glass of water for himself from the bathroom sink. He swallowed it down in large gulps, his body craving hydration. Though his head ached and his muscles felt thick, a feeling of relief and anticipation enveloped him and any physical pain dulled in comparison.

He hesitated before making the dreadful call to his parents. It was only 7:30, but he was sure Luke would have called him if anything had changed. Once he told his mother, there would be no rationalizing with her. He dialed the number slowly hoping for his father.

Twenty treacherous minutes later, Mickey stepped into the shower as thoughts of how to reunite with Gwen swirled in his mind. He dressed quickly and headed down to the bar kitchen to put some breakfast together. He wanted to show Gwen that he could pull himself together. When he heard a knock at the door, his heart skipped. There stood Gwen – it had been real. She was a sight, like coming up for air. He invited her in but she hesitated. "I made some breakfast for us." He offered smiling tentatively as he could not yet read her expression.

"Mickey, we need to talk, seriously. It might be better if we do it somewhere...neutral." Her tone dropped his hopes like a lead balloon.

"Okay." He reached out to cup her face in his hands, but she turned from him. "Gwen, I promised and I stand by my promises."

"You promised it once before, if you recall." The truth stung.

"You were gone. I couldn't handle it like I thought I would be able to. Everything lost meaning. The bar kept me going for a while, Gwen, but even that wasn't enough. Please, let me touch you."

"Neutral ground." She repeated. God, didn't she feel it any more? The space between them was electrified, magnetic. He had to physically restrain himself from the force that pulled him towards her just to respect her wishes.

Upstairs, the phone began to ring.

"I have to get that. Please, don't move." He told her and bounded up the stairs.

It was Luke. He rambled on about suitcases and babysitters almost incoherently. Mickey could only make out every other word or so until Luke breezed over the words "summer home" and Mickey thought his heart might have stopped beating.

"Whoa." Mickey interrupted. "What did you just say?"

"Her therapist said she left to come and tell me about her recollections..."

"Recollections? Of a *summer home*?"

"Yeah. She must have headed directly to my office... and...Mickey, I think she *saw* me."

Mickey's head spun. Gwen, back in his life if he could only get her to stay there. Luke, screwing around on his baby sister. Maggie. REMEMBERED.

"Luke, I think we've got bigger problems than that."

"What are you talking about? Do you...you think she went to the summer home the doctor was talking about? Where is it, Mickey? I'll go right now!"

"Get in your car and get yourself here. We'll go together."

If Maggie was on Echo Island, she would need all the people he could get. He hung up the phone and turned to see Gwen looking at him curiously.

"What's going on, Mickey?"

In a quick movement, he had Gwen by the back of her neck, his mouth crushing down on hers. She responded, turning his body to liquid, a feeling better than any amount of alcohol had ever given him. Her arms went around him and grabbed a hold of his shoulders. His hands touched her face, starving from the lack of it for so long.

"You do still want me." He murmured, never breaking from their embrace.

She pushed him back. "Mickey, stop. I'm trying to be rational here."

He moved his head in for more, but she backed away.

"Screw rational, Gwen. Hasn't a year been long enough? Look, I don't care if you want to stay in Ireland. I just know it hasn't been the same without you. I'll do whatever it takes."

"If this is how you feel, why didn't you come back?"

"'Cuz I'm a stubborn jackass. I thought you'd turn me away. And that would have been worse than the break up itself. But, Gwen, I haven't stopped thinking of you. Not for a moment. Let me kiss you again."

Gwen put a hand up to ward him off. "No. You cloud my judgment. Mickey there's still something you don't know."

"What?"

"Not here. I need you to come with me. To neutral ground, remember?"

Mickey came back to earth. "Gwen." He sighed. "There's something else going on too, that may interfere with my plan to beg you to take me back for the next several days until you hopelessly give in. I seem to be in the midst of a potential family crisis."

"Was that what the phone call was?" she noticed the different mood in his eyes immediately. Mickey nodded and swallowed hard.

"Maggie. She took off on Luke with the kids yesterday. I have to help find her."

"Do you have any idea where she might be?"

Again Mickey nodded. "She's *remembering*. I think she's gone to the cottage."

A gasp escaped Gwen's lips, understanding immediately what Mickey was saying. *Ohhh, this complicated things. I can't show him Mara with this on his mind.* "And you're going there. To find Maggie."

"I can't leave you again. I won't. I'll prove to you I'm sober for as long as you need me to. I'll leave the bar and move to Ireland if that's what you want.

"But Luke is on his way here and I need to take him to the cottage. Please say you'll come with us, because I don't think I can bear to let you out of my sight."

Gwen was torn between the look on Mickey's face and what waited for them all down the road at an IHOP. She didn't know how long they'd be gone, how Danny would feel about this…

"A day or two, Gwen." Mickey had read her thoughts.

She bit down on her lower lip. "I have to get some things. I won't be gone long."

"Luke won't be here for a few hours. I've got to get coverage for the bar. You'll come back?" Gwen nodded. "You wanted me to see something too. We have a little time. Where is this neutral ground?"

She shook her head at him quickly. "No, no. It's fine. It'll wait until we get back."

"You sure?" She nodded emphatically.

Chapter Thirty-two

A warm breeze drifted over the island, and a haze clung to the earth. On it was the promising scent of a thunderstorm by day's end. For now, it was just enough to darken the waters to a midnight blue and send an intermittent sway through the pine boughs. Several windsurfers tried to capitalize on the perfect conditions and the effect created splashes of various bright colors against the gray day. Occasionally a golden ray of sun broke through the cloud barrier, sending a beam of hope onto the water.

Owen gathered pinecones as they walked, tossing them toward the lake when it came into view between the trees. Quinn was unaccustomed to the rough terrain and frequently asked to be carried and then put down again. Trying to keep up with his older brother frustrated him until his grunts of determination would turn to tears. Finally, Maggie settled them all in a clearing for the lunch Edna had the kitchen staff graciously pack.

Her thoughts tossed back and forth between her newfound memories and Luke. During her morning's rest she attempted to establish her own hypnotic state several times, but her mind would not release any further details. Instead, she turned again to the questions most in need of answers: What was the piece that was still missing? What happened here and when? Who knew about her past and would they share with her what she now craved?

She considered calling someone. Mickey had always been honest with her. Or had he? Perhaps Aiden knew the answers – but would he tell her? Was that what he had meant that night at Mickey's opening? Or would he just turned away from her again? She didn't think she could stand that.

In her memory of the island, Patrick had seemed different to her. Her thoughts as she relived that scene, were that he seemed withdrawn and remote. That wasn't surprising to her now, in fact, it was one of Patrick's trademarks. But then, it had seemed very unusual. He had even cried. Maggie couldn't remember Patrick ever crying – though clearly her own memory could not be trusted. Sean was angry with him for something. Something that had been his responsibility. Was that memory the key? If it was, then certainly Patrick would remember. Would he discuss it with her? Was he truly on this island as Edna seemed to believe?

She wouldn't call Kit or Sean. The anger at them that she was sure she was past resurfaced and she refused to consider either of them.

She wanted to talk to Luke, needed him with her. The thought of him drained her heart of what little warmth it had and left her feeling more alone than she thought she'd ever been. She had erased the image of him in the elevator from her mind. Blocked it out – as she was learning she was exceptionally good at.

All she had of Luke right now were the two beautiful angels seated beside her, contentedly staining their lips with strawberries. Guiltily, she thought of how frantic Luke must be. Not that she was gone, perhaps that even relieved him.

But the idea that she had taken the boys would put him in a panic. Especially with her track record.

She would call him when she got back to her room, she decided. Just to let him know the boys were fine – no more. She had some more thinking to do before she could really talk. And so much more to remember.

Aiden stepped easily over thick roots and chipmunk holes. Patrick wanted to call Shauna and Davis, and he had taken the opportunity to rediscover the island on his own. It had developed quite a bit during his absence. Several outbuildings had grown up out of the dense foliage. Patrick had informed him that they were all extensions of Echoes. His was the only private residence on the island. At one time, he could have walked its entire circumference and seen no one, now he crossed paths with a handful of others, enjoying what they considered solitude.

He came to a highpoint on the island, overlooking the beauty of Lake Opinicon spreading out before him like a satin carpet. Two loons bobbed along in the water a short distance from the shore, keeping watch over their nest. Down the hill a young woman ate lunch with her children, the older boy's laughter floating on the breeze like a dandelion seed. The woman's thick, auburn hair tumbled over her shoulders in waves and she laughed as she pulled the boys in for a playful hug. The sound rang in his ears.

It took Aiden a few moments to register the idea that he was seeing his own two nephews; Quinn for the very first time. His heart raced with both excitement and fear, he couldn't seem to catch his breath. It was as though he had suddenly found himself walking in the midst of a dream. He wanted to run to her and from her, so instead he remained where he was, like a statue, watching her play with her children.

After a few moments, they began to gather their belongings together. Aiden knew they would need to pass him to return to the house, where they must be staying. He stood, still frozen in place, until she turned toward the trail and he could finally see her face. The years that separated them fell away. She looked so much the same – her complexion a soft peach, her eyes gentle, intriguing even from where he stood. She may have lost some weight, but nothing extreme. As she smoothly hoisted Quinn into her arms, Aiden stepped forward from beneath the shadow of the pine where he stood, bridging the distance he had created between them physically if not emotionally. A protective arm went around Owen as Aiden walked slowly toward her.

As he neared her, her face registered curiosity, suspicion, confusion and finally shock. Her mouth dropped open slightly and then closed tightly again.

"Hi Maggie." He said simply, wishing away the pain he had caused her so that he could hug her like any brother might do, and ruffle the hair of his nephews. Instead, they stood arm's length apart, regarding each other as strangers might.

"Aiden." She replied, the surprise coming through in her voice.

The reunion was awkward at best, and Aiden thought to release the tension by changing its focus. "Pictures don't do justice to these two princes of yours."

Maggie held Owen's head against her thigh and smiled thinly at the compliment. A shroud of bitterness returned to her features when she spoke, sarcasm laced the edges of her question. "You have pictures?"

"Mickey's the typical boasting uncle."

"So you've kept in touch with Mickey?" He couldn't discern whether he detected curiosity or jealousy in her tone. Or both.

"Yes. Well, no. I mean, Mickey sent pictures after Quinn's baptism. And Halloween and Christmas, and...well, you get the picture." When she remained silent, he discarded humor for sincerity. "Maggie. Please. Forgive me."

Forgive you for what exactly? She wondered, *for cutting me out of your life or for keeping me in the dark about my own childhood? What exactly do you regret?* But she could not bring herself to spit those angry words at him. There were accusations to be directed at so many people in her life yet she was unable to let any one of them out for fear she would never stop. "And apparently you've kept in touch with Patrick too. Edna thought she had seen you with him. I told her that was impossible. That you haven't spoken to any of us in years. I guess that wasn't the case at all."

"You talked to Edna?"

Maggie set Quinn, who had been struggling in her arms, at her feet and placed her hands on her hips defensively. It angered her that he seemed more focused on her visit with Edna than defending his silent treatment of her. Which, it seemed, was more exclusively hers than she had thought. *Could it worry him that she had learned something from Edna?* "Yes. Aiden. Does that bother you? Is there something she might say that would be catastrophic?"

His eyes narrowed slightly between suspicion and curiosity. "Like what?"

She lifted Quinn back onto her hip and took Owen's hand in hers. As he began to protest that he wasn't ready to go, Maggie stepped briskly past Aiden and headed for the lodge. Fury raged within her. Years of not speaking and this is how they finally reunite. A quick I'm sorry and then a grilling. *How dare he ask her questions about her conversations with Edna. How dare he ask her anything!*

Aiden was left standing alone on the hilltop. *Well, that went well, champ.* How many times had he wanted to see Maggie again, to repair the damage that had been done, to be welcomed back into her life? Instead, he was left staring after his sister with the burning regret that he had sealed himself away from her for too long, a nagging sensation that she was desperately in need of his help, and the belief that she was even more desperate to refuse it if offered.

Chapter Thirty-three

Maggie found Edna in the office at the back of the house. Owen and Quinn were being supervised in the main greeting area watching television. She knocked gently on the opened door. Edna peered up through her spectacles and smiled warmly. "Come in, dear." Maggie did and took a seat on the loveseat against one wall of the cramped room. She watched Edna straighten papers on the desk. "Oh, this mess! I'm sorry, I just never seem to find the time to organize things in here." Papers were shuffled into piles and the piles were placed into drawers. When she looked back at Maggie, the distraught expression she found stilled her hands. "Honey, what is it?"

The familiarity of Edna's manner calmed her some and gave her the push she needed to speak. "You were right about Aiden. He is on the island."

"Well, that's wonderful." Edna clapped her hands together. "Are you worried about me because you'll be staying at Patrick's now? I completely understand that you would. He's your brother for goodness' sake. But perhaps we could call it even if you would all come for dinner in the dining room." Maggie was shaking her head.

"No. No! I'm not staying at Patrick's! I haven't even seen Patrick yet. I haven't spoken to Aiden in years. He cut himself off from the whole family. At least, I thought it was the whole family until today. Turns out it was just me he was ignoring." Tears burned once more and the frustration of two days of constant crying fueled her anger again. "Edna," her voice softened to a whisper but there was fire beneath it. "What happened here? Why is this island, this house, so unfamiliar to me and yet familiar at the same time? What is everyone keeping from me?"

Edna paled. Maggie was certain she would refuse to answer, so she made her plea once more. "I need to know, Edna. Can't you tell me anything about why my parents sold you this house? About why we've never come back? You knew us at one time, like we were your own family. Even when I couldn't remember you I remembered your scent, your warmth. You made me feel safe the last day I was here. You held me in your arms. I know that and yet I don't know *why*! Can't you tell me what you were protecting me from?"

Tears glistened in Edna's gray eyes as she recalled the day that the Callaghan's fairy tale world had shattered into pieces. She could feel Maggie's thin frame molded against her own, see the wide horrified eyes of Mickey and Aiden, sense Patrick's shame. The little girl who had once come to her for snacks or games or a gentle hug, was now before her again, this time seeking answers.

Aiden came through the cottage door as Patrick was fixing himself a cocktail at the bar. The phone conversation he had with Shauna had gone better than the one with Davis. Hearing the screen door slam, he reached for another glass and filled it with ice. Before he could finish pouring, Aiden was upon him.

"She's here."

Patrick didn't know what Aiden was worked up about but he had been formulating a particularly elegant, though cynical, toast and fully intended to share it. He turned, with both glasses raised, extending one arm toward Aiden. "A toast," he began, "to those we have underestimated. And to those who underestimated us." He raised the glass to his lips and let liquor burn his throat. "This world hasn't seen all the Callaghans have to offer yet."

"You've got that right." Aiden replied and downed his drink as well. "Maggie's on the *island*."

Patrick set his glass on the bar and poured another shot. "I thought she had blocked this place out, Dr. Freud."

Aiden ignored the sarcasm. "Well, she's clearly remembered it somewhere down the line. She may remember a lot more than that. She was pretty angry with me."

Patrick took Aiden's glass from him and refilled it. "Well, now, why would that be? Hmmm, it couldn't be that you haven't spoken to her since Mickey's place opened, could it?"

"No shit, Pat. I'm not an idiot. There was more to it than that, though. It was as if she wanted me to slip up and tell her something. I think she's realized that we've been keeping something from her."

Patrick paced out to the deck and leaned against the white wood rail, peering over the lake to the far shore. How the hell could Maggie have remembered now, after so much time? This was his escape. No one had come here for years. He was the only one. He alone, remained true to the pain of the memories here. Then, he goes and invites Aiden back into his life and all hell breaks loose.

Aiden had never been one to let anyone's feelings lay dormant. He knew the resentment was more from being told he'd burn in hell by Davis than the news Aiden brought with him, but at the moment, he was unable to separate the two. His words from the night before came back to haunt him. *If it's time to stop running, Pat old-boy, prove it.*

"Shit." He finally responded to Aiden who had followed him onto the deck. "Next thing you know it'll be a god-damned family reunion."

Aiden ran a hand over his stubbly chin. It was the same Patrick he'd always known. Stubborn and pig-headed and thoroughly unteachable. The fragile foundation of brotherly bonding began to slip again. He followed Pat's gaze out over the lake and was reminded of a moment during their childhood.

"Do you remember the first time Dad let you drive the big boat?"

Patrick only shrugged.

"You took Mickey with you to go talk to some girls up the lake. I begged to go with you but you said I was too little. You told me to go play with the younger kids."

"Yeah, so?"

"So, I hated you for that. But I did go hang out with them. And I actually had a great time, because with them I got to be the oldest. I was looked up to. It was like I was you."

Patrick remembered always feeling like Aiden was an unwanted tag-along. He had always thought that when he got just a little older, he wouldn't be such a pain. Someday he wouldn't mind including Aiden more. But that day never came. That was his fault, and Maggie's. His for letting it happen and hers for unknowingly making them all pretend that it didn't.

What was the point to this now? That he was an ass then too? That Aiden never felt loved by him? Why was it all resurfacing now, when his life was already falling apart? Should he have foreseen that if he continued to return to Echo Island that eventually his demons would come back for another shot at him?

Now Maggie somehow remembered the cottage. *Now* he had begun to let Aiden back in his life. He may have started this series of events into motion all those years ago – and hated himself ever since, but it was who he was now. Just as he seemed to be taking a step forward, to be moving from past to present, Maggie arrived with her memories and her needs and threatened it all again.

The old anger burned brightly once more. Anger at himself, at Maggie, even at Aiden, for bringing him close to a change he could never realize. Davis clarified it for him when he told him what a fuck-up he was. Shauna had expressed it when, crying on the phone she told him she didn't even know who he was any more. He looked at Aiden who steadily returned his gaze.

"Great story, Aid. I'm sorry. In my intense stupidity I missed your moral. Let me guess… I'm an asshole? Or is it 'Spend time with those you love before its too late'? What's your point?"

Aiden could hear the bitterness seeping out of Patrick's words like thunder muffled by thick, dangerous storm clouds. The dark fury within rattled at its cage, threatening to break free.

"There is no moral. God, Pat, it was just something I remembered. Look, if Maggie is remembering things, she'll be asking questions. She'll be talking to Edna, if she hasn't already. It may be time for all of this to be out in the open, but do we want Edna to be the one to have to do it?"

Patrick remained silent, his eyes as deep as the lake.

"Shouldn't it come from her family?" Aiden prodded.

There was always a moral, Patrick thought sullenly. That's what he had always hated about those children's books Mom used to read to him at bedtime. He enjoyed the reading part, but afterward she would wrap her arms around him and ask, "What did this story teach us?" He could never answer that question right. He used to try and try to find just what Mom was looking for in an answer, but she always ended up telling him. Eventually, he would just shrug and let her explain. But Aiden was right, again. Edna should not be the one to fill in Maggie's gaps. They had been the ones to steal them from her. Well, maybe they didn't steal them – but they made sure she'd never gotten them back. Aiden was asking him to retrieve Maggie. And once again, he worried that he would miss the moral here.

"Fine." He spat. "I'll fucking go get her."

Chapter Thirty-four

By the time Luke arrived at Mickey's a small group had gathered. Gwen had taken care of what she needed to – which Mickey assumed meant gathering her things and checking out of wherever she was staying. Kit and Sean had arrived unexpectedly. Kit was beside herself, of course. Mickey regretfully told them what Luke had shared about Maggie's memory of the cottage and of his plans to drive Luke there. They immediately insisted on going as well.

It wasn't the way Mickey had ever planned to introduce his parents to his true love – uncertain still if she would even have him and shadowed by concern for his sister. Kit tried dutifully to be interested in meeting the Irishwoman, but it was clear her heart and mind were elsewhere. Gwen took it in stride and made herself useful by keeping the coffee coming.

He didn't share the news of Luke's infidelity with them. There was no need to complicate matters any further. That was for Luke to work through with Maggie on his own – if they did, in fact, find her. He could see that Luke hadn't slept or eaten. His face was unshaven and pale, his eyes bloodshot and sunken. Mickey couldn't yet bring himself to comfort the man physically, but his words were gentle.

"We'll find her." Luke nodded and accepted hugs of sympathy from Kit and Sean, the far-off glaze never leaving his eyes.

Two hours later, they were through customs and Mickey navigated the narrow twists and turns of country road. The rain splattered upon the windshield in fat drops as he continued north. The sky above him was ominous and though the sun had not yet set, there was darkness all around him.

Beside him sat Gwen, caught up in the family's heartache and worry. She knew the background surrounding what was happening, the one other time she had seen Mickey cry was the night he told her the whole story. The fear and pain had been so sharp that night as the story tumbled out of him, so tangible, she almost felt it had happened to her. Now, there was comfort only in the knowledge that she was able to be with him at a time like this. It somehow seemed that fate had led her back to him just in time.

In the back seat Luke, Sean and Kit sat mostly in silence. Quiet tears slid from Kit's cheeks, tears that had been locked away for many years. Sean looked straight ahead of him, a look of grim determination on his face. Tonight the ghosts of the past would be released from their prison.

Luke stared out his window into the stormy clouds, fretful and filled with questions he could not ask. In the course of one day, his life had taken on a new meaning and all that truly mattered to him now was having his wife and sons back safely in his arms. He felt isolated from the other passengers in the car, separated by the secret he held on to and the one they kept as well. No one had discussed the details of either, only rushed to their destination made more vital by the phone call with Aiden.

That had been a shock for Luke too. Aiden, whom he had only met a few times and never had any sort of relationship with, was the one person who knew where Maggie was. Was it this island that had driven Maggie away or Luke himself? He looked to the skies for a solution, but was answered only by a jagged streak of lightning ripping the sky, followed by a low threatening growl.

Sean reached for Kit's hand, reassuring her with a gentle squeeze. Her response was a deep sigh of fear and possibly resignation. Mickey heard it and broke the silence. "It's time, Mom. We knew this might happen and now it has. We'll get through this."

"I don't think I'll get through it, Mickey." She replied grateful for his supportive words but too overcome by sorrow to recognize it. "We thought it was best. We thought it was the right thing. My God, what have I done?"

Sean folded her into his arms. "You protected your children, Katherine. The best way we knew how. Do not take this on yourself. We are all here to right our wrongs." The weight and reality of his words hung heavily in the stale, damp air.

"I tainted his memory. I erased him, for Christ sake. I put it away and allowed him to disappear..." her voice broke away and she covered her face in shame.

Sean looked pityingly at Luke. *How different would he see me if he knew my part in Maggie's disappearance?* Luke thought guiltily, but no one other than Mickey considered for a moment that Luke might have been the reason Maggie had run off. "There are some things that Maggie doesn't remember, Luke. Things that her mind blocked out – and we allowed them to remain gone. It might be best if you understood all this before we get there."

Thunder shook outside the car and the rain pelted its windows violently, dropping like thousands of needles. Mickey turned the wipers to high and shook his head. "They won't be running the ferry in this mess."

"They will for us." Sean corrected him.

Patrick climbed the steps to the lodge with slow determination. It was early evening, though the thick gray sheet of clouds made it seem later. Crickets and cicadas created a buzz through the trees making the heavy air seem charged. A few guests sat on the enclosed porch in Adirondack chairs. They spoke of the impending storm or their recent fishing trip – inane and trivial matters in Patrick's mind. He glanced at them as he moved, with a mixture of disdain and jealousy. Their biggest concern was whether dinner would be chicken or fish.

He strode into the greeting room, past the stone fireplace and leather couches, the postcard rack and the books on "Exploring the Rideau Canal". The front desk was vacant and the door to Edna's office was closed. There had been a handful of times before that Patrick had treated the lodge as his own, and he did so now, sliding behind the counter and rapping loudly on the door. Without waiting for a reply, he opened the door and stepped inside.

Edna sat at her desk facing him. Maggie faced Edna and turned to see who had caused the intrusion. Patrick – dangerously handsome and tall, with broad shoulders, his dark hair flecked with copper. The look on his face was strange to her, however. Patrick looked anything but controlled and remote as he usually did. His deep blue eyes flitted from her to Edna with what she thought might be a hint of panic beneath them. Droplets of sweat gleamed on his forehead under the harsh fluorescent lighting of the office. For a moment, he appeared lost, somewhat unsure of what came next. When he finally spoke, his voice thundered through the little room.

"What the hell are you doing, Edna?" he demanded.

Edna pushed away from her desk and rose to her feet. Next to Patrick, she barely reached his elbow, but she faced him with a straight back and stern look. "Watch how you speak to me, Patrick. I once changed your diapers. Maggie and I were just talking. She's looking for her past."

Maggie stood to protest Patrick's rudeness, but he lunged for her with a startling suddenness, seizing her by the arm and pulling her toward him. She was caught so off-guard that it silenced her momentarily.

"What did you tell her?" he hissed angrily.

Edna walked to within inches of Patrick, looking upon him as though she towered over him instead of the other way around. "I told her she needed to see *you*."

Patrick did not have a response for her this time. He spun and dragged Maggie from the room. She tried to yanked her arm free as he pulled her through the greeting room and onto the porch. Guests looked on from the Adirondack chairs. He held tight.

"Let me go!" she screamed nearly tripping down the steps to keep up with his pace. "You can't keep it from me forever. I have a right to know about my own life!"

If Patrick heard her, he showed no sign. His pace never slowed, his grip never loosened. Thunder tumbled across the sky, a gust of wind blew Maggie's hair over her face and Patrick continued on. She cleared her view with her free hand and stubbed her toe on a root. "What happened here? Why did we sell the house? Why has all of this been kept from me?" The questions came fast and furious. "What do you know, Patrick?!" Patrick said nothing.

Maggie finally escaped Patrick's grip when they reached the bottom of the porch steps. "Let go!" she repeated yanking her arm from his grasp. "You can't just drag me around the island – the boys are still inside. I am not going anywhere with you!"

Patrick looked at her face, flushed with concern and confusion and anger. Slowly, the anger he had tried to direct at her drained. He was eighteen again, with the new realization that he would be the reason her life changed forever. He was the catalyst to creating the Callaghans as they were today.

"I'll give you your answers! At my place, with Aiden there. I'll make sure Edna keeps the boys occupied. But the discussion you're looking for needs to happen with *me* not her."

"You know everything, don't you?" she asked him.

Patrick nodded. "Will you wait here while I make sure Edna's okay with the boys for a couple of hours?"

Maggie started to nod and then paused. "Do you promise to tell me everything if I come with you?"

The world they had built would certainly come crashing down if Patrick were to let go of the secrets they had so carefully covered all these years. Kit and Sean were sure to disown him. Yet, in the back of his mind, he couldn't help but believe that this responsibility truly should fall to him. If it hadn't been for him in the first place… "I promise I'll try. Wait right here?"

Maggie nodded.

The charm of Patrick's place was lost on Maggie. She was oblivious to her surroundings as they walked up the stairs and into the cottage. She and Patrick had not spoken any further on their walk, both of them cautious of what was certain to come. She sat on the couch and Patrick handed her a glass of something strong. That was when she noticed Aiden, sitting on a barstool like an onlooker. More outrage bubbled up from within her. Aiden had warned Patrick that she was closing in on the truth. He had been the one to send Patrick running after her.

"You *both* know everything, don't you!" she shouted and the bite of her own words brought a sting to her eyes. She looked down at the glass in her hand and swiftly turned it up at her lips. Fire filled her mouth, her throat, continuing on all the way down to her gut. "You both know the answers to all these questions while I've been running around like a lunatic trying to figure it all out myself!"

Patrick turned from his place at the bar. "Maggie, please understand." He started. "It was done for you. Mom and Dad wanted to protect you."

"Mom and Dad know? And…then…Mickey too?" Maggie bit down against the threat of tears. She wanted to appear strong not weak.

Both men nodded somberly.

"Everyone?" she gasped. "I've been seeing a therapist, going through hypnosis, accused of being crazy…losing my *husband* to another woman…and you all know *why?"* She felt the world slip from under her feet. The betrayal she felt by Luke now magnified to everyone that she had ever thought cared for her. Everyone except her boys. Only Owen and Bryan Quinn were true.

Patrick or Aiden started to speak but Maggie put a hand up to silence him. "Wait." She stood slowly, in a daze and walked out on to the porch. The clouds had thickened in the sky casting shadow over the entire lake. Most boats had driven back to the safety of their docks. The water was dark and choppy, unsettled, much like her heart.

She looked at the grounds around her. The pine needle carpet and moss-covered rocks. Memories flickered like candles of chasing frogs and building forts and yet the one piece that she was missing remained just out of her grasp.

She turned back to Patrick and Aiden who hadn't moved.

"What am I still missing?" It was more of a demand than a question. Aiden shifted uncomfortably and took a step toward her, but Patrick placed a hand on his chest.

"Please let me. Maggie. Seventeen years ago, I was supposed to watch you. Some kids up the lake offered to take me skiing, though and I went. I left you alone. Sort of."

"Pat…" Aiden began.

"I'm getting there! Give me a minute!

"Maggie, the piece you're still missing is who you were with that day. You blocked it out all these years. You're missing …Shane."

Shane.

Bryan Shane.

The memories tumbled back into place with that one single word. Shane. Her younger brother, *their* younger brother! How had she forgotten that she'd had a younger brother!

"He died here, Mags. On this island. That day." It came from Aiden with a deadly calm.

Shane had died here and she had no memory of it all this time. The whys began to riddle her mind and at the same time she felt a self-betrayal that snaked its way over her body until it squeezed at her heart.

Her knees went weak and she stumbled. Patrick was there quickly to catch her. Slowly, he led her back to the safety of the couch.

Maggie stared ahead of her, unseeing. "How did he die?"

Aiden took her glass and refilled it before speaking again. He sat down next to her. "He drowned. You were the only one there when it happened."

"Aid, stop." The fear in Patrick's voice came from a place that could not relive the next part of the story. The part he should have been there for. The part that, were it not for him, none of them would have to be doing this right now. "This is not right. Mom and Dad need to be a part of this. We can't continue this here. Not now."

"Mickey called your cell phone while you were gone. They're all on their way here now." Aiden replied. "Mom, Dad, Mickey, Luke. They've been worried about Maggie and I told them she was here. They're all coming."

Patrick responded to Aiden, but Maggie could no longer hear him. Her world tumbled. Her mind was unable to hold the past and the present simultaneously. Her thoughts jumped to Luke and to what she had seen on the elevator – was that just yesterday? She saw him as he had been the last time they had spoken, the arguments they'd had, the accusations. Now he was coming *here*. What would she say to him? Could she even stand to look at him again? Did he know about Shane too?

Her mind jumped back to Shane. Aiden had said that she was with him when he died. But she still couldn't remember that at all. There was no face, no feeling, no memory. Why couldn't she remember even now when she knew the truth? She found the glass on the table before her and drank it, oblivious to the burn this time. Aiden and Patrick continued to argue as though she were invisible.

"Did you think what it might do to your mother to bring her back here after all this time? You always think you know what's best for everybody! You don't, Aiden!"

"I knew you well enough to help you with the mess you'd gotten into at work. Let's remember that you called *me*. You asked *me* to come up here. I was doing fine, living my life away from the denial you've all surrounded yourselves in. Just fine!"

"Bullshit. Mickey told me you were at his bar. You can't even cut yourself off from us without screwing it up. You could never do anything without messing up somehow."

"This isn't even about me. You're the one who's played victim all these years. Now you want to take control of this situation, why? So that you can blame yourself for it too?"

Maggie turned and walked out of the cottage leaving her brothers to argue.

She didn't know how long she wandered around the island before reaching the lodge. She only knew that the last traces of light were to the far west, streaking the sky with a thin brush of purple on the horizon beneath the steel gray. And it had started to rain. She thought of her parents and brothers, wondered what it must have been like to not talk about Shane whenever she was near. It now made more sense to her why she had been sent away to school when no one else had. It didn't excuse it, but at least there had been a reason.

She thought of Jamie and desperately wanted to call her and beg her for one more memory. She thought of Luke on his way here with her parents and Mickey. She thought of Owen and Quinn blissfully unaware of the chaos going on around them. Maggie realized she had been away from them for some time now, and though Edna had assured Patrick the boys would be fine if she needed time alone, it was the thought of them that sent her running back to the lodge.

The late dinner was over and the last few lingering guests were headed to their rooms for the evening. The porch had cleared too, with the impending storm. Edna was overseeing the clearing of the dining room and kitchen but caught a glimpse of Maggie through the double door leading to the greeting room. Worry lines creased her forehead as she rushed to check on her.

"The boys have been fed and read to. They're having their dessert in the room off the kitchen." She explained.

"Thanks." Maggie replied dully. The immediate relief that her children were fine only made room for the thoughts that had plagued her all day. "I'm sorry that Patrick was so… awful."

"Not at all, dear. Are you all right?"

Maggie wandered past Edna without responding to collect the boys and get them into bed. When they got back to the room they were staying in, Aiden sat waiting for them.

"Mommy, who is that?" Owen asked curiously.

"That's your uncle, baby." She replied wearily as though there wasn't a single drop of emotion left within her.

"How come I never saw him before?" Maggie looked at Aiden.

"Ask him." She replied.

"Maggie..." Aiden began, "I'm so sorry about all of this. I'll go if you want me to. But I would really appreciate the opportunity to explain some of my actions to you."

Maggie nodded slightly. She was too tired too argue, too confused to question.

"Please come back to Pat's and stay there tonight with the boys. There's room. And... we *are* family."

"We're not a *family*, Aiden. We are so *far* from being a family! But we used to be...and I think that's even worse."

"Maggie, please. We have a chance now to be a family again."

She looked at him as though he were crazy. "I've been lied to my *whole* life Aiden. Every one of you knew and not *one* of you treated me like family would."

Aiden took Maggie's hand in his own. He went back to a place seventeen years in the past.

"You were gone, Mags. After the accident, there was nothing behind your eyes. You shut it out or something. You would say nothing for days and then you would just start screaming and none of us could stop it. It was...well, it was worse than what happened to Shane in a way. You had to be hospitalized. The day of Shane's funeral, mom and dad had to admit you. We thought we'd lost you too.

"They gave you medication and it calmed you. You were gone for two whole weeks, and when you finally came home, part of you was back. You were almost the old Maggie again, except for one thing. You remembered nothing. Mom and dad decided that for the time being, we would allow you to forget.

"No one thought it would be forever. It was just best at the time. But you seemed to build a new life for yourself and we kept letting you forget. We all made mistakes. That's obvious now. But at the time..."

The room fell silent. Owen and Quinn sat close to Maggie, seeming to know that she needed them near her. She felt their warmth, wrapped her arms around them and held them close. They were her source of strength.

"Will you come back to Pat's?" Aiden asked again.

Maggie looked at the brother she barely knew any more. "Did you only stop talking to me, Aiden?"

Aiden longed to tell her how he had spent years trying to convince the family to be straight with her, to the point of shutting them all out. That it had been for her that he did it and not because of her. But it seemed, somehow, disloyal to the rest of them. They had all simply tried to do what they believed to be right.

"No." he replied instead. "I shut myself off from everyone. Mickey kept sending me pictures of your kids and Patrick's kids. He'd leave me messages updating me on everyone from time to time. Patrick just contacted me recently. He needed my help with something and I saw a chance to maybe put things back together."

"Was it this that made you go away?"

He would defend and protect his family, but he would not lie any longer.

"Yeah."

Maggie's body drooped with exhaustion. There was still so much more to know, to remember, to ask. Not tonight.

"Come on, Mags." Aiden said, helping her stand. "You're exhausted. Hey, boys, do you want to go see Uncle Pat's cottage?"

Owen nodded emphatically and Quinn smiled in response to Aiden's sudden excitement. "How 'bout a ride on my shoulders, Quinn?"

Chapter Thirty-five

Sean spoke to the ferry master quietly and convinced him to make one final run in the thunder storm. Kit and Sean huddled together, trying to brace themselves for the sight they had believed they would never see again. Luke looked out at the disappearing lights on the shoreline behind them numbly, as though going in reverse might undo everything. Gwen and Mickey found some privacy at the stern of the boat, for some brief solitude.

"Are you going to miss a flight home by coming with me?" Mickey asked her searching for a hint of her thoughts. They huddled under hoods in the rain.

"No. We got open-ended tickets not knowing what it might take to…" she covered her mouth.

"We?" Mickey's eyes narrowed suspiciously.

Gwen buried her face in her hands. "Danny came with me." She admitted.

Mickey wasn't sure what was meant by this admission. Why hadn't Danny come with her to see him? Why wouldn't she tell him he was *here*? He searched for a sign from her, but her face remained covered.

Then it hit him, like a lightning bolt. Gwen and Danny were *together* now. His head swam dizzily and his stomach rolled. He grasped the rail of the boat to steady himself. Gwen peaked at him through her fingers.

"Mickey? I'm sorry, I was going to tell you he was with me, but everything happened so fast. There wasn't any time!" Mickey held his unsteady free hand in front of her face to stop her from continuing. He faced the sky, to let the rain pelt him.

The pain of losing her hadn't prepared him for this. He wanted to scream at her, or beg her, or even act like it wasn't driving a knife straight through him, but no words would come. His legs weakened beneath him and he gripped the rail tighter.

"Mickey?" Gwen asked again, noticing the green hue to his face. "It isn't that bad. You were supposed to have seen him this morning. You know, on our neutral ground. Why do you look sick?"

"You…" He couldn't say it, could he?

"and…" one more heartbreaking word.

"Danny?"

"What about us? He….Oh my God, Mickey, no!" she burst into laughter. Her hood fell back from her face, drenching her in the downpour. When she could finally speak, she looked at him, still chuckling. "Mickey, we're not together! Is that what you thought?!"

Mickey could only stare back at her, looking for the truth in her eyes. "Mickey! He's like my brother. He's your best friend! It's nothing like that!"

Finally, Mickey leaned forward holding his stomach that still threatened to empty.

"Jesus, Gwen. Don't do that to me." Her laughter echoed around them, clashing with the thunder.

It was late when they finally arrived on the island. Patrick came down to the dock to greet them. He quickly explained that Maggie was okay, but that she was finally sleeping. This would have to wait one more night.

There was no room in Patrick's cottage – it certainly hadn't been built with this many visitors in mind. He thought of his two Adirondack chairs and almost laughed aloud at the irony. Edna had one guest cottage available for them, though. After much apologizing on Patrick's part, she agreed to move a smaller group to her one honeymoon suite free of charge, to accommodate the crowd Patrick had coming.

Kit was uncomfortable enough to be back on the island, now she would be a guest in her former home. *At least it's not the main house*, she thought. Edna had probably taken that into consideration.

Patrick looked at Luke as he led them all to the guest cottage. "There's room for you, of course.. The room I put Maggie in has a double bed and the boys are in sleeping bags on the floor."

Luke was torn between the possibility of seeing Maggie tonight and the concern that she would turn him away.

"I'd like that." He replied, unable to resist the sight of his boys and the chance to make things right with Maggie. "I won't wake her." Patrick nodded, sympathy thick in his expression for his brother in-law.

Maybe Maggie hadn't seen after all…

Chapter Thirty-six

"The haunting, wailing call lulls you half-awake..."

The woods were dark and still as Maggie made her way through stray branches and tree roots. She could hardly see her own hand in front of her face, but her body willed her on and her mind told her the way. Like a sleepwalker, unconscious of the journey, no thoughts were coherent. The trees rocked against the wind, the rain pelted her face and arms as she ploughed through the underbrush to reach the rocky clearing. She couldn't feel the sting of it. Peering down the steep, jagged cliff into the darkness, she could only hear the patter of rain , but in her mind it was deep blue, reflecting a cloudless sky above. She teetered on the edge.

Atop the perilous bluff, water trickling in a thin line down her back from the tip of her ponytail, she eyed the water below victoriously. She had done it. Her brother had dared her and she had done it.

Cliff jumping. Just like the older kids did.

Turning her challenging gaze upon Shane, her lips turned up, she taunted. "Your turn."

Shane looked hesitant. It was so far down to the water. But he wouldn't turn Maggie down after she'd done it, she was a girl.

Pat and Mickey would pick on him the rest of the summer if they knew he was too scared to try something a girl had done.

He swallowed hard and peered over the edge. When he looked back at Maggie, his face had taken on as much false confidence as he could muster.

"Sure. It's just water." He took a few steps back and drew in a deep breath. "See you in a few." Clenching his teeth and fists, Shane took three running steps and was airborne.

Lightning cut through the sky followed immediately with the deep, rolling bass of thunder. She could see the splash he made when he landed.

Maggie watched him plunge into the water below. His body was so rigid, he'd practically done a pencil dive. She chuckled at the realization of how scared Shane must have been, his resolve, though, was stronger than the fear. Pat would be proud of him.

The ripples from the jump began to clear, tiny bubbles popping up from where Shane had entered. He should be coming up… come up…

Her pulse began to pound in her ears as she waited for her brother's head to break the surface. If he was playing a mean trick on her…

It was taking too long. Maggie turned to look in all directions around her. No one. They were too far from the house for her to run and get Daddy.

"Shane!" she began to yell toward the water below her. "Shane, come up!"

Panic ripped at her chest and Maggie's body began to shake. "Help!" she screamed. "Someone! Please!!" Her voice was swallowed up by the silence of the island. No one would come.

Maggie backed up a few paces and ran at the edge of the cliff, her tender bare feet beating against the rock. She jumped from the edge and plummeted into the cool black waters.

Below the surface, she peered into the hazy, green dimness, pushing away the seaweed until she found him. His eyes were open and they met hers full of complete and utter terror. She almost gasped. She reached him quickly. Almost to his waist, Shane was submerged in the mucky bottom of the lake. His dive must have been deep enough that he hit bottom and sunk.

Maggie wrapped her arms around Shane's chest and kicked, trying to pry him from his muddy trap. He didn't budge.

She surfaced quickly for the air that her lungs ached for and dove again toward her baby brother.

This time, she wrapped her legs around him tight and aimed with her arms toward the surface of the water.Again he wouldn't budge, held in the clutches of the lakebed.After a few moments she had to surface once more.

Again she dove downward.

His eyes still gazed at her, but the panic was gone. They seemed to glaze over and were slightly cloudy. She reached for him but he shook his head, as though telling her he knew there was no escape.

She covered his mouth with hers and blew air into his lungs. He writhed and twisted violently and Maggie was frightened, not knowing if she was helping him or not. She surfaced again and repeated her actions, desperate to keep him alive.

When she returned this time, Shane was calm. His hand floated slowly up toward her, reaching out to her. Maggie grasped hiss hand and held tightly to it. She watched as her brother slowly closed his eyes. She stayed as his body went limp. She didn't let go, couldn't let go of him. Even as her body demanded air, she held on, her salty tears mixing with the lake water. The world around her began to grow dark, her lungs and throat burned with the demand for air.

And still she clung to him.

Aiden woke to a boom of thunder. The storm outside bellowed, the ground by his window was littered with scattered leaves and stray branches. Lightning crackled through the sky so brightly he could glimpse the lake, dark and brooding. He heard Quinn call out, frightened by the storm and heard Luke's sleepy voice trying to soothe him. When his next cry sounded more desperate, Aiden rushed across the hall to his room.

Luke leaned over Quinn's frame swallowed up by an adult-sized sleeping bag. He sensed Aiden's presence and turned toward the doorway.

"He's okay. I got him." He gestured toward the bed. "She's not here." There was no surprise in his voice – it had become all too common.

It took a moment for his words to break through Aiden's sleepy fog. Maggie was gone. Owen slept on sofa cushions in one corner, oblivious to the howling winds and piercing rains against the house.

"She's *gone?*"

"Yeah." *She probably woke up and saw me here,* he thought. "She's probably sleeping downstairs." *Or out in the storm.* Luke stroked Quinn's hair gently while he spoke.

Patrick's form filled the doorframe. The storm seemed to have everyone up. "She's gone." Aiden whispered.

"What?"

"She's gone." He hissed. "Maggie's not here."

"She's probably in the kitchen or something. No one would go out tonight, right?"

Luke was silent.

Aiden shrugged. "Go check. Please."

Patrick disappeared, returning only moments later. Quinn seemed to be settling back to sleep, so they stepped silently out of the room closing the door behind him. "She's not in the house." Even as Patrick said it he was pulling a dark green rain slicker over his head.

"Pat, it's a big island…" Aiden began to argue, though he knew it would make no difference and was glad for that.

"Do you have any doubt where she's gone?"

Luke could only look on.

"But, that's at the far end of the island. In this storm?"

Patrick looked at his watch. "Seventeen years ago today, Aiden, Shane died. Maggie has returned there to remember, I'm sure of it. This time, I will be there."

Climbing the slippery rocks of the southern cliffs, Patrick heard Shane's name tear through the storm-soaked night. He raced up the steep incline using hands and propel him on the climb. Reaching the cliff's edge he peered downward into the inky darkness. White caps sprayed angrily and slapped at the shoreline. The flashlight beam scanned, big sweeping movements over the surface until it passed a figure bobbing against the waves. He brought the light back to settle upon Maggie, her fiery hair darkened to rust. His mind rewound to hearing of the moment when Mickey had found her seventeen years earlier. When it should have been him. The name pierced his ears again, and at first he thought it had come from his own memory.

His heart raced madly. Maggie could be having one of her nightmares, or reliving the memory. If that were true, the only thing that had kept Maggie from staying down there with Shane that day had been Mickey. He screamed her name but got no response. He watched her disappear beneath the water.

Without another thought, he ripped the slicker off his body and dove. He broke the water only feet from Maggie. On his way back up, he encircled her waist. The shock of it had Maggie flailing. "Shane!" she screamed again, clawing at Patrick's arms and face. "Let me go! He's still down there! Shane!"

Patrick struggled to get a hold of her abusive limbs while aiming for the shore.

"Maggie, it's Patrick!" he sputtered through mouthfuls of water. "It's over. It was years ago. Shane's gone." She continued to fight him as he dragged her toward shore.

"No, Mickey, he's down there. Please, he's dying!"

Patrick's eyes had adjusted enough to the darkness enough that he could see her in shadow, but in that moment a bolt of lightning lit up the sky and he saw the glaze in her eyes. He grasped her firmly and shook her shoulders hard. "It's Patrick, Maggie! I'm not Mickey. That was years ago. You're okay now." He reached the rocky shore and dragged her onto a bed of pine needles where they collapsed together.

Maggie was silent for a moment and then Patrick heard her muffled sobs. He pulled himself slowly from the rocky ground to wrap her in his arms.

"I couldn't save him! I dared him to jump. I knew he shouldn't and I dared him anyway. I did this to him!"

"Shhh." He comforted. "Maggie, it's not your fault."

"He was scared…so scared! But he was brave. I had to keep coming up for air and he…he couldn't. I pulled with my arms…my legs…he wouldn't come up. I could see his eyes down there."

Patrick heard this part of the story for the first time. It was one that only Maggie could tell. It was what he had been so afraid to hear and yet what he had wanted from her that afternoon when their father laid all the blame on him – to know what she had gone through because of him.

Patrick held onto her while she cried for her brother for the first time in seventeen years. He clung to her and she to him, soaking wet. The thunder continue to shake the ground and trees around them, but neither noticed.

"I tried to pull him, but he wouldn't come up. I tried to breathe for him, but…he wanted my hand. I held his hand and then he died. I let him die." The sobs shook her body.

"No, you didn't. You kept him from dying alone." Patrick's heart burned with emotion as he imagined what his sister had witnessed at the bottom of that lake. He didn't know until this moment what the memory had been for Maggie.

He wondered if anyone could have carried on with that memory at twelve years old.

"You stayed with him, Maggie. My God, how frightened you must have been but you *stayed*."

Maggie's shivering intensified. "I…didn't want him to be alone. He…wanted my hand."

Patrick got to his feet and lifted Maggie in his arms.

"I remember it all now. Every moment of it. I…can still feel him there. I can still see his eyes." It came out in ragged, choked breaths.

"I'm taking you home now." He cradled her like a child, believing that this was what he would have done, should have done, that day. She let her head rest on his shoulder. "You're incredibly strong and brave, Maggie. It must have been such a comfort for Shane to know that you were right there by his side."

Maggie clung to Patrick, exhausted. The tears continued to stream, mixing with the rain and lake water. She was asleep in his arms before they reached the cottage.

Chapter Thirty-seven

Maggie rubbed her weary eyes with the back of her hands. She could feel her pulse pounding in her temples and her head felt too heavy to lift. She couldn't remember getting back to Patrick's, but she realized she could remember everything else. She propped herself on her elbows and saw bright daylight shining from behind the curtains.

"Maggie?" She turned at the sound of her name to look into the exhausted and deeply saddened eyes of her husband. The true reason for Maggie's quick departure had paled against the incredible events of the past few days. Now, gazing upon the haggard form of the man she had stood beside upon the altar, who held her hand and pressed it to his cheek during two childbirths, what she witnessed two days earlier came flooding back in one last debilitating wave.

Tears would not come now – for either one. They were both too emotionally drained to begin the pending battle with lachrymal weapons. Before him, he saw the woman who had supported him when he had nothing, had worked two jobs to provide a roof over their head, undergone hours of pain, tears, and sweat to provide him a legacy in his two precious sons. Before her stood the eyes of her sweet, feisty Owen and the mannerism of her genuine, comedic Quinn.

So much had been invested in the relationship, so much energy. What would it come to now?

"Where are the kids?" Maggie asked in a near whisper. Although what she wanted most right now was to curl up next to Owen and Quinn and sleep for days, she knew that there was much to be settled before she could rest again.

"They're out playing with their new-found cousins. Shauna showed up this morning."

He sat down next to her and she pulled herself up and away from him. Though he was afraid of the answer, he needed to ask. "Maggie, what made you leave?"

She closed her eyes and breathed deeply. "You." His greatest fear was realized in that simple word. "I was coming to tell you that I had remembered the island, that I was figuring things out and that we might be okay." He reached out to touch her hand but she pulled away. "And I saw *you* in the elevator." There was no emotion in her voice. Only truth.

Luke hung his head. "Maggie, it was…"

She shook her head vigorously and then regretted the quick move when the ache became a throbbing pain. "Don't tell me what it was or what it wasn't. I can't think straight anymore with everything that's happened!" She pushed herself up and off the bed. "Please, Luke. I can't do this right now. I've only just remembered watching my little brother die before my eyes. I just remembered even *having* a little brother. My entire family is probably downstairs right now, waiting to justify to me how they let that happen. I can't…" She looked at Luke and then looked away, it hurt too much to see his face. "I needed you and you needed someone else." She slipped on a pair of jeans from the end of the bed. "And right now, you will just have to wait."

"I can't, Maggie, please."

She turned to him her face alight with anger. "You can't do this for me? You were practically *attacking* someone *else* in an *elevator* at your office building!" He felt the blow of each emphasized word and wasn't certain the entire family downstairs hadn't heard it too. "And you can't let me have just a few moments? I did everything you asked me to. I let you take the boys off without me. I started seeing Dr. Cooper. I even sat through four horrible days while my parents critiqued every breath I took. For what, Luke?" she circled the bed shaking her head. "To discover I had blocked out a brother for seventeen years and my family kept it from me. Oh, and just as an extra bonus, my husband's *screwing* someone else!"

"It wasn't like that, Maggie." But she was at the door.

She looked back at him showing the exhaustion and sorrow that still plagued her. "Luke, shut up."

Everyone was gathered in the living room. Even Luke had followed shortly after her, though he stood in the doorway, knowing he did not quite belong with the others. No one made a sound when she entered the room, as if unsure of who should speak first. Maggie sat on the couch between Mickey and Patrick, laying one hand on each of their knees for stability and leaned back into them. "I remember it all." She said looking from Sean to Kit and back. Neither could find any words. "It's been coming back in bits and pieces for the past few weeks. Last night when Patrick found me at the cliffs I remembered everything.

"I don't want to be angry. I was…still am, but I'm so tired of being angry." She glanced at Luke. "What I don't understand is *how*. I think I can get the why, even if I think it is a horrible excuse for a reason. I repressed the memory, and everyone else allowed that to happen. You all thought it would put me back together. But I can't fathom *how*? How could you all allow him to be forgotten? How could you strike him from any conversation, from our pictures? The work it must have taken. The effort that must have been involved in removing him from everything!" Kit had begun to sob. "Was I sent away because it would be easier?" She promised herself she would not cry now and she stopped herself from saying anymore to bite back the tears that stung her throat.

Kit moved to kneel at Maggie's feet and placed her hands in Maggie's lap. "Honey, no. After what you had been through, Maggie, after what you had seen! It was a blessing for you to have forgotten. Who was I, as a mother, to make you remember? I lost my baby, and I will suffer an eternity in hell for killing his memory as well, but I still had you! It was all I could think of to do." The tears flowed freely down her cheeks. "You went to Dylan for a fresh start. A chance at a normal life. We thought it was the only way at the time."

Kit turned to look at Aiden, Mickey and Patrick. "You all suffered so at the expense of what I did. The whole family did. But by the time I realized the pain it was causing, I didn't know how to undo it.

"Aiden. You knew in your heart the only way to move on was to confront the pain and we wouldn't let you. And rather than hurt us to heal yourself, you backed away. And we let you feel hurt and blame for that. We did that to you and I will never be able to make up for that.

"Patrick, I watched you blame yourself all these years. I watched you distance yourself from us emotionally so that you couldn't cause hurt. But Patrick, it was *not* your fault! You were a child too. Please stop taking the blame upon yourself, because we all miss you so terribly.

"Mickey, you tried to be the rock. When Patrick went to school and Maggie to Dylan you tried to keep our family together with your light. And we turned away from your attempts. We chose to stay in mourning, rather than heal under that light. And so you ran away and started drinking to heal your own pain.

"All of these things stemmed from my horrible, terrible decision to allow Maggie to forget. And I can never make up for that. I just ask that you please let us try to be a family again." She placed her head on Maggie's knee, broken and bruised.

"Kit." Sean finally spoke. "You cannot take this all on yourself either. The decision was not yours alone. We did this together. And you made every effort to keep the family close. I was the one who pushed the family away...blaming Patrick, resenting Mickey...blaming my anger on Aiden."

"Are the lies done now? What else do I need to know?" she asked of no one in particular. The room was silent for a long moment.

"Maggie," Sean began. "We are done with the lies. I think there will be many moments when questions come up for you as your memory strengthens. I promise you, when these questions come you can ask anyone of us. We will be completely honest with you. No more hiding behind the truth. Not even in the name of protection."

Maggie nodded slightly.

Maggie looked around the room at her Callaghans. They were a broken family. A terrible decision made amidst horrible grief had broken them all. At one time, they were that family Maggie had always dreamed of. Perhaps that is why she worked so hard to create it as an adult. She hadn't dreamed it at all. She realized that she was not the only one whose life had been entirely altered by that one decision made. It had made Patrick the sullen, distant man he was. Anger and guilt had festered within him and yet, he continued to live with the deception in protection of her. Mickey had fought to keep the family together, to maintain some shred of the closeness they had once shared. He tried so hard with no success and it had eventually driven him away. Driven him to drink. But it had also driven him to Gwen. Looking at the two of them – had it all been the wrong road to take?

And Aiden. Aiden had wanted so badly to make the family whole that he made repairing broken people his profession. He had become an expert at it. And when even that expertise could not help those he loved the most he shut them out – not in anger, as she had once thought, but in hurt. He was unable to watch what it was doing to them – but not willing to break the vow of silence they had sworn him to.

And here they all sat willing to still take the blame for it individually, to save the others from that responsibility. But it was not a time for blame, not any more. Was it possible for them to become a family again now? Could they heal what was broken within each of them?

"We'll remember him now." Maggie said softly and she could feel her heart become peaceful. "We'll make up for the years he was forgotten." She slowly placed her hand on Kit's hair and began to stroke it gently.

"And we will never forget him again."

"I promise you that, Maggie." Kit whispered. Mickey smiled softly. "You know, I think he might be proud of us, finally."

Shauna and Patrick were first to separate themselves from the group. Mickey and Gwen went for a walk around the island. Aiden took the kids out to play and Kit and Sean decided to finally visit their old place and pay their long overdue respects to Edna. It left Maggie and Luke alone.

"Maggie…I can't ever take back what happened. I couldn't understand why you were so distant. I thought you were…turned off by me. Michelle listened at a time when you and I couldn't seem to talk to each other. It was all a big, huge mistake."

Maggie winced upon hearing her name. Michelle had been to their house. She had chatted with Maggie at office parties. To hear *who* he had been kissing so passionately only made matters worse.

"It *was* a mistake." She wouldn't look at him. "We both made mistakes. We didn't communicate, we didn't share our feelings. I realize that I am at fault in all this too. I was erratic and unreliable." She stared out the window, at Aiden playing tag as he carried Quinn and Ashleigh around on his shoulders. Her eyes remained dry but her heart broke for her darling boys and the broken family they would have to face now.

"But I didn't look for any of those things we had lost in someone else." She finally turned to face him. "I need some time to myself. This is all just too much for me right now. I don't even know who I am and I can't fit our screwed up relationship into that right now."

"Maggie, let me help..."

"No! I am going to learn this on my own. I am not going to be that dependent, needy person I have been any more."

"What are you saying...it's over, just like that?"

Maggie took a step toward him, but couldn't bring herself to get any closer. "Not over. Not necessarily. I just need...I need you to leave me alone for a while. To try to get everything straight in my head before we try to look at us."

"A while? You mean a day? A week?"

"I don't know, Luke! A while! You need to figure out what it is you feel for...her on your own and I need to figure out... a lot."

"A separation." Luke said flatly. "You want me to move out. I don't feel anything for her, Maggie – I swear it!"

"Luke," she spoke slowly, finding herself in a role reversal with her husband. She was now the voice of reason and logic. "You don't feel nothing. What I saw was far from nothing." She swallowed hard against the image that filled her mind. "I am asking you for some time. Call it separation if you want, I don't care what it's called. After what you did – I think this is the least you could do for me."

Tears filled his eyes and he dropped his head into his hands. " I'll do whatever you ask, Mags. Whatever you need. Just don't shut me out completely. Let me try."

Everyone was invited to dinner at Echoes that night and though the conversation was uncomfortable, it was, perhaps, one of the more normal family meals they had shared in ages. Stories that included Shane were told by all for the first time, everyone making certain he would never be left out again. Kit wanted Aiden to catch everyone up on his career, his personal life, his love life. He laughed at that, but admitted to having a potential relationship.

Maggie looked around at what her family should have been all these years. Close, in everyone's business, loud. She still felt like an outsider, but realized that they had mourned for 17 years. Every time they were not able to speak of Shane, they mourned. Every birthday of his that passed, every anniversary of his death, they had thought of him.

That time had just begun for Maggie. She intended to make up to Shane all the time she had lost by remembering him now. Maybe then, she would be able to be a true part of her family.

Chapter Thirty-eight

It seemed to take an eternity for Mickey to get his parents home so that he could be alone with Gwen, but finally they were waving goodbye to Kit and Sean in the driveway and pulling away.

They'd had a little alone time on the island, but Gwen had maintained a safe distance from him the whole time, nearly driving him mad. He knew he could only prove his sobriety over time. He just hoped that she would give him enough of it. He thought about selling the bar and following her back to Ireland. It would break his heart to do – but his business wasn't enough without her. If it meant a lifetime of building drafts for Danny and living his days out above "Bunns" to keep Gwen in his life, he would do it.

"I called Danny from the last rest stop and he's going to meet us at the bar." Gwen told him.

That meant even more time before he could be alone with Gwen. Not that he didn't want to see his closest friend. He still got a slight chill when he thought of how he had imagined them together. He smiled genuinely at Gwen, though more at the fact that he had been off the mark on that than her announcement.

"Cool. It'll be great to see Danny again. So long as you're sure I was wrong about you two." Gwen's attempt to smile at his joke fell short and a new set of worries cropped up in his mind. "He's taking you home, isn't he?"

Gwen looked out the window. "Can we stop somewhere and talk for a minute before we get there?"

A hard lump formed in Mickey's throat. He found the closest parking lot and pulled in. This was it. Whatever else had been weighing on her mind, keeping her distant. He was about to understand. He turned the car off and faced her.

"What is it Gwen? I don't think I can wait any longer." He was all seriousness now, and it was uncharacteristic of him. It made her nervous.

"Mickey," she started. She had played the conversation out in her mind a hundred times over the past two days and was determined not to let fear or pride get in her way now. "You're really off the sauce, right?"

"Absolutely! I haven't even thought about it, Gwen. Honest." She looked at her hands. "Look, I know I still need to prove it to you, but just give me some time. Stay here a while and I will..."

"I believe you, Mickey." Her eyes moved slowly back to his. "You've just been through a hell of a time up there. And Patrick has a kilo of liquor, believe me." Her head shook back and forth slowly. "You don't have to convince me anymore. As long as I have your word."

"I swear it." Mickey placed a hand over his heart. Gwen nodded, satisfied. "There's something else, isn't there?"

Again Gwen nodded, this time her eyes glistening.

The words tasted bitter on Mickey's tongue. "It's still over, isn't it?"

"You may want it to be when you've heard." A single tear broke loose and snaked down her cheek. Mickey reached over, tenderly, to brush it away. Her eyes closed at his touch, sending two more tumbling. He wiped them away as well with his thumbs and held her face.

"Never. Please tell me."

She opened her eyes and looked straight into his. "When you left...I...well, I didn't know at the time. And once I did know I couldn't...I was afraid..." she broke off, angry at herself for stumbling so. "Oh, God, Mickey! This is so hard! I don't want to trap you. I'm afraid you'll change how you feel but stay anyway!"

His hands still on her face, he pulled her closer to him into a gentle kiss. Everything he felt for her was poured from his lips into her heart. He pulled away to kiss her nose, her eyes, before pressing his forehead to hers. "Open your eyes." He told her. She could feel his warm breath on her skin. "I have no idea what the hell you're trying to tell me. But how can you *not know* how I feel?" He kissed her again, lingering this time as though it might be his last opportunity. "If it's another guy, if you want me to move to Ireland. Gwen, as long as you still want me it doesn't matter."

"I know you feel that way *now*." His closeness was making her dizzy. She longed to sink into him, to feel the wonderful electric burn of his mouth on hers. "I can't breathe." She groped for the door handle and tumbled out of the car, gulping fresh air in hopes of clearing her mind of wanting him. Mickey quickly followed.

Frustration edged his emotions as she paced little circles on the other side of the Jeep.

"I can't take much more of this, Gwen."

She whirled to face him. "You're talking of forgiving me if I slept with another man, of abandoning your bar to move across the world. Because that's the kind of person you are. Because you would sacrifice anything, even your feelings to do what's right for someone else. In a moment, you may *hate* me – but you would still do the right thing! That's what I'm so afraid of! What I've done..."

"WHAT. HAVE. YOU. DONE?!" It echoed across the lot. Now he could appreciate the space she'd put between them because he was certain he would have shaken her had she been close enough.

"After you left," she started again, slowly, annunciating each word carefully so she would only have to utter them once. "I found out that I was pregnant."

He didn't move.

"I never told you. By the time I could think straight, I was, afraid you would feel trapped. You would come back even if you didn't want to. I didn't want that..." she tilted her face to the sky before looking at him again. "Mickey. You have a *daughter*. She is six months old and her name is Mara. She's waiting for us with Danny."

Silence.

It seemed an eternity that Mickey stood there, unmoving. Gazing at her with his mouth slightly open.

She wanted to say more. Wanted to explain herself, to tell him how many times she had planned to call, wanted to call. But she knew that once again Mickey's solid footing dropped out from beneath him and she didn't yet know where he was likely to land.

Now she wanted that passionate kiss, his arms locked around her. *Now*, with him knowing what she had done, what she had kept from him, she wanted the promises he'd been making since she arrived.

As she watched and waited for what seemed an eternity, she decided she would settle for just about anything. Anything but the expressionless face across from her.

Should she run to his side or run away? Embrace him or let him be alone? Any sign from him, she would obey. How quickly the tables could turn.

It felt like hours, though it had likely been no more than a minute or two, but she could take no more. "Mickey? Say something. Anything. Tell me to get away from you or yell and scream. *Something*."

"Mara?" He whispered. She wasn't sure if it was a question or a statement.

Gwen nodded. "Mara Michelle Callaghan." She started babbling, afraid of more silence. "Michelle, because it's the female version of Michael. She has your eyes. And your smile. I think she may be getting your sense of humor too. She's beautiful. But…I don't want you to do something out of a sense of duty."

"What *do* you want?"

"I don't want you to feel trapped."

He shook his head. "Not what you don't want. What do you *want*?" His words were backed by emotions Gwen knew he was carefully restraining.

"I want *you*. I want *us*." He searched her eyes for truth. "What do you want?"

Then he smiled. "I want to see our daughter."

Chapter Thirty-nine

Aiden was anxious to put the work day behind him. Finally, he had been able to reschedule his roof-top date with Colleen. He still needed to stop and get steaks and margarita mix, maybe even buy some candles – was that still considered romantic?

He shut down his computer, putting away a few files while it logged off. He was slinging his messenger bag over his shoulder when the phone rang. He considered letting it go to voicemail, but something told him it might be important.

If this is Pat with another emergency, he thought, *so help me...*

"Aiden Callaghan."

"Mr. C? It's Tommy."

"Hey, Tommy. What's up?" he tried to hide his surprise.

"My mom got arrested again. They're sending me and my sister back to foster care."

Aiden's heart sank. How much more pain would this kid have to face? "Tommy. I'm so sorry." He said sincerely.

"They'll split us up." His voice was strong, but Aiden knew how hard this had to be for him.

"You're coming back here first, right?"

"Yeah. I got another two months there. But she ain't getting' out this time, Mr. C."

Aiden didn't ask what the charges were. He knew it would be either sale or prostitution. Tommy had been down this road before. "I'll talk to your foster care worker, Tommy. I'll do everything I can to keep you and your sister together. Got that?"

"Yeah."

"How are you holding up?"

"M'okay. I kicked Asshole out. Told him with my mom gone I'd go to the cops on him. He was gone that night. Didn't want to take care of two punk kids, I guess. Coward."

"Who are you with now, Tommy?"

"I'm at the jail. They're bringing me back there tonight."

"Will you come see me tomorrow morning?"

Tommy laughed and Aiden shared the silent joke. A few months ago, Aiden wouldn't have even asked the question. Tommy would never have come voluntarily.

"Yeah, Mr. C. I'll stop by."

Aiden smiled. "Good deal. I'll see ya tomorrow."

"Yeah. See ya."

Aiden replaced the receiver and looked up to find Colleen leaning in the doorframe. His heart sped; he didn't realize how good it would feel to see her until she was there.

"Shit!" he exclaimed and her face fell.

"Again?" Exasperation.

Aiden came around his desk to where she stood.

"Naw. We're totally still on for tonight. That *is* how I got you to kiss me for the first time, though."

"Kiss you!" Colleen crossed her arms in front of her. "You kissed *me* in case you forgot!

Aiden flashed his teeth and shrugged. "You say so. Come with me to get the steaks?"

Colleen smiled back at him. "Sure."

"Margarita mix too. I'm thinking 'bout getting you drunk tonight." He snaked an arm around her waist as they headed for his car.

"Really? That's too bad because I don't kiss drunk." She fit her body with his as they walked.

"Hmmm. May have to rethink that then." He opened the car door for her and waited while she slid in before crossing to his side.

"Hey, Colleen?" he asked as he turned the engine over. "How crazy do you think it would be for a single guy to take on a couple of juvie foster kids?"

Colleen's brows shot up as she looked at him. That would be classic Aiden. "Really crazy" she replied.

"Really?" he asked. He backed out of the lot and pulled into traffic, thoughtful. "Cool."

Patrick sat before the judge. Sweat made his collar itch uncomfortably and he ached to loosen his tie. When he was done with all of this, he swore he'd never wear a three-piece suit again. Shauna sat behind him, her head high and her shoulders squared. She had not left his side once through this ordeal.

"You are being sentenced to nine months community service. Your securities license is hereby revoked. Mr. Callaghan, you will not practice financial advisement in the State of New York again. Is this understood?"

"Yes, your honor. Thank you, your honor."

"You are free to go."

It was as though a huge weight had been lifted from him. He wanted as far away from the financial world as possible and that was exactly what the judge demanded. He turned to Shauna, relief flooded her face. She beamed at him and threw her arms around him in an uncharacteristic display of affection. His attorney clapped him on the back and they shook hands congenially. It was over.

As they drove home, Shauna took his hand in hers. "It was what we'd hoped for, Pat. Everything we'd secretly hoped but were afraid to say these past months."

Patrick leaned over and kissed her head. "McAvoy thinks they'll accept my time with Habitat for Humanity." He explained his conversation with his attorney before the sentencing. "That puts me three months in already."

"Did you call Edna this morning?" she asked, squeezing his hand tighter. He pulled into the parking garage and slid into his reserved spot.

"I did." A grin escaped his lips. "I told her if things went well, we'd make her an offer by the end of the day."

His grin was contagious. "Well, I guess we better make another call."

Chapter Forty

Shortly after returning home from Echo Island, Luke moved out of the house. It was agreed to be a temporary arrangement. The weekend he left, he took the boys out for the day and Maggie used the time to drive to her hometown. She found the small gravesite she had never known existed. The headstone read simply:

Bryan Shane Callaghan
June 7, 1975 – July 6, 1986
Beloved son, brother, friend
Guide him to Your Light

The grave was well cared for with fresh flowers in pots on both sides of his headstone. A polished wooden box was wrapped in a plastic bag and tucked in between the pots. Maggie lowered herself to her knees and gently removed the box. Its hinges were slightly rusted, but the wood looked new. Carved into the top were Shane's initials. Slowly, Maggie opened the lid, afraid of what she might find within. A few old photographs lay on top, the first of Shane when he was a baby. The colors had faded some as though sunlight had shone on it many years ago. Beneath that was a picture of

Maggie holding Shane. She had been about three at the time, and both of them had big, goofy smiles on their faces. The last picture was more recent. The entire Callaghan clan had gathered in front of the cottage for a family picture. The moment she saw it, the memory returned to her, vague but real. She studied Shane's face closely, allowing his return to her memory to strengthen and deepen. How could she ever have forgotten that sweet face, that insistent tag-along, *her* baby brother? Tears escaped silently to dampen the ground where he lay.

Beneath the photos, Maggie noticed a piece of notepaper folded several times and badly dog-eared. She hesitated, feeling intrusive, before she opened it to see what it held. Her mother's handwriting covered the page dated January 19, 1987. Through blurred vision, she read the desperate words:

My dearest Shane,

Darling boy, my missing you never fades. You are on my mind always. I know you are in a peaceful place, but I selfishly still want you here with us. You seem to have been the glue that held our family together because we have all fallen apart with you gone.

If it is true that you are watching over us from above, please do not be dismayed at how we are managing. It is the only way we know how. Speaking of you is still much too difficult for your brothers and your sister has suffered so much. It is as though we lost part of her when we lost you. Do not feel you are forgotten, because that will never happen. Even Maggie, I know, still carries you with her in her heart somewhere, just as I am certain that you took a piece of her with you.

I sometimes wonder if I will ever stop feeling that I can't go on. I am angry at God, you can tell Him that. I am no help to Daddy, and I feel like I'm losing your brothers. Maggie's gone away to school – we are just a shell of what we used to be! We have sold the cottage. It no longer holds any joy for us. Oh, Shane, we want you back!!

Be strong for us, as you always were, deep inside. We will need your guidance to carry on. I pray to you now, that our family will someday heal from this.

I am leaving you your baseball cards and some pictures of better times. I know you cherished them. I will visit you often and forever, but you are always in my heart.

Mom

Maggie put the note back, on top of the baseball cards and closed the box. So recently Maggie hadn't even known that this grave existed. Feeling safe, in the company of her brother, she blew the dust from the lid of her memories and unlocked the top. Images of Shane's magnetic smile danced before her eyes. The sound of his voice was music in her ears and the touch of his hand...

Clouds covered the warm face of the sun, darkening her memories. His hand still felt cold and wet. The smiling little face before her suddenly took on a look of terror. Silently, his eyes bore into her soul, pleading for her help. Maggie lowered herself before the headstone and lay down over her brother. As she rested her head on the ground, she could almost feel her cheek against his. "I'm so sorry, Shane. I couldn't save you. I tried but I just wasn't strong enough. I couldn't even save you a second time by keeping you alive in my heart. I turned away from you.

"I'm here now. I'll never close off my mind again, I promise. I'll keep your memory with me forever. I can see you in Quinn every day so I know a part of you lives on."

Epilogue

"How and when the male and female rejoin
after a winter's separation remains a mystery."

July 4, 2004

Patrick flipped burgers on the grill while Shauna and Kit covered the picnic tables in festive checkered cloths. Maggie and Aiden sat with Mickey and Gwen under a shady pine tree and listened intently to a minute-by-minute account of their recent visit to Ireland. Sean was at the dock with the children, fishing and frog-hunting.

The lake buzzed with the sound of boats and wave-runners, as this was one of the summer's busiest weekends. Children were towed behind Bayliners on large tire tubes and skiers worked on their spray. It was a perfect day for families to be together. Maggie and Gwen rose from their cool spot to get the rest of the food from Patrick's cottage.

Patrick and Shauna were interning with Edna, part of their two-year plan to purchase "Echoes" when Edna decided to retire. Shauna had found a new voice in the relationship, becoming an equal partner with Patrick, and was quite skilled with negotiations.

The price had been haggled over for some time. Ironically, Edna was asking *less* than Patrick wanted to pay. In late spring, they had finally settled on a number, with the stipulation that Patrick and Shauna spend two summers under Edna's mentorship before taking sole ownership. During that time, revenues were to be shared. Edna had been kind enough to give them this special weekend off – at least until Patrick led the grand fireworks display behind the house that evening. They would spread blankets over the scratchy ground and watch the sky sparkle and pop. Owen and Patrick Jr. had been looking forward to it all day.

Maggie heard the children returning from the lake as she returned from the cottage with a bowl of potato salad. Their laughter permeated the air. Sean's deep voice could be heard behind them all. "Glad you could come." Maggie heard him say as the voices grew closer. "Plenty of food to go around and I'll bet Mickey's got a Harp's on ice for ya. And there's your girl right over there."

"Thanks, Sean. It feels good to be back." The voice flowed like warm liquid down Maggie's spine. She had asked Luke to come three weeks ago, but he had told her he didn't think he could. She had fought to keep him out of her mind all day.

Shortly after their separation Luke left his law firm and accepted a job as a corporate advisor in Boston. Maggie had worried that his move had been Luke's way of lashing out at her. When he didn't move back after several months, she realized it had been more than that. He did come every weekend, though, and sometimes mid-week, to see the her and the boys, but for some time it seemed that he and Maggie made no progress toward reconciliation.

Then, he called her in the dead of winter and asked her out on a date. He actually began to *court* her and Maggie regained some of her hope that she had lost for them. They took long walks along the Dover or talked for hours under their own gazebo. They made love again. They even talked about moving closer to Maggie's parents and brother as they worked on rebuilding their family. Maggie felt certain Luke would appreciate the opportunity to spend this long, holiday weekend as a family. Instead, he seemed more stubborn than usual, assuring her he needed to be in Boston that week.

At the sound of his voice now, she spun her head to see if it was really true, her long braid whipping around behind her. Luke caught her eye and smiled his crooked smile, making her heart flip and race. He walked to her and enveloped her in a gentle embrace, drinking her in.

"Surprise."

"Where have you been?"

"I had a few things to take care of at home first." He said. "I finished up a little earlier than I expected so I could join you. That okay?"

Maggie smiled, enjoying the feel of him close to her, and nodded. Luke lifted her feet from the ground in a firm hug and bent his head to press his lips gently over hers. She responded quickly and completely, the heat in the kiss setting off the little moths in her stomach.

"I moved my stuff back home." He whispered through the kiss and delighted in watching her eyes spark with surprise. "And I quit my job in Boston. I was thinking we could look at some of the real estate in New York. Hope that's okay."

"Better than okay." she smiled, brushing her lips with his. "I'm really going to need you around the house. The boys are getting so busy and it's only going to get worse from there."

"All you need me for is housework?" he asked pulling back slightly in mock hurt.

"Well, we *are* going to be busy." She teased. "You know with a move...and... Luke... you know that fabulous night we had a couple months ago? After you took me to the play and dinner?"

He kissed her neck. "Mmmm. Course I remember. You were kinda crazy, in fact."

"Yeah. Crazy's the word I'm thinking. See, I haven't exactly been using anything. Nothing was going on for so long, I just...didn't bother."

Luke's head jerked up to look into her eyes, see if she was teasing him again.

"Maggie, are you...?"

"Mmmhmm. And I'm thinking it might just be a girl this time."

Made in the USA
Lexington, KY
08 March 2012